Not My Will

Not My Will

Francena H. Arnold

MOODY PRESS

CHICAGO

*To Dad and the youngsters—
whose faith in me gave me
the courage to try*

1

Alex and Jean Stewart stood by the playpen and, with arms about each other, watched the determined efforts of the tiny girl inside to reach the ball that had rolled away from her. She could not crawl, but she reached and wriggled and hunched herself toward it with a great effort. Inch by inch she struggled, panting with exertion until at last, when she had achieved her desire and held the treasure in her dimpled hand, she was too tired to play, but fell asleep instead with a smug little smile on her face.

The two watchers laughed at her efforts and cheered when she won. Then, as they looked at the little sleeper Jean said, "Isn't she a persistent mite? She is that way about anything she wants. She worked all during her ride this morning to catch the Tinkertoy that I had hung on the hood of her carriage. But she finally got it."

Alex smiled proudly at his tiny daughter, then sobered at a sudden thought that came to him.

"I hope she won't be like her Aunt Ruth," he said with a note of pain in his voice.

His older sister Ruth had been a laughing, lovely girl, dear to the hearts of her parents and younger brother. She had a sunny disposition, and the old home echoed to the laughter of the brother and sister. During those years Alex Stewart was sure that whatever Ruth did was right. Now, looking back from the vantage point of later years, he realized how much she had imposed on his boyish affection and the strong love of her parents. When she had set her mind to a course of action she would willfully pursue it, "against wind, tide, or flood," her mother used to say. And the remonstrances of her parents, and the frequent punishments that came her way, were equally unavailing. At eighteen, against the pleadings of her whole family, she had married a man unworthy of her.

For fifteen years now Ruth had borne with a bitter, unbroken spirit, the results of her wilfulness. Her husband had been dead several years but his influence on her life remained. She was still attractive and could have married again had she wished. She had money enough to have permitted her to live a life of varied interests and pleasures. But the bitterness of her spirit poisoned her entire outlook. The sins of one man had aroused her contempt for all men. The energies that should have been used for good were consumed in hatred and scorn, and the laugh that had once been so gay was now cynically sharp.

And so a tone of regret crept into Alex Stewart's voice as he admitted that baby Eleanor, even in such small matters as lost bottles and straying balls, seemed to partake of the determination of Ruth Stewart Edwards. He brushed back a soft golden ringlet from the baby brow and spoke again.

"A strong will is an asset if rightly used. Ruth could have become a beautiful woman—probably a happy wife and mother all these years—if she had used that will in a better way. I don't want to *break* Eleanor's will, but it's going to be a job to control it!"

Jean, the wife and mother, straightened the blanket over the little one and, as they turned away, said in a tone of quiet faith, "We must pray much for our lovely baby, that the heavenly Father will guide her and give us wisdom to train her."

Before the little playpen was exchanged for a walker, however, a short trip away from home ended in a tragic railroad accident; and baby Eleanor was robbed of both parents. Aunt Ruth was the only relative left in the world to care for the mite. At first she was appalled at the task that confronted her of rearing the little orphan. But the heart that had thought itself closed forever to affection opened slowly but surely to the touch of baby hands, and soon Aunt Ruth was lavishing upon this delectable little morsel of humanity all the pent-up love of her intense nature.

She began to plan and dream again—she who had thought her dreams were all past. She was glad now for the wealth that had only burdened her before, for with it she could give Eleanor every opportunity that she had once desired for herself. This baby was hers—all hers—and she would mould and shape the young life in the way she desired it to be, and no one should say her nay!

Then began the struggle that was to last more than twenty years. And yet, despite the clash of wills, there was strong mutual love between the little girl and her aunt. The sore and bitter heart of Ruth Edwards attached itself fervently to the orphaned child, and she poured out the accumulated affection of her childless life on Eleanor, who returned in full measure all her devotion. Ruth learned to play games with Eleanor; they worked together over difficult arithmetic problems; they laughed over amusing incidents at school or at play.

And they fought. Not with angry words or loud disputation but with strong determination on both sides. Of course, when Eleanor was tiny, Aunt Ruth usually had her way, and the clashes were rare, for so great was her love for this little girl that she crossed her only when necessary. And when Eleanor did set her heart on the nice bright red penny candy in the store window, auntie took away the sting of refusal by buying a whole box of delicious and expensive chocolates. However, there were several memorable clashes that left both participants really ill.

One never-to-be-forgotten struggle came when Eleanor was in the first grade and sat in front of a red-headed, toothless, and altogether fascinating little boy named Jackie Dennis. Jackie was entranced by Eleanor's bobbing brown curls and showed his devotion by small gifts of gum balls and pencils; and one day he presented her with a ring he got for a penny at the school store.

The little gilt ring precipitated a crisis; for when Eleanor arrived home from school that afternoon she proudly displayed it to Aunt Ruth and made the startling announcement that when she grew up she was going to marry Jackie Dennis. She was totally unprepared for the storm that descended upon her head.

"You must never think of that boy again. You must not walk to school with him anymore; you mustn't even speak to him," Aunt Ruth commanded in closing.

"I will if I want to," replied the stubborn little girl.

"You *must* not."

"But I *will*."

This struggle lasted for weeks and was still current when school closed. But it was pushed into the background by the fun of leaving the big city for the cabin in the woods to which they retired each summer.

In September Aunt Ruth had a surprise for Eleanor. They were not going back to the big house on the boulevard. Aunt Ruth had bought a beautiful new brick bungalow in the suburbs. One of the very nicest things about it, Aunt Ruth told Eleanor, was that Mike and Mary, the couple who served as cook and handyman, would live by themselves in an apartment over the garage, thus leaving the two of them living alone together. "And that's what we've always wanted, isn't it, dear?"

To Eleanor the new home was almost as good as fairyland. The lawn was lovely and green and the garden full of flowers. There were big trees with many kinds of birds, and inside the house Eleanor had the prettiest little room all to herself.

Of course, Eleanor had to go to a new school. She had been living in the new home a whole month before she realized that Aunt Ruth had won and she wasn't seeing Jackie Dennis anymore. Then she was furious.

"I'll run away," she resolved, "I'll find my way back to the boulevard and find Jackie and go live with him forever and ever."

But before she had time to carry out her plan, Aunt Ruth gave her a bicycle, which she very much wanted; and in the fun of learning to ride, her anger faded. She met new playmates at school, too, and with so many new and engrossing interests to engage her attention, Jackie's red hair and gum balls were at last forgotten. But a bit of resentment lay in her heart.

Then, when Eleanor started high school, she met Dale Truman. The freshman class was planning a Halloween party in the gym, and Dale asked Eleanor to attend with him. In delight she came to Aunt Ruth.

"Aunt Ruth, our class is going to have a Halloween party in the gym, and the nicest boy, Dale Truman, asked if he could take me to it. May I go with him?"

Her heart sank as she read her aunt's face even before she spoke.

"No, Eleanor, I do not think it would be wise. If you would like to have some of your girl friends in for a Halloween party at home, you may."

"But, auntie—"

"Now, Eleanor, you mustn't try to argue. Auntie knows what is best for you." This with a disarming smile.

"I don't care. I want to go. All the girls are going, and lots of them are going with boys. I think it's mean!"

"We won't discuss it any further," said Ruth Edwards, setting her lips in determination.

That night Eleanor sobbed out her disappointment into her pillow. Suddenly she remembered something she had not thought of in a long time; a little boy with his front teeth out, looking in vain for her at school. The long-buried resentment flamed up. She was naturally a straightforward child, and although very determined in her efforts to achieve her desires, she had always struggled openly and fought fairly. Lying in bed, with her cheeks wet with tears, she looked back over many incidents of her childhood and realized that most of the lovely toys and delightful trips had been bribes.

"Mike would say she drew red herrings across the trail," she whispered. "She's been cheating all these years, and the only way I'll *ever* get anything like other girls is to do some cheating myself! It won't do any good to coax. She won't change her mind. If she'd sell the house in town and move out here just to get rid of Jackie, she'd take me to Europe to keep me away from Dale! I'll just *have* to cheat, too."

This sudden determination made her cheeks flush in the dark. But, although she knew it was wrong, she did not consider giving up. Lying in bed she made her plan and finally fell asleep with tears on her cheeks.

Several days passed, and the party was not mentioned. Then one morning at the breakfast table, Eleanor asked casually, "Auntie, may I stay all night tonight at Rose Martello's? She needs help with her English. Her folks don't speak English, and it's hard for her."

"Who is Rose Martello, dear?" the careful Aunt Ruth questioned.

"Don't you remember? She's the tiny girl with black curls who played the piano so beautifully when the girls were here yesterday."

"Oh, yes, I remember. But is she the kind of girl I would want you to associate with intimately? And does her mother want you? Rose seems all right, but I don't like your going there when I've never met her mother."

"She *is* a lovely girl, auntie," Eleanor hurried on. "Mrs. Martello is nice, too. We've been there twice after school. But they are Italians, you know, and her mother doesn't talk much English. She is bashful because of that, so even if you did call on her she would probably not want to see you. When Americans come there she stays in the kitchen and makes Rose talk to them. But she has been so nice to us girls, and I'd really like to help Rose."

And so Aunt Ruth consented, not knowing that Eleanor had selected Rose of all her friends as the most likely partner in deceit and had offered her a dollar for each night she might spend at the Martello's. Good Mrs. Martello, who made friends of every casual acquaintance, would hardly have recognized herself in the descriptions Aunt Ruth received—descriptions of herself that kept that lady from calling on her—and would have been shocked to know of the money that Rose was spending on ice cream and candy.

And since Aunt Ruth, always proper, insisted on Eleanor's returning Rose's hospitality, this bargain was very profitable for Rose in all respects. Her marks, at school, too, rose steadily, for Eleanor—to mollify her conscience—insisted that Rose really study on nights when she was paying dollars of self-denial out of her allowance for the privilege of attending this or that party with a boy from school.

At another time Aunt Ruth might not have been deceived by this clumsy subterfuge; but she was relieved to have the subject of Dale dropped so readily and was glad to have Eleanor transfer her interest to a girl friend—even a foreign girl. She would hardly have believed it if she had been told that Eleanor's head was not bent over a book in the Martello's parlor but was tossing gaily at Dale's quips at a party or basketball game.

Eleanor tired of Dale, of course, but then there were Gordon and John and Allan and others in succession. She was pretty, and she was popular—even despite a very strict code of behavior which she had imposed on herself to help salve her conscience. "When I'm out with the boys I'll act as if Aunt Ruth were along," she told herself, and with characteristic determination, she did it. And so the boys respected her and thought of her not only as a lot of fun but as the right kind of girl, too.

All through high school Eleanor deceived and disobeyed, even though she loved Aunt Ruth and they had wonderful times together.

"Aunt Ruth is grand," Eleanor commented to one of her girl friends, "but on this one subject she is just plain *crazy*. The easiest way to get along with her is not to tell her. Then her feelings aren't hurt, and we don't have any trouble."

Years later Eleanor was to look back to this high school episode with heartsick regret, realizing that it was the foundation for the heartache and tragedy of later years. It might have led to disastrous results at the time, had it not been that in her senior year she found a new interest and discovered a new world—the world that lives and moves outside and beyond the sight of ordinary human life, the marvelous world seen through the lens of a microscope.

The new science teacher at the high school had a captivating personality. He loved his work and with fascinating skill opened to Eleanor's view marvelous works of nature. He recognized in her a real student and was delighted to give extra time and effort to her. Professor Thorne showed her how the wonders seen through the microscope could be caught and held by the camera; and from that time on, Rose and the boy friends were forgotten. Aunt Ruth was delighted with this hobby and offered to Eleanor added inducements of money and equipment. One whole room in the attic was equipped for photography, and between this and the wonderful laboratory at school, Eleanor's days and evenings were divided. She and Aunt Ruth went on trips to secure specimens, and it was not long before Aunt Ruth was as enthusiastic over her new world of science as was Eleanor herself.

One day Eleanor confided her hopes for the future. "I am going to be a scientist, Auntie—a really good one, of course. I get sick of folks talking as if the boys would all have careers and the girls would only get married. I'll show them! I'm better now at this than any of the boys, and I'm going to be the best there is. No husband or babies for me!"

Ruth Edwards's bitter heart was gladdened by that remark. She determined to send Eleanor to the best colleges and universities in America. Then they would go abroad. There should be no limit to the opportunities Eleanor should be given to encourage her in the work she had chosen to do. At long last Ruth had real use for her accumulated wealth and was glad it had not been dissipated by extravagance. Eleanor—educated, talented, brilliant—would show the world the superiority of the intellect of woman over that of mere man. "No husband or babies for me!" Ruth still heard the words. If Eleanor had chosen science as her first and only love, then she should have every opportunity to worship at its shrine!

So man proposed. But God, as always, disposed. That fall, when Eleanor was ready for college, Ruth was not well. A visit to her doctor sent her home with troubled brow. Eleanor, not being able to extract much information from her, went to see the doctor herself and left with the knowledge that Ruth had an incurable disease. At least the doctor said it was incurable. But they would not believe that it was so. They consulted other doctors. So began a struggle of four long years against death. They visited hospital after hospital, clinic after clinic. As a last hope they took a trip of 3,000 miles and returned with heavy hearts and saddened faces, not to the brick bungalow but to the cottage in the woods. There, with faithful Mary and Mike, they awaited the inevitable.

As the days passed, Eleanor's spirit rebelled. "Why do I have to give up all I have in the world?" she asked herself. "Other girls have whole housefuls of families. Why should kind, good Aunt Ruth have to suffer? Why must anyone suffer?" Sometimes she lay awake at night pondering these weighty questions, and she thought about them many times during the day. Ruth glimpsed the struggle, and one night as Eleanor sat by her bed she said slowly, "Dear, I hope you are not going to feel too badly about all this."

"I *can't* feel too badly. It just isn't *right!*" Eleanor responded heatedly.

"Well, there was a time when I felt that way too. I'm not an old woman and I still want to live, especially since you are with me. I want to help with your work. But lying here in the long nights, I've done lots of thinking and wondering. I've been pretty headstrong. All my life I've wanted my own way and fought to get it. Having made one big mistake, I let it turn me from the right way."

Eleanor patted her arm. "It has been a *good* way, auntie dear, and I can't feel it's right for you to have to go."

Ruth shook her head. "I tried to make it a good way, but I wanted it always to be *my* way, and the selfish way is never a good way. I have lived entirely for myself, and the world is no better for my being—yes, I know I've cared for you, but that has been pure joy for me. It has cost me nothing, and I have received everything."

She was silent for a minute, then continued wistfully, "I wish I could go back and try again. I would try mother's way instead of my own. She lived first of all for her Lord, then for others—and last, for herself. She was happier than I have ever been."

Eleanor did not speak, and Aunt Ruth went on, "As I have lain here thinking of my life I have realized how futile it has been compared to mother's. I had a better education than she had, I've had more money to spend in one year than she had in her lifetime. Yet she faced death as if she were confident of God's leading in both the past and the future and could leave everything to Him. I haven't let Him lead me in the past, and I have no assurance He will want to take over the case now."

Mary, standing by, murmured with a tender voice as she straightened the tumbled pillows, "Oh yes, He will! I know Him, and it's glad He'd be to lead any lamb that called Him."

But Eleanor did not dare speak, lest the bitterness in her heart overflow. She did not want to grieve this dear aunt so obviously near death. And if Aunt Ruth could get any comfort by returning to her childhood religion, let her do it. Eleanor had nothing against religion. It was a rather good thing for the weak and those in trouble. She was sure there was a God somewhere whose duty it was to help people who weren't able to manage their lives alone. But if He did govern the affairs of mankind as Mary often said, Eleanor felt He was being very cruel to her just now. Hurriedly she kissed her aunt goodnight and went to her own room to cry herself to sleep. Waking in the middle of the night she saw a light in the invalid's room and, donning robe and slippers, hurried in to find her aunt propped up on her pillow writing.

"I couldn't sleep," Ruth smiled, "So I am writing a letter. Mary has been with me, and she is a rare comfort. Don't worry about me, dear. I am not afraid now, and I feel much better. Don't let me forget to have you call Mr. Hastings in the morning. I want him to come out and discuss some important business. There's no time to waste. Run along back to bed, dear. I am feeling sleepy now. I will put this aside and turn out the light."

Eleanor turned away with a heavy heart, and after the house was dark again she lay through the rest of the night, sleepless and rebellious. When she looked into the room the next morning Aunt Ruth was sleeping quietly. Out in the kitchen Mary sang softly as she prepared breakfast,

> "There is a fountain filled with blood,
> Drawn from Immanuel's veins;
> And sinners, plunged beneath that flood,
> Lose all their guilty stains!"

When she saw Eleanor she said, "The poor tired dear was sleepin' so sweet I had no thought to wake her. We'll let her get what rest she can from the naggin' pain. She'll rouse soon enough."

But she did not rouse. The doctor came, but there was nothing to be done. Before the day ended, the tired body of this solately reconciled child of God was freed forever from the pain that had tortured it, and her spirit was safe at home in the Father's house.

On the table lay the unfinished letter. Its first words, "My dear, dear child," told Eleanor that it was meant for her, but it was only after the funeral that she could force herself to read it.

My dear, dear child:

I may not have another chance to talk to you, and there is something that must be said. If I could turn back and live the past over again, I would try to teach you many things I failed to give you in these years when I had the opportunity. My sense of values is strangely altered in the light that has just come upon me.

Of one thing I am not sorry. That is the plan for your future. As I have lain here I have begun to see a purpose in all this pain. This world is full of suffering, and this disease that has shattered me has contributed a share of it. No one has yet mastered it. The one who does will do more for mankind than I could do if I lived a thousand years. I am not predicting that you can do all this. But you can help. With your slides and glass you can join the ranks of those who battle disease, and help to conquer it. If my going inspires you to do this, I am glad to have suffered.

But I want to say more than this. Mary has talked and prayed with me. I have found the right way at last, I am sure, for I have found Christ. If only I had known Him long ago! I cannot urge you too strongly to commit your path to Christ. He will be the friend and guide you need, for He will never fail you, my child.—

The letter was never finished, but Eleanor did not care. She had what she thought was the expression of her aunt's last wish, and her soul leaped to the challenge that it offered her. Then and there she dedicated her life to a battle with pain. What Aunt Ruth might have said had she been able to finish her letter did not matter. And the important business that she had wanted to discuss with her lawyer was not remembered again until years later when Eleanor wondered how her life might have been changed had her aunt been able to have that talk.

In a few days the lawyer called and in the presence of Mike and Mary read the will. There was a generous bequest to these faithful servants; enough to enable them to return to the place of their youth and spend the rest of their lives in comfort on the little farm they had dreamed about but never dared hope to acquire.

Everything else was given to Eleanor. Now she was free to continue her studies, to pursue the course to which she had pledged her life.

Long months ago Eleanor and Aunt Ruth had planned the course Eleanor was to follow—years of school and then laboratory, and Eleanor had always thought she knew all Aunt Ruth's wishes as to her future. But the last paragraph of the will surprised her.

"This sum of money is to be kept in trust by the said administrator of the estate, and the income given to Eleanor Stewart only until her twenty-fifth birthday, at which time the entire principal shall be turned over to her with no restrictions. If, however, at any time prior to her twenty-fifth birthday, Eleanor contracts a marriage, she shall forfeit all claim to the estate, and the entire sum shall be paid to the Xenia Laboratories to be used in medical research."

The old lawyer glanced with troubled expression at pretty Eleanor, but she hastened to reassure him.

"Don't let that worry you, Mr. Hastings. Auntie and I understood each other. I have a great work to do and shall never think of marriage, I assure you."

2

The next two years flew happily by. Eleanor might have been lonely had she stopped working long enough to think about it, for she made no friends and few acquaintances. No place on earth offers such seclusion as a great city. In a small town, everyone knows everyone else's private life and feels free to question and discuss at will. But among the millions of tiny atoms composing the population of a large city, one atom can easily escape notice altogether.

Eleanor chose a university in just such a city. Having been out of school for several years she was older than most of the students and had little sympathy with the light-hearted frivolity of the average youth about her. Her purpose in life was so compelling, her absorption in her work so complete, that she did not feel at all the currents of campus activities flowing and eddying about her. She was a good student and gave careful and diligent preparation to all her studies. English, psychology, and math however, were to her only necessary and uninteresting tasks that must be done as a part of her preparation for her life work. But in the biological laboratory she was in her element and utterly happy.

Old Professor Nichols, world-renowned scientist, author, and teacher, took an unusual interest in her. Professor Thorne, Eleanor's high school teacher, was a favorite former pupil of Professor Nichols and wrote enthusiastically of Eleanor's abilities and interest. And the professor, who had long ago abandoned hope of making any real impression on hundreds of the young folks who filled his lecture rooms each day—at night they appeared in his dreams as conglomerate masses of saddle shoes, lurid neckties, and sloppy sweaters—found in her just the assistant he needed to aid him in the great task to which his remaining years were dedicated. He hoped to publish a textbook that would give to future generations the truths he had so painstakingly acquired during his years of study and research. He had longed to find someone to help him—someone who could catch his vision and materialize his dreams. Eleanor, with her skill with microscope and camera, and with her quick understanding, seemed to have been sent to him for that specific purpose. Together they labored in the laboratory or darkroom, often far into the night. He rejoiced over her patience and persistence and was thankful to the kind Providence who had sent him such an invaluable helper.

Still Eleanor puzzled him. "Miss Eleanor, why *do* you work so hard?" he asked one day, watching her flushed face and too-bright eyes bent over the specimen before her. "Don't you ever go to any of these—er—functions most of the young people are so enamored of attending?"

"Never," replied Eleanor promptly.

"I am overjoyed to have you evince such an interest in our work, especially since my own eyesight is growing less reliable all the time. But—er—even if I am half-blind, I am aware that anyone as attractive as you should spend some time in the company of gentlemen somewhat younger than I. Don't you know any?"

Professor Nichols was surprised by the earnestness with which Eleanor answered.

"No, I don't know any and, frankly, am not interested. I don't want even to think about men. I said I would give my life to work, and I will. I always do as I say and always shall!"

"Well, Miss Stewart, I admire your courage and determination, but that is a strong statement to make." He laid down his work and looked at her intently as he said, "A long life has taught me that we can't always do as we will."

"I think we can, if we will hard enough," insisted Eleanor, adjusting her microscope with precision.

"Even considering that there are forces against which our own wills are powerless?" continued the old man, his eyes keenly upon her.

"For instance?" she inquired coolly.

"Well," he replied slowly, "there might be lack of money, for one thing. Failing physical powers are another. Or there is —death. Surely your will could not conquer that."

"Oh, of course I'm not silly enough to think that. But before I chose my lifework I had met death—in fact, it was one of the signposts on my way. My aunt's death gave me the inspiration to devote my life to fighting the disease that killed her. Through her death I also inherited the money that will make it possible for me to educate myself for this work. And as for physical disability, I'm not afraid of that for a while. I intend to live quietly, study hard, and keep my mind on my purpose. And I *will* achieve it. I never give up!"

"Well, Miss Eleanor," replied the professor soberly, "may God bless you in your ambition! I have devoted my whole life to a cause which I considered worthy, but now that I am bested by blindness and age, my prayers will be with you as you carry on."

Eleanor lifted her head. "Prayers?" she inquired with a smile.

"Yes. Don't you pray over your work?"

"Why, no. Why should I? I do my best. How could prayer help?"

"Prayer is difficult to explain to one who has not experienced it. To me, the One who framed all these things with which we work, 'without whom was not anything made that was made,' is so all-wise and all-good and all-powerful that I need Him on my side. I feel so utterly weak and insufficient when I stand before His wonders that I just have to pray to Him for guidance in my work."

Eleanor bent over her task in silence for a few moments. Then she spoke, with some hesitation.

"I think I understand you, and yet I can't see it that way. I believe in God, of course. Studying science has made me sure of Him. Such a wonderfully ordered and designed universe never came by chance. I respect His laws too highly to not believe in

21

Him, but that is as far as I can go with you. Those laws are unchangeable and control everything. I think if I work hard enough I'll find the ones I need. But," she concluded triumphantly, "it will take *work*, not prayer."

The old professor did not reply. The years had taught him that this bright head bending diligently over the table would have to be bowed under difficult circumstances before Eleanor would really understand his meaning. Further words were useless. He merely said gently,

"If the day comes when you need help, Miss Eleanor, perhaps it will comfort you to remember that your old professor prayed—not only for this work—but for *you*."

It had been a long time since anyone had shown any personal interest in Eleanor, and this unexpected kindness touched her deeply. When she spoke there was a break in her voice.

"Oh, I do appreciate that, and please don't think me hard. I'm really not. I do get lonely, and I wish I had time for other things. If I could believe in prayer, maybe I could pray and let God do the work and I could rest sometimes. But I don't think things get done that way. This is my job, and I'm going to do it myself. I do care for your interest, though, and if anyone's prayers are answered, yours will be." Then she smiled as she concluded, "You pray, and I'll work."

"Seriously, Miss Eleanor," the professor said, "you would work all the better if you took an evening off sometimes to go to a party or some such affair."

Eleanor valued this friendly old man's advice, and, since she really had been lonely, she began to make friendly overtures toward some of the young people for whom she had previously been too busy. Soon she was accepting invitations to parties, concerts, and plays, and only then realized how much she had missed the social life she had known. Professor Nichols was right, and she did work better after occasional playtimes.

3

Christmas was approaching—her second Christmas in college. *It means nothing to me,* she thought. *When Aunt Ruth was here it meant parties and presents, but now if I get any presents I'll have to buy them myself!* Her thoughts flew back wistfully to Christmases she had known at the cottage in the woods, with the candlelight church service at midnight and whenever possible sleigh rides through the starlit night around the frozen lake. Then she thought of last Christmas Eve, which she had spent in the laboratory at work. It had been two o'clock in the morning when she had looked up triumphantly from the finished slides, having captured a rare and hitherto unphotographed form of life after weeks of pursuit. At dawn she had crept into bed and slept through the whole day.

"This year I'll spend all Christmas week in research at Newton Library," she promised herself. Eager to begin, she made a special trip to the library before school closed, hoping to leaf through the wonderful volumes in anticipation. But there was a sign on the door, "CLOSED UNTIL JANUARY SECOND FOR REMODELING."

Now what shall I do with myself? Eleanor wondered as she crossed the campus on the way back to her room. So intent was she on her own thoughts she hardly noticed a cheery woman who looked at her keenly and then halted beside her.

"Why so glum, young lady?"

Eleanor looked up quickly, then smiled.

"Why, Carolyn Fleet! I didn't recognize you. With that red cap on, I thought you were some little freshman out for a lark."

"Well, I'm not—and you haven't answered my question."

"I'm disappointed," Eleanor admitted. "I had planned to spend all next week in research at Newton Library—and now I find it closed."

"Why, what a thought! You can't mean it. No one works Christmas week!"

"I do," Eleanor corrected her. "Or at least I wanted to."

"I'm glad you can't," Carolyn said flatly. "That's no way to spend Christmas."

"I haven't any other way," said Eleanor. "I haven't any family. I can't think of another thing to do."

"Let me think for you. I can show you how Christmas should be spent, given the proper wherewithal."

"Well, go ahead and suggest," continued Eleanor with a slight show of interest.

"First, for myself, I would like to go back East for Christmas where my mother and father are keeping my two youngsters while Fred and I study here. With Christmas coming on I wonder more and more whether even an education and a salary raise are worth being away from Jerry and Dottie during the holidays. Of course, I know they are," she added hastily, "but if I don't do something for somebody or his children, I'm going to sit and howl all Christmas week. So I think I'll adopt you and some other homeless youngsters and make Christmas merry for you in spite of yourselves!"

"Well, I'm willing to be an experiment." Eleanor smiled.

As they parted Carolyn said, "A two-room apartment may not be the best setting for a Christmas celebration, but it's all I have to offer. Now if only I had an ancestral farmhouse nearby —but all my ancestors were storekeepers in Connecticut."

That night, as Eleanor lay in bed, the idea came. Before she was dressed the next morning she telephoned Carolyn and asked excitedly, "Would a big log cottage in the woods do as well as an ancestral farmhouse, Carolyn?

"Do!! It would be perfect. But who has one?"

"I know of one less than two hours' drive from here that we are free to use. As Christmas is on Monday there will be a long holiday. Can you use it?"

"Eleanor," said Carolyn with earnestness, "you are nothing less than an angel from heaven! Just leave it to *me* to show you a good time. How many folks can you put up overnight in this made-to-order cottage?"

"Twelve, by squeezing a bit. I was there once for a house party so I remember. The owner says we can use it, but we will have to bring our own linens, as the house hasn't been opened in two years."

"Len, you're a honey. And whoever the owner is, tell him I love him. I'll get a crowd together right away. I'll be the official chaperone and go around and gather up an assortment of other young people stranded here for the holidays."

Eleanor looked forward to the house party with mixed emotions. After Aunt Ruth's death she and Mary had closed the cottage, and she had not been near it since. She had thought she would never want to go back again, but now she found herself looking forward in keen anticipation. It would be wonderful to see the woods blanketed in snow, to watch the moon rise over the sparkling pines and birches on the hills, and to skate out on the lake with the wind fighting against her. It was exhilarating to defeat the wind!

Plans were finally completed. Eleanor and the Fleets would drive to the cottage on Friday evening and make preparations for the others, who would arrive after work on Saturday afternoon.

All Friday afternoon Carolyn and Eleanor shopped, and when they stopped at the laboratory to pick up Fred Fleet, the car was loaded with fruit, cakes, all kinds of good things to eat, decorations, games, blankets—everything they could think of to make a perfect weekend.

Fred bounded down the steps three at a time, followed by a tall, blonde young man wearing a leather coat and cap, whom Eleanor recognized as the assistant to Professor Merritt in the biological laboratories. Fred opened the car door and then made the introduction.

"Carolyn, Eleanor, this is Chad Stewart. He is going to do the heavy work while I boss. Chad, this is my wife, Carolyn, and this is Eleanor Stewart. Quite a coincidence, the same name, isn't it? I doubt you are of the same family, though. Chad is of the royal line—Bonnie Prince Charlie, you know. Eleanor is just plain middle class Scotch-Irish, of the very best kind, though. Climb in back, your highness, and ride with the lady while my wife and I do the driving up here."

So began the great weekend, and simultaneously began something that Eleanor came to know as her Picture Gallery, in which hung one portrait after another of Chad Stewart: Chad drawing deep breaths of crisp, tangy winter air; Chad lifting quiet, worshipful eyes to the hills as they came into view; Chad swinging an axe with powerful strokes that told of years spent in woods country; Chad carrying in great armfuls of pine logs to pile in the fireplace; Chad and herself walking quietly along the aisles of the snow-clad forest cathedral or silently watching the moon above the eastern wood.

All the members of the house party were a jolly crowd, and every hour was packed full of fun. Truly, Carolyn knew how Christmas should be spent, as she had declared.

But after the first evening, Eleanor and Chad lived in a world apart. Whether tramping through the snow or sitting about the fireplace, singing or roasting apples, Eleanor and Chad found themselves side by side, almost unconscious of the presence of the others. As the twilight of Christmas Eve drew on, the young people gathered around the fire, singing carols and playing games until ten o'clock. Then Eleanor remembered that there was traditionally a midnight service in the nearby church, so off they all trooped to attend. The solemnity of the service subdued the hilarious group, and they returned quietly. Eleanor and Chad loitered behind the others and hand in hand climbed the hill overlooking the lake. They were quiet for a moment; then to relieve the silence Eleanor said, "This is the highest spot in the state. I used to think it the highest in the world."

"Have you been here often?" asked Chad.

"Yes, every summer. Don't tell the others, but this is my cottage. Father and mother left it to me when I was a tiny baby, and Auntie brought me here every summer."

"This is certainly a great place! Didn't you love coming here?"

"Yes, and I still do. When I was little I would climb up here and look and look and try to see Father and Mother in heaven. Sometimes I thought I could see the gates." She smiled.

Chad's voice was quiet. "This seems like heaven right here to me—just you and I together alone on the hilltop!"

Eleanor's laugh was a bit tremulous. You're not asking much of heaven."

Chad laid a reproving finger on her lips. "It's more than I deserve, young lady." Then his tone changed, and he reached out for her hand as he said, "Eleanor, I know this is—well—precipitate. But since I first saw you on Friday, I haven't been able to think of anything else except how sweet you are. I love you, Eleanor Stewart."

Eleanor drew a quavering breath but said nothing. After a moment, Chad continued, "I know this must all sound crazy. I never intended to make love to any girl for years to come. But I do love you, and I must know—do you care even the least bit for me?"

Still no answer. Chad waited anxiously, then said in a husky tone, "Forgive me. I've made you angry. Oh, I didn't mean to, but I couldn't help it. You're so sweet, and—oh, please don't!" For Eleanor was crying. Clumsily he fumbled for a handkerchief and, wiping away the tears, continued, "I'll go away tonight and never bother you again. I'm such a clumsy chap. I don't know how to make love!"

Eleanor's sobs continued, so in desperation Chad gathered her close in his arms and whispered, "Please tell me. What is it, dear?"

In a broken voice Eleanor replied, "You're so *dear*—and —it's been—so long—since—anybody—really cared—for me— I—just couldn't—stand it!"

Chad held her close as he laughed happily.

"From this minute on you can know there's someone who *does* care for you more than his own life. Do you love me too, Eleanor? Will you marry me someday when we can manage it?"

For a moment there flashed through Eleanor's mind the thought of Aunt Ruth's will—of her plan for a life devoted to work—of the brilliant career she was to achieve. But Chad's arms were around her, his cheek was against hers, and when she looked up she could see the pleading in his eyes. She was lonesome and hungry for love, and he was very dear!

So there under the wintry sky they pledged themselves to each other and went downhill together. To the others they gave no sign nor word of explanation; and when they returned to the city not even Carolyn and Fred knew how matters stood between them.

4

Through the weeks of January and February, Eleanor worked as never before. But now her evenings belonged to Chad. Occasionally they attended social affairs, but they preferred to take long walks and talks together, just getting acquainted with each other. Eleanor described vividly the several years of travel she and Aunt Ruth had spent together between her graduation from high school and her entry at the university. She explained how Aunt Ruth's death had directed her choice of a profession. She described her dreams for the future; a brilliant career, a laboratory of her own. Now she would work with him on the isolation of this dread disease germ.

Chad, in turn, gave graphic pictures of his childhood on the farm, attending the district school, helping his doctor father with the chores. He described his younger brother, Bob; his lovely sister Connie; and the baby sister, Mary Lou. He unconsciously gave Eleanor glimpses of small economies that she had never known, such as walking to and from high school in the nearby town. She clasped his arm and pressed it close the night he told of his father's death and the five years that followed, years of farm drudgery lightened only by the dream of someday getting an education that would enable him to hang over the gate the shingle CHARLES E. STEWART, M.D.

"I didn't expect to start to college this soon," Chad said. "But Bob says he is through with school, and fortunately his choice of lifework is farming. Then, too, Mother has turned the house into a sort of convalescent home. She's great at putting folks back on their feet. So I found it possible to get away sooner than I had hoped. Add to that the fact that Mother had promised Dad that I should come—and here I am. And here *you* are," he finished suddenly.

"Lovely lady, I certainly didn't plan on you. I wasn't going to even think of women until the old shingle was nailed up good and tight."

"Are you sorry?" Eleanor smiled quizzically.

"I'm not sure," he teased. "I haven't had a really coherent thought since Christmas."

"I didn't plan for you, either," Eleanor said seriously. "I was going to travel the long road alone, Chad. I was brave and big. Now I have no desire to go on without you. And yet—you are a disturbing element. When I'm away from you I can't work —very well—and when I'm with you I can't work at all."

"If we could only get married!" Chad twisted a lock of his hair as though he expected it to stir up in his head an answer to the whole problem. "It will be years before I can support you. By that time you'll probably be tired of having me around."

"You know better," Eleanor said soberly. "I don't change, Chad. I'll be there to hand you the nails when you hang up the shingle."

"But six years!" Chad exclaimed in dismay. "That's— that's half a lifetime!"

Eleanor said nothing. Chad would have been surprised could he have seen the pictures flashing through her mind. One showed herself on her twenty-fifth birthday, with the family lawyers handing her all the papers entitling her to her complete inheritance. Following that, the picture of herself and Chad being quietly married in some little chapel. Then, herself paying for both her education and Chad's. There was no sense in both struggling along separately!

Strangely enough, she had never told Chad of Aunt Ruth's peculiar will, and hence he had no idea that she was really wealthy. She lived in an ordinary little furnished room, dressed simply, and had no extravagant tastes. She longed for the intervening two years to pass so that she might have her money and be married to Chad. She could not afford to sacrifice her future by marrying him now, even if he had asked her. Her dreams of medical school and of the battle against disease were too sweet to her. The money she must have—but she wanted to marry Chad too, and as time went on Eleanor began to be irritated by the thought of waiting until her twenty-fifth birthday.

A vague resentment against Aunt Ruth began to take root in her heart. "What right did she have to bind me this way?" Eleanor demanded of herself one sleepless night. "Just because *she* hated men, why should *my* life be spoiled?" She turned and tossed, finally falling asleep to dream that Aunt Ruth's arm was reaching out from the grave, holding her in a viselike grasp, and she herself was crying out, "She cheats! And I can cheat too!"

The next morning a thought was implanted in her breast. But she bided her time.

When Chad, tired from a morning in classes and an afternoon in the laboratory, broke out one evening with impatient rebellion against their lot, Eleanor thought a moment and then offered a solution to their problem, "We could get married now, Chad."

"What do you mean? I can hardly pay my own expenses."

"Well, look, dear," she spoke rapidly, "I make enough to live on here, and you earn enough to keep yourself. It wouldn't cost any more if we were married."

"But my wife shan't support herself!" he said almost viciously. She stroked his hand. "Isn't that rather silly? It's not as though I were going out scrubbing floors to earn my money. Whether I'm married or not, I want to keep my job with Professor Nichols. If you were making enough money to support us both, would you want me to give up my job?"

"No," he said slowly. "But I still don't like it."

Eleanor hung her head. "I don't like being all alone in the world either."

Chad drew her close for a moment, then continued protestingly, "Folks would think I'm a regular leech! They'll say I can't support you so you have to work!"

There was Eleanor's opening.

"No one need know," she replied quietly. "I'm quite sure Professor Nichols wouldn't like it anyway. He's a dear old soul but a childish one, and he would probably expect my work to suffer. So why tell?"

"Lovely lady, I want you desperately for my wife, but when the day comes I want the whole world to know about it. I don't like secrecy."

Eleanor ignored him and continued, "Our 'ould Mary' would have called me a shameless hussy. But I see happiness, and I want it! Chad, don't think I'm wicked, but we could do it. You could live in your room all week, and I in mine, and no one would suspect a thing. But every weekend we could go to our wonderful cottage and live in our own little world until Monday morning."

Chad's eyes glowed. "It would be a little heaven on earth, and no mistake," he agreed. "But I can't do it. I just can't."

For a whole month they battled. Eleanor's face became pale and strained and there were shadows under her eyes. Chad was quiet and grave. Then one day they were walking across the campus and Chad was reading aloud a letter from his mother. One paragraph in particular seemed meant for them:

Today is my wedding anniversary and I have been thinking much of your father. We never intended to marry as soon as we did, but I was alone and needed him. We went ahead—and I have never been sorry. For thus I had a greater share in his work, and the things we suffered together are my sweetest memories now.

"There, now, you see," Eleanor said quickly, "*he* didn't let *his* pride keep them away from happiness."

"True," Chad admitted thoughtfully. "But when they were married they let everyone know. They didn't hide it like a crime."

"They didn't have any reason for hiding it. We have. For the sake of our work it seems better for us not to appear to be married. And I've been thinking lately that fate must have decreed it so. That's why we have the same name. We can do it, and no one will suspect." Her face glowed as she continued, "Think, Chad, of the beautiful days we could have together every weekend—and a real honeymoon during spring vacation!"

Chad drew a long breath. In the shadow of the great tree above them, he grasped her shoulders and looked straight into her eyes.

5

Spring vacation. Spring in the woods, with the earth smelling pungently damp and little green shoots pushing through the mold; with the streams running bank full, and the ground springy underfoot; with returning birds busy with nest-building; with new life triumphantly breaking forth on every side.

"Wake up, Len! Let's go for a walk before the sun is up. If we hurry we can beat him to the hilltop!"

They scrambled into their clothes and raced through the woods. The sun was just peeping over the line of hills on the horizon. Silhouetted against the crimson light, the church tower looked large and dark, and the red glow through the belfry caught Chad's fancy.

"God's light, through His church," he whispered.

Eleanor was awed. The beauty had not reminded her of God. She leaned against Chad and looked up at his bare head, the spring wind rushing his hair, his eyes shining as he watched the ascending sun. In after years Eleanor would linger long over this portrait in the Picture Gallery.

Back to the cabin they raced and dropped laughing and breathless on the steps. As Eleanor began to pin up her hair, Chad said, "It's too cool to be without a fire. I'll get that axe I impressed you with last winter and cut some wood, while you scramble some eggs for breakfast."

"While I scramble some eggs, did you say?" she asked.

"Certainly. Didn't we bring some?"

33

"Yes," she said doubtfully. "I guess we did. But, Chad, I can't scramble eggs."

"Can't scramble eggs? Well, where've you been all your life? What did you eat while you were there?"

"I've eaten scrambled eggs lots of times, but I never cooked any."

"Couldn't you just look at them and guess how?" Chad teased.

"No. I don't even know how to get the crazy things open."

Chad threw his head back and laughed so loudly that a stray hound sneaking out from under the porch drew back in alarm. Eleanor's cheeks flushed.

"Is that so funny?" she asked in annoyance. "Did all your other girls know how to cook?"

"Why, certainly. I thought women were born knowing how to scramble eggs. Say, you aren't peeved, are you?" Chad looked tenderly into the pretty, pouting face.

"I don't like to appear incompetent'" Eleanor said quickly. "I'm sure there are some things I can do."

"Sure there are. You're the cleverest little germ isolator I know." Chad patted her head consolingly. "But it so happens I want eggs for breakfast, not germs."

Eleanor jumped up, smiling again. "I can learn to scramble an egg just as well as any of your other girls ever could."

Chad arose, too, and drew her close as he laughed softly. "Bless your jealous little heart! I never had any other girl in my life. The only women I have ever loved before were my mother and Connie and Mary Lou. And you don't have to scramble eggs. I can do it well enough for both of us."

"No, sir, you shan't do the cooking in this family. If I can get a germ under the slide, I can get an egg into the pan. To the kitchen—ready, march!"

She tied on an apron, and Chad slipped into one, too, "just in case you miss your aim." Then he said, "Lovely lady, I'm sorry if I hurt you with my teasing. Bob and I have always teased Connie and Mary Lou, and I just do it without thinking. Don't you really like it?"

Eleanor smiled ruefully. "I guess I don't like to be reminded of my ignorance. And I never had anyone to tease me before. I'll have to get used to it, won't I?"

"In a month you'll love it," Chad assured her. "Now, as for the eggs, I could do this for you, but instead I shall lend my moral support."

The first egg broke all over the table. The second ran through Eleanor's fingers to the floor. The third broke into the bowl properly. But by the time there were four eggs in the bowl, there were three on the floor and table.

"How shall we ever clean up this mess?" asked Eleanor in dismay.

"Easy," responded Chad promptly. He went to the door and whistled, and the hound came loping up the steps and into the kitchen. In a few minutes he had departed, leaving behind only clean egg shells.

"As for the floor," Chad promised, "I shall scrub it with my own little hands."

Never again in her life did Eleanor break eggs into a bowl without remembering Chad leaning his elbows on the table and saying, "Not too fast there. And not too rough. Eggs are like women—handle them gently, but firmly."

That evening they sat side by side before the crackling fire of pine knots in the big living room. Eleanor had found a basket of pine cones in the store room, and now, as she threw them on the fire one by one, she began to talk to Chad of the difficult hours she had spent here before Aunt Ruth's death. He drew her closer as he realized how lonely her life had been and how many of the joyous experiences of youth she had been denied. He had long ago discovered deep within her the possibilities of a wonderful womanhood, and her capacity for love humbled him, knowing it was all poured out on himself. Restrained with others, she talked freely to him, and as he sat and watched her, he wondered what sort of woman she would have been, given a normal childhood.

"A penny for your thoughts." She smiled, brushing her hands on her skirt after emptying the basket.

"That's a small sum for such priceless thoughts. However, I'll *give* them to you. Believe it or not, I was thinking of you and wishing I could take you home and show you off to my folks. Let's do it, Len!'' he exclaimed impulsively.

"Oh, no," she cried in panic. "I can't, really, Chad. You wouldn't want to do that, would you? Some day I'll be proud and happy to go home as your wife. But not until I'm done with Professor Nichols's work. He'd not like it at all. Oh, you won't tell, will you?"

Chad was surprised at this outburst. "Of course not, if you feel so strongly. I guess we would have tough sledding if you lost out with the Professor. I promised, and I'll keep my word. But I want to walk in the front door with you and say to them, 'Look what *I* found.' That's what Bob and Con and I used to say. But none of us ever had such a find as this!''

"What do you suppose they would say?" queried Eleanor. She was glad to get Chad to talking about his family, instead of that dangerous topic.

"Let me see." Chad pretended a deep study. "Con would bite off her nails in jealous rage. Bob would be sure to break his engagement to Marilyn. Mom would ask if you could milk cows, and when you said, 'Oh, so that's where milk comes from!' she would die of shame on the spot.''

Eleanor's chin elevated. "I could learn to milk if I wanted to.''

"Of course you could, but if you're real smart you won't want to. I shudder to think of the oceans of milk I've coaxed from that herd in my day.''

"Aren't there such things as milking machines?"

"Listen to her!" Chad addressed the leaping flames in the fireplace. "Pretty soon she'll be telling me the difference between clover and alfalfa.''

After a moment's silenced during which Chad got his hair pulled for this piece of impertinence, he continued in a softer tone.

"Joking aside, honey, they'd all love you to death. Mom would be happy to think her son had married so well, and you and Con would be chums from the start. Bob is quiet, but he's a deep one. He and I used to tease Mom by singing a song to her, 'I want a girl just like the girl that married dear old dad!' Guess we meant it, for Bob went and proposed to Marilyn, who is very much like Mom, and I often see things about you that remind me of her.''

"Thank you, dear," Eleanor said seriously. "I don't know your mother, but I know that's a real compliment, and I treasure it.''

Chad went on. "There's one member of the family, though, who will adore you for two reasons. First, because you're you. Second, because you're mine. That's Mary Lou. I'm her special big brother, and all I say and do are just right to her. Poor little girl. You know, she never saw Dad. She was born the night he died. Some day I'll tell you all about that. It was hard, and I can't talk much about it yet. But I guess that's why I feel the way I do about Mary Lou. To have had a dad like ours and never to have known him!''

Eleanor held his hand tightly. When she spoke, her voice was shaky.

"I never remember seeing either my mother or father."

Chad looked down at the bright head and said tenderly, "And you didn't even have any brothers or sisters to make things easier.''

"No one but Aunt Ruth. She was as sweet as she could be, but I used to want other children so badly.''

"I think every child has a right to a big family," Chad mused. "I used to say I'd have at least a dozen of my own, but that was before Dad left us and I found out just what it means to keep them fed and covered with clothes!''

"Just think, Len," he continued, "Some day we'll have children of our own. I guess every fellow wants a son, and I certainly do. And I want a cuddly, lovable little girl like Mary Lou. But I'd want her to be like you, too, so I could get acquainted with the little girl I never knew, who grew up to be the big girl I adore!''

Moonlight on the lake. The weather had turned warmer, and as they sat there, Chad sang softly under his breath. Eleanor had noticed that his favorite songs were hymns. Now and then she joined in a hymn she knew, but many of Chad's songs were new to her—short little choruses, mostly about loving Jesus Christ and serving Him.

"You think a lot about God, don't you, Chad?" she asked once.

"Not as much as I should, I guess. Out here in the woods with just you and me and the stars, He seems pretty near. When I'm at home with Mom and the others He seems to be sitting right in the parlor with us. But when I get so busy at school, I'm sorry to say I forget Him sometimes. I'm rightly thankful for Christian parents and for the training I got. I am a Christian, even though I don't talk much about it. But college has changed some of my ideas and mixed me up on others. When I get through school and have time, I'll have to clean up my spiritual life like Mom cleans up her darning basket. I'll sort out all the ideas and mend the holes and put everything in order."

Eleanor had listened with interest and now she exclaimed, "Well, I never could make God seem real. Aunt Ruth never let me miss a Sunday at church, but I invented a game. I locked my ears tight against what the preacher said, and as I look back now I can't remember a single word I ever heard."

"Aren't you a Christian, Len?" Chad asked soberly, with disappointment in his voice.

"Yes, I guess so. In my heart I believe that Christ died for sinners. But all the ideas that used to satisfy me seem to be so obsolete on the campus. And, anyway, I have found out that to succeed in any real big work you have to give your whole heart and mind to it. I believe that the work we have chosen to do will be of immeasurable benefit to the world. That is a religion in itself. And it leaves not much time for going around saving souls or things like that."

"Bob and Con both take their religion more seriously than I do," Chad remarked. "They were just born good. Bob has a class of boys at Sunday school that is the talk of the town. Con speaks well and is always being elected president of something or other. She and Bob sing beautifully and often are invited to help at meetings in other places."

"Didn't you ever sing with them?"

"Not by invitation." He laughed. "They don't think much of my ability. When Mary Lou and I want to sing, we go to the woods."

"I like to hear you," Eleanor insisted loyally. "And I like those choruses."

"You're prejudiced, Mrs. Stewart. By the way, I like that name."

"So do I. It means the only real happiness I've ever had in my life."

"Are you happy now, Len?" Chad asked in a low tone.

"So much it hurts."

"God willing, dear," he said with a kiss, "I'll keep you that way."

* * *

Rain was falling in sheets on the shingle roof. Eleanor and Chad were on the floor before the big bookcases, looking through old books covered with the dust of years.

"Listen to this, Eleanor," Chad said suddenly.

"When I was in high school, we studied *Lady of the Lake*, and last night when you stood for a moment on the hill above the lake, I thought of that, and I just now found this description of Ellen—

> "With head upraised and look intent
> And eye and ear attentive bent,
> And locks flung back and lips apart
> Like monument of Grecian art,
> In listening mood she seemed to stand
> The guardian Naiad of the strand.

"It fit you so well that I decided you were Ellen, my Lady of the Lake."

"I'm yours all right," she said smoothing the golden waves of hair back from his brow. "But I was never called a Naiad before."

"I'm glad of that. No one else should have the right. But let's see what else Scott says about you.

> "And ne'er did Grecian chisel trace
> A nymph, a naiad or a grace
> Of fairer form or lovelier face

39

"Hm, he meant you, sure enough. He was just born a century or so too soon. He was a mystic and had a vision of futurity and saw you in it."

She laughed at his nonsense, and he continued to read,

> "A chieftain's daughter seemed the maid
> Her satin snood, her silken plaid
> Her golden brooch such birth betrayed.
> And seldom was a snood amid
> (*What is a snood, anyway?*)
> Such wild luxuriant ringlets hid.
> (*Yours* are *wild when you've been up on*
> *the hill in a wind.*)
> Whose glossy black——"?

"Hm, that doesn't fit. I'll have to doctor it a bit—'raven's wing'—no, it has to be altered—I'm not very good at poetry —but wait a minute—ah, here it is:

> "Whose shining locks to shame might bring
> The plumage of the cardinal's wing."

Eleanor gave him a push that tumbled him over backwards as she cried, "I am *not* red-headed."

"Not red-headed? Well, what are you then?"

"Just—just—*almost* red-headed," she admitted with a laugh. "And if I'm Ellen of the Lake, who are you? Fitz James?"

"Not on your life. I'm Malcolm, the guy that got the lady. Don't you remember the end? Poor Malcolm was chained to Ellen for life by the king's necklace! And if *his* Ellen were half as sweet as mine, he didn't want to ever be unchained. Ho-hum, it's almost eleven o'clock. Come on, Almost-Red-Head, let's call it a day."

From that night on, Chad seldom called her anything but Ellen; and when they went back to the city, the little volume of Scott went with him.

6

Eleanor had thought that they would spend the summer at the university, going to the lake for the short vacation between terms. But in early May, Professor Nichols began to talk of a trip East to do some work with a Dr. Kinsolving at the Xenia Laboratories.

"And of course I want you to go with me, Miss Eleanor," he informed her. "You are my second pair of eyes, and in that way you can keep on with the illustrations you are preparing for the textbook."

For the first time Eleanor began to question the advisability of their impulsive marriage. She was eager to go East with the Professor and take advantage of the opportunity of working in the wonderful Xenia Laboratories, but how could she leave Chad? Every time she saw him he was dearer, and she was sure he would not want her to leave him for the summer. She pondered long over this weighty problem, but it was solved for her in an unexpected way.

One evening when Eleanor met Chad for dinner, she immediately perceived that he was troubled. As they sat at the table, he handed her a letter from home. She read—

Dear Son:
I would rather do almost anything than write this letter to you. Your schooling has already been much delayed, and I had hoped you could go on with no further interruptions. I know you had

planned doing some hard work this summer. But I have no one else to turn to, and I know you'd want to help.

Bob fell yesterday and broke his leg. A rung of the haymow ladder gave way. Mary Lou found him unconscious at the foot of it, and it almost frightened her to death. He is at the hospital now, resting as well as we can expect. But he is beginning to fret already about the work. Uncle John can't carry on alone. He means well, but you know him. We can manage for a few weeks until school is out, but I fear you'll have to come home for the summer's work. You know how I dislike to ask this, and Bob and Con are heartsick over it. Only Mary Lou is pleased. All she can think of is that you're coming home. That's enough for her. Between sympathy for Bob and joy over the prospect of seeing you, she's almost torn in two.

I must hurry into town now. We will write every day. Don't worry, for the doctor says Bob will be all right. And I know that God's hand is in this, as in everything. It is comforting to rest in Him.

Mother

Chad took the letter away from Eleanor again and placed his big hand over her smaller one.

"Listen, Ellen," he said pleadingly, "I just have to go to Mother. She needs me. Old Bob is probably worrying himself into a fever over all this. But I can't think of leaving you here alone."

Ellen laughed. "Why, I stayed alone last summer, and it didn't worry you."

"I didn't know you then," he corrected her. "But somehow I remember a sort of dissatisfied feeling all last summer. That must have been why."

They both laughed, then Chad's face resumed its serious expression.

"Ellen, won't you go home with me? You'd love it. They'd all love you, and in spite of Bob's illness we would have a wonderful summer."

"Chad, how could I?" she cried. "We'd have to tell we're married."

"I know it, honey, but that wouldn't hurt, would it? I can't leave you behind, and I can't stay here when they need me."

Chad's face brightened. "Let's do away with this secrecy and tell the whole world," he suggested eagerly. "If the old professor wants to fire you, we'll struggle along somehow."

Eleanor was touched by the longing in Chad's voice. But she knew a reason, of which Chad was unaware, why their marriage must remain a secret. So studying intently the pattern in the tablecloth in order not to see the pain she knew would come into her husband's eyes, she said, "Oh, Chad, we can't! Please don't tempt me with any more descriptions of summer on the farm with you. I'm having an awful time trying to be wise and sane for both of us. We would enjoy the summer, but there would be a price to pay later. Remember our work, dear."

"Lovely lady, you're right as usual—but what will you do here alone all summer? That's what I don't like."

Drawing a long breath, Eleanor looked up into his troubled face.

"Fate seems to have taken care of that problem. Professor Nichols has decided to go East this summer to do some work and wants me to go along and help him. I don't want to go and leave you, but now it will be all right. He really does need me."

Chad demurred again. "It still isn't right," he argued. "After all, we are married, and those weeks apart will be endless. Now if only Mother didn't need me . . ." he mused.

"But she does need you, dear, and Professor Nichols needs me. We'll both go where duty calls us, do our work well, and look forward to a happy reunion in the fall. We can write often, and the time will pass quickly."

"It will drag, and you know it," Chad said emphatically. "But you are right about duty and all that." Then his eyes flashed as he continued, "Some day, Ellen, I'm going to take you home with me—and I hope it won't be long."

"And I'll go gladly and proudly, dear," she replied. "But just now we have a goal—a worthwhile one—to work toward. Some day we'll tell the world!"

At the railroad station, when it was actually time for Chad to leave, Ellen's resolution almost failed her. Together they stood in the middle of the great waiting room, and Ellen tried to think of the bright, casual things she had prepared to say to

Chad. But they were all gone. Instead, a little voice inside was whispering to her.

"Speak the word," it said. "He could still buy you a ticket and take you with him. He doesn't want to go without you. Think how nice a whole summer with him as his wife would be. Think of his family, waiting to meet you. Speak the word, and when the train pulls out you'll be sitting beside him on the seat. Just say, 'Chad, let's—'

"Chad, it's time to go," Ellen almost screamed, to drown out the maddening little voice. "Good-bye, darling. I'll see you in the fall." Choking back the tears that were threatening to come, she drew his head down and kissed him, gave him a push through the gate, and almost ran from the station.

7

After the first pain of separation had worn off, Chad was genuinely glad to be at home again. He had missed his family more than he had realized. It was good, too, to be active again in the outdoors, after two years of confining study; and it was good to know that by keeping the farm running he was contributing to the rapid recovery of his brother.

But along with the joy of reunion with his family, there came to Chad an uneasiness about the state of his own soul. So many things about the farm reminded him of his idolized father, who combined care of souls and bodies in one ministry of healing, and who talked freely to his two sons about his ideals for manhood as he busied himself at farm tasks between calls on his patients.

Driving the tractor across the fields one sunny morning, Chad pondered one statement of his father's that kept recurring to his mind, "A man isn't fit to be a doctor who can't doctor souls as well as bodies. Sometimes if you cure the soul, the body will take care of itself."

"If Dad were here he'd say I'm not fit to be a doctor, then," Chad told himself. "My soul certainly needs some doctoring before I can do anything for anyone else's. I couldn't even take care of the soul of a—a cow! All the folks here think I'm so wonderful, but if they only knew the spiritual mess I'm in!"

One event after another drove a barb into Chad's tender conscience. On Saturday night Bob seemed troubled. "What's the matter, old boy?'' Chad asked him. ''Is there something I can do for you?''

''You could, but I don't know if you would,'' replied Bob hesitatingly.

''If it's within my powers, I promise it in advance.''

''Well, it's about my Sunday school class that I'm concerned at present.'' Bob smiled at the look of dismay that crept over Chad's face. ''You asked for it, remember. Will you teach it for me until I set back on my feet?''

''I promised—and I will. But I fear I can't do a very good job of it.''

''You'll have to get the Lord to show you how. I couldn't teach them at all if He didn't map out everything for me in advance.''

Late that night Chad's head was bent over his Bible and the quarterly. *But,* he thought, *the Lord isn't showing me how. Bob must have a better acquaintance with Him than I have.*

On Sunday afternoon Connie said, ''Chad, I have charge of the meeting tonight, and just for a little variety how would it be if you took fifteen minutes or so to tell us country young'uns about mission work in the big city, also about some of the big churches you have visited there?''

''Mission work?'' Chad asked blankly.

''Yes, you know—some of the well-known rescue missions, neighborhood houses, or wherever you've been. We'd like to hear about it,'' Connie said eagerly.

''Con,'' said Chad with a show of assurance he did not feel, ''I've never been to any of them. They really work us at school, you know. As for big churches, I've visited a few, but that was a long time ago, after I first went down there, and I couldn't describe them very well now.''

''Oh, all right,'' replied Connie in disappointment. ''I suppose you *are* busy. But if I were right there in the same city, I'd make time to see some of the things people are doing for the Lord.''

Chad retired behind a book he had picked up from the table and did not answer.

Mary Lou was Chad's faithful follower all through the day, devoting to him as much time as she could squeeze in between her little household duties, always faithfully performed. Even when he struggled at night over the family bookkeeping, Mary Lou sat at his elbow perfectly quiet, now, and then patting his arm or running to get him a sharp pencil at his request.

One day she stood in the barn watching him milk. He looked up to see a troubled expression on her face.

"What's the matter, Susie?" he said. "All the troubles of the world dumped on your little gingham shoulders?"

"There's something that's bothering me," she replied seriously, "and I wish someone would help me."

"Suppose you tell brother," he suggested. "If it's what to name the kittens or whether to make your doll's dress pink or blue, I'm not sure I could help you, but I'll try."

Mary Lou smiled. "It's nothing like *that*. You're so funny sometimes. This is something the minister said that I don't understand."

Chad's face lost its laughing look. "I'll help you if I can, Mary Lou. But I can't do anything for you until you tell me what it is."

"Well, I don't understand at all how God could be in heaven and still be in Jesus Christ, like the Bible says. If all God was in Christ, was He out of heaven?"

Chad whistled softly. "Whew! What a little theologian we are turning out to be!"

"I don't know what that is," Mary Lou said soberly.

"A theologian?"

She nodded.

Chad's eyes twinkled. "A theologian, my little sister, is an individual who devotes the majority of his time to an endeavor to acquire an adequate and practical and thorough knowledge of the Infinite and Almighty."

Mary Lou looked amazed but simply said, "Oh," politely. Then eagerly, "Well, what's the answer to my question?"

"Why don't you ask the minister?" Chad evaded.

"I would, but I'm afraid it would hurt his feelings to think I didn't understand his sermon."

"I would advise you to try and see." Chad smiled. "Bigger folks than you don't always understand what he is talking about, and he knows it."

"Do you ?"

"Do I what?" he parried.

"Always understand what he is talking about?"

"To tell you the truth, no," Chad admitted. "Some of it goes right over my head, too."

"Well, I thought they taught you everything in college," said Mary Lou in a disappointed tone.

"Honey, they don't have time for everything, so they just squeeze in the most important things," Chad said carelessly.

"God is the most important," Mary Lou rebuked him.

"I mean for a doctor to know."

"You said Daddy said God is the most important for a doctor to know, too." The blue eyes were searching him gravely.

"Little sister," said Chad rising, "don't ever change. Now let's go into the milk house with this nice fresh milk."

All that night he saw a pair of solemn blue eyes looking straight at him and heard a serious little voice saying, "God is the most important."

Every evening after the day's work was done Chad would drive to the hospital and there tell Bob all the news of the farm, ask for his advice on various procedures, and try to cheer up the restless lad as he fretted at his confinement. One night he found Bob with a white face and hands that trembled as he took the daily paper Chad had brought.

"What's your trouble, old fellow?" asked Chad, setting down the basket of summer apples he had picked that day. "You look a bit unsteady."

"Listen, Chad," he said uncertainly, "what if these doctors aren't telling me the truth? This leg ought to be well by now. What if I never walk again? Am I going to be a cripple? Have they told you anything you're keeping from me?"

"Not a thing, Bob," was the cheerful answer. "You'll be frisking around like a spring lamb in just a few weeks now."

"Maybe they're not telling you then, either. Every day they come around with that same old cheerful line, and I'll bet if I were dying they'd pat me on the back and say, 'Coming along fine, Stewart!'"

"Well, what do you want them to do?" Chad smiled. "Pull a long face and tell you in a sepulchral tone that you are marked for an early grave?"

"No, but—oh, if they'd just tell me some of the actual facts in the case I'd feel better. They don't tell me anything! They just smile those eternal smiles, and all the time I can feel they are thinking, 'Poor fellow! He'll never walk again!'"

"Bob, you've been alone so much you're brooding," said Chad earnestly. "Now you mustn't think these things. Believe me, I know what I say when I tell you this leg is going to be helping you climb into the tractor in a few weeks now."

Bob clutched his brother's hand pleadingly. "Chad, won't you pray with me? I've been lonesome for Dad all day and thinking how he used to pray with us when we were in trouble. Won't you take his place tonight?"

Chad was ashamed and perplexed. Clearly Bob did not realize that he had grown away from many of the family customs and habits, for he was now waiting expectantly for him to begin. He knelt by the bed and began in a faltering voice.

"Our Father which art in Heaven, be with us here tonight. Help us to feel close to Thee. If we have grown away from Thee at all, bring us back again. Father, please help Bob to trust Thee to bring him back to health and strength in Thine own time and way. And Lord, wilt thou heal him as quickly as possible? Forgive us our sins, we pray in Jesus' name. Amen."

"Amen," echoed from the bed.

As Chad rose from his knees, he could see that Bob's troubled brow was clear again. He clasped his hand, said quietly, "I'll see you tomorrow, old man," and quickly stepped from the room, his feelings in a turmoil. But his prayer had been sincere, and if God had heard it He would straighten him out spiritually.

The best part of Chad's summer was the opportunity to be with his mother again. Mrs. Stewart was a busy woman, for the big house had four or five convalescent boarders all the time, people needing rest and special care. Even though there was a woman to do the kitchen work, and Uncle John (once a patient) was the indispensable handyman, Mother and the two girls were busy from morning until night. Yet somehow she managed many a quiet time to talk with this big boy, her firstborn.

During these quiet talks, Mrs. Stewart's discerning heart soon discovered that Chad's joy in fellowship and service for his Lord had been dulled, that the new interests and the work of college had crowded out the Savior who had bought him. She had spent many hours on her knees in prayer for Chad while he was away and now realized that God had sent him back to her for a while to have his spiritual experience refreshed, to give him an opportunity to rededicate his life to the service of Christ.

One evening Chad and Mrs. Stewart walked together to the quiet graveyard where the Doctor Dad lay. It was a small plot of ground on a hill behind the church. In one corner under a great elm was a rustic seat, and here the tall son and the gray-haired mother sat down after having stood at the grave for a few reverent moments.

"Precious unto the Lord is the death of His saints," Chad quoted from the simple tombstone. "The Lord certainly must have loved Dad dearly. He was one of His saints, wasn't he? I don't ever expect to meet a better man."

"Dad was no more of a saint than you are, son," was the quiet reply.

"I? Why, I'm no saint at all, Mom."

"Aren't you a Christian, Chad?"

"Why, of course! You know that when I accepted Christ years ago I *meant* it."

"Any saved person—any child of God—is a saint. But I must admit that we sometimes forget that. Dad didn't forget, Chad. Every hour of every day he lived completely for his Lord, joyously yielding his life to his Master's control. You children have a wonderful heritage in that."

Her quiet voice broke with the last words as if memory had brought fresh realization of loss. Chad patted the workworn hand that lay on his knee, and the two sat in silence for several minutes. Mrs. Stewart lifted her heart in prayer for guidance before she spoke again.

"How is it with you and the Lord, son? I have been watching you all summer, and I don't believe you are happy in your Christian life. I am sure of your salvation, but I believe you have lost the joy of it since you left us for school. Am I right?"

"What makes you ask that?" he parried.

"Oh, mothers have eyes and ears, and their hearts are tuned to any little disturbances in their children's lives. What has come between you and your Lord?"

Chad had picked up a large twig and was now trimming the tiny stems from it. His answer came slowly.

"I don't know—honestly, I don't, Mom. I didn't realize there was anything wrong until I got home here. Now everything seems to be pointing accusations at me. There are so many things here that remind me of Dad and bring his training and teachings to mind that I am realizing more every day how different I am from the man he would have wanted me to be. Then Bob asked me to teach his Sunday school class, and I found out how rusty I'd become on my Bible study. And once when he asked me to pray with him I found I didn't enjoy doing it anymore. It embarrassed me to pray with him. Con and Mary Lou have both said things quite innocently that showed me where I stand, and—and—I am beginning to realize I am an absolute spiritual heel!"

Mrs. Stewart had to smile at the boyish ending of the confession, but her heart was gladdened at the sincere repentance that she knew was behind it.

"But, Mom," Chad went on to say, whittling faster as he talked: "What bothers me is that I don't know how I got this way. I don't know where the trouble lies. I used to love my Bible, and I used to pray. I'd like to again. I'd like to have a real *live* Christian experience like the rest of you have. What's the matter with me that I don't?"

Mrs. Stewart looked straight at the perplexed blue eyes and said simply, "Surrender."

Chad thought this over a minute, then he continued, "No, I don't think that's it. I've surrendered my life to Christ. I don't drink or smoke, I don't even dance or chase to the shows like most of the fellows do. I don't—"

"I fast twice in the week, I give tithes of all I possess." His mother smiled, and Chad smiled too in spite of himself. "But did he go down to his house justified because of it?"

"No—I remember that from Sunday school. The one who was justified was the one who said, 'Lord, be merciful to me, a sinner!' But I've done that, too, Mom. I'm not trusting in my own works. But having asked for and received forgiveness, then having lived apart from the things that are called worldly, why don't I find the joy I seek?''

'''Worldly' is an ambiguous term, son. Most folks think of it in connection with pleasures and amusements. But I've always thought that work and care and ambition can be just as worldly. Anything that ties us to the world rather than drawing us closer to God is worldly. Is there something that you are putting ahead of God in your life, Chad?''

''Well—I don't know. When a fellow sets out on such a program as I've outlined for myself, he has to give practically his whole time and attention to it.''

Mrs. Stewart realized that he had evaded her question, but said nothing further. Instead, she opened her shabby handbag and took out a small Testament. Opening it and laying it on her lap she said, ''It seems to me that the key to the whole situation is found in the third chapter of Colossians. We have there the picture of the believer who has found the secret of real joy. Listen, dear. 'If ye then be risen with Christ, seek those things which are above.' Have you been seeking those things which are above, son? Or have your best interests and hopes centered on what the world has to offer you? I am sure you haven't been guilty of what the world calls the grosser sins, but have you not been guilty of withholding from Him that which is rightfully His? Listen again.

'''Set your affections on things above, not on things on the earth.' Have you given Him your heart's best love, or is your profession, your desire to succeed in your calling, dearer to you than He is? Is your life hid with Christ in God?''

Chad did not answer, so the mother turned again to the Book and quoted the well-known verses that picture the believer's joyful union with Christ and the assurance of the peace that God gives in hearts that are yielded to Him. When she had finished she sat in prayerful silence. Chad was staring at the gravel at his feet, and his hand clasped tightly the watch he had drawn from his pocket. Finally he spoke hesitantly, as if he hardly knew how to express the thoughts that troubled him.

''Mom, a Christian should love Christ more than he loves anyone else, should he not?''

"Yes, son."

"How *could* you love Him more than you loved Dad? I always thought that you loved Dad with all your being."

"I did, dear. I loved him so much that I have never fully lived since he left me. But I love Christ more than that. Some day you will understand what I mean. Loving a dear one here on earth doesn't come between us and Christ at all. In fact, I know I loved Dad better because we both loved our Lord. And I know that my Lord was dearer because of the love of my husband."

Chad was silent, and she spoke again.

"Is there one so dear to you, son?"

His voice broke as he answered. "Yes, I'll tell you all about her someday when I can show you her picture. I don't want you to think that she has come between me and the Lord, Mother, for she hasn't. She is sweet and good, and I know I am better for having loved her. In fact I'm not half good enough for her."

"I know she is good and sweet or my boy could not love her. But she must not come before your Lord, dear. Come now, it's growing late. We must be getting back."

They walked to the farm in silence. Above them the August sky was full of stars, and as Chad looked at them it seemed to him that they were nearer to him than Ellen was. He longed unutterably for her presence and wished that the two of them could kneel together that night and settle their relationship to God. But she was not here, and his conscience urged him to immediate action. He must get right with his Lord himself; then he would be better able to help Ellen when he saw her again.

Mrs. Stewart's heart longed to help this tall son who still seemed so like a little lad to her, but she had learned through long years of close walking with her Master that it is often better to pray than to talk. So they walked on, over the bridge, up the hill, down the dusty road, and across the dewy lawn. As Chad was about to go to his room, she laid her hand on his arm and said, "Will you do something for me, Chad?"

"What is that, Mom?"

"Read the third chapter of Colossians again, and pray over it before you go to bed."

Chad gave her arm a squeeze. "That's just what I was going to do." Then he stepped in and closed the door.

Several hours later Mrs. Stewart wakened and noticed a thin shaft of light under Chad's door. Thinking he had fallen asleep and forgotten to extinguish the light, she crossed the hall to his room and tapped gently on the door, not expecting a reply. To her surprise she heard a muffled "Come in." She entered to find Chad just rising from his knees, the Bible open on the bed, and his eyes brimming with tears. In a husky voice he said, "I'll go to bed now, Mom. It's all right. The Lord and I are friends again."

Thoughts of Eleanor had never been far from Chad's mind since he left her, and he did not need the picture in his watch case to bring her face into constant remembrance. But now he missed her more than ever. He longed to share with her this wonderful new experience of day-by-day living with Christ and to bring her to this same "good place" of the Spirit. As he thought about her and prayed for her day after day, he began to doubt that Eleanor had ever really known the Lord as Savior. He knew she had been raised in a formally religious atmosphere and had been taken into the church with a class of boys and girls when she was twelve years old. But as he looked back and tried to recall all they had said to each other on the subject, he became convinced that she had never been born again. He understood clearly, as he never had before, just how they had let themselves get into the situation which was now proving so complicated and difficult. Had Eleanor been a Christian, or had he been living close to the Lord, as he should have been doing, their problem would have been put into the Lord's hands, and they would have waited to marry in His good time. Chad did not blame Eleanor. She did not know the Lord. He did. He should have followed his Master first and have gone to Him in his perplexities, rather than to have been overpersuaded by Eleanor. Much as he loved her, and even with the memory of the sweet fellowship of the spring months they had had together, he wished with all his heart that he could go back to Christmas and begin again, to woo and win Eleanor in a different way.

The step had been taken, however, and the problem now was their future. He loved her more than ever, and he prayed with new humility and faith for her salvation. He pondered much on the secrecy of their marriage and longed to confess it all to his mother and ask her help. But it was Eleanor's secret as well as his own, and he felt he must wait for her to join him in the confession. He knew she would not do this until she saw the whole matter in a new light. And that light would only come when she knew the Light of the World. So he prayed and worked and waited for their reunion.

One night as he drove home from the hospital, his soul seemed burdened beyond endurance. He realized anew that more important than anything else in the world is a person's relationship to God; that a right relationship can be established only as he accepts Jesus Christ as his Savior from sin. Eleanor just *must* accept his Savior! He would be willing to give his own life if that were necessary to bring it about. He stopped the car by the cemetery gate, and, going softly through the shadows to the seat by the elm, he knelt for a long time, pouring out his soul at the throne of intercession, pleading that the Holy Spirit might convict the girl he loved of her need and of Christ's sufficiency to meet that need. "Oh Father, whatever it may cost me, bless Eleanor and bring her to Thee," he prayed.

8

Eleanor's summer was also full and busy. Professor Nichols, feeling that his working days were nearing an end, tried to crowd every day as full of work as possible. Early in the morning and late at night, Eleanor's eyes and hands and mind were needed. This was no pleasure trip. The textbook that was to be the crowning labor of the professor's career needed just these weeks of work to complete it. Haste was imperative, for it might not be possible to make this trip again. So early and late they labored, putting into the precious textbook their combined labors.

Professor Nichols took no recreation and was so engrossed in his work and oblivious to all things else that he did not notice Eleanor's weariness. She never complained, however. She had found that if she worked as hard as possible all day, there was less time to be lonely.

"But I *am* lonely," she admitted to herself. "I love my work, and I want to help, but it doesn't satisfy me anymore. I wonder what the professor would think if he knew that my thoughts aren't here in the laboratory half the time but out in the fields with Chad. If only I could have gone with him!"

Letter writing helped, but not much. Every letter Eleanor received made her long more intensely for her husband, especially as she read of his yearning for her. Several times she wrote long letters in return, pouring out all her love on the paper. But the intensity of the letters frightened her when she read them over, and in the end she always burned them, sending Chad instead short, bright notes telling of her work and her admiration for the professor. She knew that these would not satisfy Chad, but she could not write more intimately without breaking down the wall she had constructed to shut in her longing to be with him.

"Why, if Chad ever got this," Eleanor told herself as she finished re-reading one of the long love letters she never mailed, "he'd come on the next train and bundle me up and take me back with him without listening to a word I could say. No siree!" She shook her bright head and began writing a much different sort of letter. "I'll make it all clear to him when I see him again."

One morning in mid-September, Professor Nichols entered the laboratory to find Eleanor already at work.

"Well, Miss Eleanor," he announced jovially, "I have good news for you."

"What is it—is the book finished?"

"It can be finished now quite satisfactorily without the aid of the equipment here. We are going to return home just as soon as you can prepare yourself for the journey. How soon can we make our reservations ?"

He was unprepared for the glad smile that broke over her face. "Oh, tomorrow—today!" she exclaimed. "I can be ready as soon as you like. Do let's go soon!"

"Well, we shall take our departure as soon as arrangements can be concluded. I suppose you are eager to take up this next year's work at the University." He beamed on her fondly.

Chad, Chad, her heart sang.

* * *

As the miles flew behind them, the thoughts of both the professor and Eleanor raced ahead. Professor Nichols, anticipating the finishing of his book, was thanking the Lord for sending him such an efficient assistant as Eleanor, whose aid had been so indispensable to him. He planned the dedication of the volume.

To my dear wife, whose faith in me inspired this volume, and to my faithful assistant, E. A. S., whose labors made it possible . . .

Eleanor was not thinking of the book. She was wondering when Chad would return from the farm. His last letter had not disclosed his plans. She sent him a wire and thought she could not bear the disappointment if he should still be gone when she arrived. The professor and his wife left the train at a suburb just outside the city, but she scarcely heard their farewells. She was as excited as any schoolgirl at the prospect of seeing Chad again.

The station was full of people milling about, but no Chad. Eleanor made her way to the street door. Suddenly she felt her purse being slipped out from under her arm. She turned to retrieve it, only to meet Chad's laughing, loving gaze.

"This your purse, madam?" He held it up teasingly.

"Oh, Chad," she gasped.

Quickly he engineered her to the sidewalk and beckoned for a cab. They climbed in; Chad gave the driver an address, and as they drove off Chad's arms went around her in a close, tender caress.

"Darling," he said. "I know this is extravagant, but you wouldn't have wanted me to do this on the 'L,' would you? Oh, Ellen, it's been a long, long summer, and I promise you a hundred times over it will never happen again. Did you miss me? Your letters didn't sound like it." He looked at her half teasingly, half pleadingly.

"I missed you so much I didn't dare put one bit of it on paper," she replied huskily. "I wrote you long letters—but they frightened me, and I burned them."

"Oh, that wasn't right," he exclaimed. "After we got into it there wasn't any way out, though. The folks really did need me, and the old professor needed you. We promised not to tell, and we didn't. But, look here, young lady," and he placed a finger under her chin and tilted her eyes to look straight into his own, "here's one decision of mine that is absolutely final. I'm not going home again without you."

"I hope you won't have to, dear. It was all harder than I dreamed it could be," she said, smoothing softly the hand that had grown hard with the summer's toil. "But it is all behind us now, and we have the rest of our lives to be together. You've done the right thing, and I've done the helpful thing, so let's not grieve over it anymore but look ahead to this year together at school. And—oh, Chad!'' Her face brightened with the sudden thought. ''We still have time to go out to the lake together for a few days before registration.''

His only answer was a kiss. Then for a time they rode together in silence, enjoying the familiar sights and sounds of the big city.

Suddenly Ellen sat up. ''Chad, this driver must be lost. We're not going the right way!''

''Yes, we are,'' he returned mysteriously. ''I want to show you something. Afterward we can go over to the campus if you like.''

A look of wonderment came on Ellen's face, and it increased when the taxi drew up before an apartment building and stopped. Chad helped her out, and the driver carried her bag up to the entrance.

''Chad, what in the world—'' she began, but he raised a quieting finger.

''Now, just wait a minute,'' he replied.

He unlocked the door and drew Eleanor inside. ''Follow me,'' he said mysteriously and started up the steps. On the second floor he opened another door, took Eleanor's hand, and pulled her inside.

''Welcome home, Mrs. Stewart''' he said with a flourish.

''Chad! What is this?'' she exclaimed, looking around in astonishment.

''Just what I said. Home. I'm the head of this house, and I'm setting my foot down. I've rented this apartment. No weekend wife for me any longer.''

Before he had even finished his speech Eleanor's comprehension returned and she had flung herself into his arms. ''Oh, darling, this is wonderful,'' she exclaimed.

Chad looked frowning into the hall mirror. ''Mrs. Stewart, if you unsettle my necktie like that again I'll take you back to the university and exchange you for a set of books.''

She laughed unsteadily and promised to be more dignified. Chad sat down on the studio couch between the casement windows and drew her down beside him.

''Rest here awhile, and then we'll inspect our nice shiny new home together.''

"Chad, we can't do this!"

"We can, and we will."

"But how? We can't afford it in the first place. And no one knows we are married."

"One person does now—the manager of this building. But no one at school will find out. After all, we are nearly four miles from the University, and when we leave there at the end of the day, our lives are our own. As for the cost," Chad went on, a little frown puckering his brow, "well, I don't feel so good about that, for you'll have to pay your share just as if you were living at your old address. I wish it weren't that way, but until we're through school, I don't see any other way. And as there was still a small discrepancy in the rent between what I could pay and what the rent costs," Chad finished smilingly, "I asked the maintenance man whether he could use a strong extra hand on Saturdays and Mondays, and it seems he can, so I'll work out the rest of the rent firsthand."

"But what if . . ." Eleanor's voice trailed off doubtfully.

"Don't tell me; let me say it. What if someone comes to see us and finds out our horrible secret? Who's been coming to see you the past two years, my girl, with you working so hard? Nobody. And the same goes for me, too. In the two years that I have roomed over Professor Merritt's garage, no other person has set foot in my room. From now on, I'm going to take up even more of your time, so you'll be an absolute social dud. So you just push all your little doubts into the back of your mind and forget them, and lean that pretty head closer on my shoulder and rest a little bit."

Eleanor sighed contentedly. "Just to be able to feel you again, and to know you're real and not a dream, makes me forget I ever was tired. And this lovely apartment—"

"'Fess up, now—aren't you glad I did it?"

"Well, of course, except that every time I think of the complications it may involve I get panicky."

"We'll take care of the complications as fast as they come to call on us. Just now let's talk about our rosy future. Do you know, every time I kissed Mary Lou this summer, I longed for the day when you and I will have our own houseful of youngsters. Would you mind half a dozen?"

"Dear me, such a few!" Eleanor exclaimed in mock dismay. "I had thought we wanted a whole dozen, all taught to behave."

Chad continued musingly. "They will inherit the tendency to be beautiful from you and to be good from my mother." Then suddenly he added, "This is a very abrupt change of subject, but what do you say we look at our house?"

The apartment was tiny but attractive, and every corner was examined thoroughly. There was a large living room, simply and tastefully furnished, with windows that looked out into the branches of a huge oak. One side of the room opened into a dressing room and bath, and from the other side one entered a dinette and kitchen.

"Why, it's just like the doll's house I used to have!" exclaimed Ellen joyously, as she stepped into the cheery red and white kitchenette.

"Well, what do you know!" Chad exclaimed, opening the refrigerator door. "The people who lived here before us must have left us a few morsels of food."

Ellen came and peered over his shoulder and saw that he had been shopping and stocked everything necessary for their first dinner in their own home.

"Wise man." She laughed. "I also observe that you bought everything ready cooked. Undoubtedly a reflection on my culinary abilities."

"Honest, I didn't think of that! I just wanted to save time on this special evening. We ought to spend all our time looking at each other, don't you think?"

"Why, of course—and you couldn't hurt my feelings if you did cast aspersions on my cooking ability. But I *will learn*, if only to show you what an excellent housewife you married."

"I married the only girl in the world for me, and that's all that matters," Chad said in a low voice.

The meal was soon ready, and they sat down, not across the table from each other in proper style, but side by side, hand in hand. When they were seated Chad put his arm around his wife, bowed his head, and said softly,

"We thank Thee, Father, for all Thy goodness to us, and especially that Thou hast brought us together again. We thank

Thee for this home, and we ask that Thy blessing may rest on it and us. May we live and work here to Thy glory. Bless this food to our use and us to Thy service. Amen."

9

Eleanor was now happier than she had ever been in all her life. At eight every morning she and Chad arrived at school and went to their separate classes. At noon they ate lunch together in a corner of Professor Nichols's laboratory, always empty except for them, and after lunch they studied for a half hour. In the afternoon Chad went to the chemistry laboratory and worked hard until five o'clock. Eleanor worked with her slides or labored in the darkroom for one or two hours, then hurried away to buy groceries and prepare dinner. She had attacked the cooking problem with precision and thoroughness and had become fascinated by the possibilities found in the cookbook. There were some dismal failures, of course, but Chad manfully ate all that she cooked. He teased her about "pop unders" and "cardboard pie crust" if they appeared, praised her for all her successes, and was inordinately proud of her progress.

Eleanor confined herself scrupulously to the budget that she and Chad had made based on their earnings at school. Her monthly income from the lawyer lay untouched in the bank, and it became a point of honor with her never to touch a cent of it, as Chad did not know of its existence and would not understand

"But I wonder what he would think," she asked herself late one afternoon, while she busily peeled potatoes and onions for a savory stew, "if he knew that I could sit down and write a check that would pay for our rent and food for a whole year? He wouldn't like it, probably—so I'll just let the money pile up."

So Eleanor practiced all the economies she knew and learned new ones to help stretch the little budget. She traded baby-tending for the use of a washing machine, and it was with elation that she hung her first washing on the line.

"If Aunt Ruth could only see me now." She smiled. "She never dreamed her darling child would come to this—for the sake of a man. Dear Auntie! I wish she knew how happy I am!"

Happiness was the order of the day in the little apartment. Eleanor and Chad enjoyed sweet fellowship studying together at the little breakfast table in the alcove, and Eleanor would one day linger long over this view in her Picture Gallery.

Yet she was unhappily aware that Chad was disturbed because their spiritual fellowship was not what he longed to have it be. The new experience he had written her about during the summer had made a difference. When he prayed before breakfast, it was not just "saying grace," as she had always known it, but a real morning prayer. He thanked God for the rest and care of the night, and committed them both to Him for guidance and protection during the day. Eleanor did not dislike this; it simply did not interest her much; and often she found her thoughts straying to work or lessons that lay ahead.

Every evening before Chad started studying, he would read a while from his Bible, which always lay within easy reach on the living room table. Often he would read aloud. Eleanor enjoyed this—but more because of her admiration for her husband's voice than of any appreciation for the text itself. However, because she saw he loved the Book, she sincerely tried to become more interested in it.

Sunday morning dawned; their first Sunday in the new apartment.

"Would you like to go to Sunday school and church with me this morning, Ellen?" asked Chad hesitantly at the breakfast table.

"Oh, I'm sorry," she replied in some surprise. "I didn't know you had planned to go. We never used to, you know. There's some reading I want to do before I see the professor tomorrow, so you won't mind if I stay home will you?"

In spite of his assurances to the contrary, Eleanor knew that he did mind, and as she stood at the window watching him go off down the street alone she resolved to go with him hereafter, even if it were going to bore her.

On the following Sunday morning Chad was standing in front of the mirror, struggling with an uncooperative necktie, when he observed Eleanor begin to don her best dress.

"Where are you going, my pretty maid?" he quoted abstractedly.

"'I'm going to Sunday school, sir, she said,'" Eleanor replied demurely getting out her powder puff, "that is, if I can find a handsome blonde gentleman to take me."

"Here's one who will be delighted." Chad fairly beamed. "If any other blonde gentlemen turn up, tell them you already have an engagement."

After a few blocks' walk, Chad stopped in front of an ugly little building cramped in between two stores on a business street. "Well, here we are," he said.

"This?" cried Eleanor, shocked.

"This is it, dear. I think you'll like it when we begin."

Instead of the cushioned pews that Eleanor had been accustomed to find in church, there were rows of straight, hard, chairs. The painted walls were adorned only with Scripture texts. The piano was battered, the song books were ragged. Eleanor began to regret that she had worn her best dress.

"What made you choose a church like this?" she asked Chad as they sat alone in the back row of chairs.

Chad smiled at her bewilderment. "I know it must seem pretty bad, but I promised Mom I'd get into some kind of work for the Lord. All the other churches around here looked well able to get along without my talents. This one seemed nearer my size and style, so I tried it, and it 'fit.' Then you asked to come, and here we are!"

"At least it's different," Eleanor admitted. "I don't mean to be critical. But they won't ask me to do anything, will they?"

"I think not. Last week they only asked me to read a verse in the Sunday school class. You could do that, couldn't you?"

"Yes," she whispered, "but I'd rather not do anything."

Chad smiled.

The room was filling rapidly, and Eleanor studied the faces about her. *They don't dress as well as the ones I know at school, but their faces are much the same,* she thought.

To her surprise, she genuinely enjoyed the Sunday school class, which was taught by a middle-aged man who knew and loved the Book he taught. His enthusiasm was such a novelty that Eleanor failed to notice the occasional grammatical error she might otherwise have heard.

But the music was an ordeal. The pianist was absent, and the nervous young girl who was conscripted to fill the vacancy managed to ruin the song service by playing with meticulous slowness in order to avoid errors. The special selection by the choir Eleanor described to herself as "ghastly."

The sermon was the first she had heard in more than two years. The preacher, a small, insignificant-looking man with weak eyes that peered through thick lenses, mounted the platform. After one look at him, Ellen resigned herself to being thoroughly bored. She almost retracted the good resolution she had made the previous Sunday, so great was her dismay.

Yet, as he spoke she became less and less conscious of the man and deeply conscious of the message. He did not use eloquence, nor did he attempt to play on the emotions of his listeners. He talked with simple straightforward directness. The title of the sermon was "Bought with a Price"; and for the first time in her life Eleanor heard a clear, understandable statement of what the death of Christ had meant to the world. It interested her exceedingly, but it did not occur to her to apply it to herself.

Walking home later through the sunflecked streets, Chad asked pleadingly, "Was it so very bad, Ellen?"

"It wasn't bad at all. It was good. I'm glad I went. But I wish I could show that poor pianist how to play. Her efforts were pitiful."

"Yes, they were pretty crude," Chad admitted. "Yet all the time I kept thinking, 'She's probably suffering more than I am. She knows it's bad, but she does it because she loves the Lord.'"

"Do you really think He knows and cares about such little things as that, Chad?"

"Yes, certainly. If He cares about sparrows and lilies and hungry beggars, He cares about everything in our daily lives. I'm finding out now how much I need Him in everything I do."

Eleanor did not answer. This was alien territory to her. She felt again a vague uneasiness that there should be this experience in Chad's life into which she could not seem to enter. She was apprehensive that God would somehow spoil her fun with Chad. For her, work and love were enough. She did her work well and did not feel as though she needed God; and could not understand why Chad did.

"But I do try," she told her conscience one day. "I listen when Chad reads the Bible, and I talk about religion whenever he wants to. I go to church and Sunday school and even to prayer meetings sometimes."

"But what do you think about when you are there?" conscience would ask.

To this Eleanor would not reply for she knew she usually thought about her work. While the sermon was going on, she planned experiments or labeled slides for illustrations in the professor's book.

And yet the seed was falling on good soil, and more and more of the truths she heard being preached and taught were sinking in. She began to feel a vague dissatisfaction with herself; to feel less sure of her own conclusions about life and its meaning. She knew Chad had something she did not possess, and she knew he was longing to share it with her. The Bible readings that had at first bored her became precious; and when Chad prayed she knelt inside the circle of his arm and felt drawn close to God. Chad did not hurry her or urge her to take any step. He wanted her decision, when it came, to be not for his sake but for the Lord's. So he waited and prayed and trusted. He saw that she was changing and thanked God for it.

On Sunday night before Thanksgiving the little minister preached again on Christ's atoning death on the cross. It was only two months since Eleanor had heard him preach the same sermon. He seemed to fear that someone who had never known God's plan of salvation for mankind would get away without hearing it. So it came into practically every sermon; and today, as on that first Sunday, he made it clear and simple. But there was a vast difference in one listener. The first time Eleanor had listened as one apart. Today it all seemed meant for her. And it came to her overwhelmingly how much she needed this Savior. She forgot all the people around her, and, bowing her head, she came face to face for the first time with the question of her own relationship with the crucified One. Chad saw the bowed head and the tears that softened the proud little face and rejoiced at this sign of the Spirit's working. But he did not question Eleanor. He knew she preferred to settle the matter alone. When she was ready, she would tell him all about it, and they would rejoice together. So he concentrated on the exams that filled the next few days and waited patiently for the happy time he felt was very near at hand.

10

Except for one short trip to the lake in a borrowed car to bring back some dishes and linens to the apartment, Chad and Eleanor had not been there since the beginning of school. Weekends there were household tasks for Eleanor and maintenance work for Chad. Eleanor longed for the cottage, however; and on Tuesday evening as they munched popcorn and bent over their books in the dinette she said, "Chad, do you think you could beg off from your work here for this weekend? Wouldn't it be grand if we could go to the lake tomorrow night and stay until Sunday or Monday? It would make up for some of our lonesomeness of last summer."

"Lady, what an idea!" Chad cried enthusiastically. "Sure I can get off. I put in a lot of overtime when the engineer was sick, and if he wants me to I'll put in more later. I have been wishing we could go but was afraid you'd think you had to work."

"No, Mrs. Nichols thinks I look tired and has ordered a rest. So—if you can go—the party is on. Oh—" a sudden thought made Eleanor's face fall "—your mother won't expect you home, will she?"

Chad picked up the darning basket that sat nearby and began to play with the spools of cotton. His face was sober and a bit troubled as he replied, "No. She knows I can't afford mid-year trips home. I had a letter today though, and they want me to come Christmas if I possibly can. Bob and Marilyn are to be married, and Bob wants me to be best man."

"Can't we manage the expense some way?" Eleanor asked quickly. "You really ought to go for the wedding." She longed to add, "Just let me pay for it," but knew that was impossible.

Chad was still whirling the spools around his finger. "Ellen, if we can raise the carfare, will you go with me and let me show my family my wife?"

"Oh, I *couldn't*! I know how you feel, dear. I don't like this secrecy, either. But we agreed, you know, and we've gone too far to go back now. I *wish* things were different, but—we can't tell folks yet." Her voice was shaky and she upset the basket and spilled the socks all over the floor as she reached for Chad's hand. "Please, darling, you go without me. Next year I'll do it. Truly I will. But I just can't now."

"Don't get so frightened, honey. I won't do a thing against your wishes. But this is final, and you might as well understand it," he said firmly, kissing the hands clinging imploringly to his. "I don't get the idea of your being so upset at the mere mention of going home with me as my wife. But I will not go home anymore without you."

Ellen's heart contained a mixture of emotions, but she decided it would be best to let the whole subject drop for the time being. She did not reply but began picking up the scattered contents of the mending basket, and in a minute Chad spoke again.

"There's something I've been intending to tell you. I have a surprise for you. Even though to the casual observer you are not supposed to be my wife, I have responsibilities to shoulder, so I have taken out some life insurance. I took out enough to protect you if anything should happen to me. The policy came today. Here it is. You'd better take care of it."

Ellen opened the large envelope. When she saw the amount of the policy, she was startled and shocked. "Why, you shouldn't have made it so large," she cried. "How can you pay it?"

"I wanted it large enough to keep you comfortably if you had to get on without me. It will be hard to pay for a few years, but I sold my sorrel colt to Bob, and that covered the premium for the first year. After that I'll just have to hustle to meet the payments. Mother has a small policy which would pay for any burial expenses—" He stopped abruptly as he saw her look of terror. "Darling, don't look like that! We have to talk about things like this sometimes. As I was saying, Mom has Bob and the girls to look after her, but you're all mine, and I'm going to look after you the best way I know how!"

"I love you more than ever for thinking of this," Eleanor said, whisking away a tear that had fallen to the table. "But let's put the policy away and forget about it. Anyway, if you should die, I'd want to die too!"

"Well, my love, I don't think you'll have use for the policy very soon—unless you try too many new dishes on me for Thanksgiving dinner! By the way, I think we can borrow my professor's old car again. I fixed the starter for him last week, so he'll probably feel indebted to me. We can load it up with all the 'makin's' of a real feast!"

So the invitation for Christmas was not mentioned again. But Eleanor now knew that the matter of the secrecy of their marriage would become increasingly troublesome unless Chad understood once for all that it was not a mere whim on her part that sealed her lips. She resolved that the next time the subject came up, she would tell him of Aunt Ruth's strange will.

* * *

The day before Thanksgiving was cold; and as Eleanor descended from the streetcar at the corner, a few snowflakes stung her face. Chad had apparently arrived home first for the familiar old car was parked at the curb, and as she turned in at the walk Chad came through the door with his arms full of bundles.

"It's about time you arrived, my lady," he greeted her. "I've loaded my suitcase and those cans of cookies and all that stuff you left on the table. Are your comb and toothbrush packed?"

"I'll be ready in ten minutes. We'd better take our heavy coats. It's down to twenty degrees now, and that lake can be the *coldest* place."

Chad carried down Eleanor's suitcase while she followed with her cameras. They stopped at the market long enough to buy groceries to last through the holidays, then headed toward the lake and the cabin in the woods.

71

* * *

From beginning to end it was an ideal holiday. The cabin was dark and cold when Ellen and Chad arrived; but a fire was already laid in the fireplace, and in a moment it was snapping and crackling merrily. Then Chad ran downstairs and built a fire in the furnace, and soon the whole house was warm despite the chill wind outside. All night the wind roared about the cottage, and when they wakened it was to a world wrapped in white.

"Oh, Chad, look! Isn't it grand? Snow for Thanksgiving! I never knew it to come so early before!"

"I like it because it reminds me of last Christmas—only I like it even better now without all the other folks around."

Eleanor dimpled. "Once or twice I was glad of having a few folks around to shelter me. You courted so fast I was afraid and ran away."

"Yes, you did—not! You were almost as smitten as I was. You still are a bit peculiar, but I liked you then, and I like you better now—even if you are peculiar."

"You're a conceited man, and I—love you," Eleanor finished with a tone of finality. "Do you realize we've been married about two-thirds of a year? It's time we stopped talking like honeymooners and began to be bored with each other, isn't it?"

"Lady of the Lake, get me straight on this," Chad said earnestly, looking straight into the little face, "I didn't marry you because it seemed the wise and prudent thing to do. I married you because I had lost my head over you. I love you more every day—hence I lose a little more of my head every day. I expect to wind up as a modern Headless Horseman if I stay around you, which I intend to, and so the honeymoon will last as long as we do."

"You're sweet."

"I'm hungry, too. Forgive me for introducing such a crass note into this beautiful conversation, but when do we eat, and will it be breakfast or dinner when it arrives?"

"We'll have breakfast, then go for a hike in the woods. That will give us a good incentive to get dinner."

After breakfast they donned their heaviest wraps. Chad made a trip to the basement and came back carrying a pair of

72

Mike's old galoshes, only slightly too large, and something else that Ellen hailed with delight.

"My old coaster! I haven't seen that sled for years. Oh, what fun we're going to have!" Then she noticed the galoshes and said, "That gives me an idea. I'm sure Mary must have left a pair around here, too."

A search of the closets yielded a pair of overshoes that were wearable with the toes stuffed full of paper. Chad also found an old leather coat of Mike's and a cap which made him look like Daniel Boone. Ellen seized on a discarded knitted scarf of Mary's and a pair of fur mittens she had once owned. Then together they floundered out into the wonderful white world.

Dragging the sled behind them, they climbed to the hilltop. There Chad sped down the snow on the side facing the meadow and made a slide that led down over the slope almost to the road beyond. Again and again they sat on the sled and flew down the hill, laughing at an occasional spill in the snow and rejoicing in the clear, cold air.

"I used to think this was fun, even though I had to slide alone," panted Eleanor. "But I didn't really know what fun was, I can see. There isn't any fun alone at all."

"Another thing that's no fun," said Chad meditatively, gazing at the blue sky, "is starving to death. Once there was a man in the Russian wilderness—"

"All right, all right," Eleanor laughed. "We'll go back and get dinner. I know a hint when I hear one."

Chad pulled Eleanor on the sled all the way back to the house and spilled her into the big drift by the door, after which he pulled her out, brushed off the snow, and kissed the cheeks rosy with cold.

"Now for that much-heralded dinner, my love. I hope it doesn't take as long as Mom's Thanksgiving dinners do. She always begins about four thirty in the morning."

"It won't," Ellen assured him. "The chicken—excuse me, the turkey—has already been roasted, and I have only to warm it up, according to the man in the delicatessen. The potatoes will cook in half an hour, and all the other things come out of cans. Our Pilgrim ancestors would be shocked—but our feast will suit us, so let them worry!"

Chad set the table, opened the boxes of cookies and cakes Eleanor had baked, emptied the canned cranberry sauce into a festive cut glass dish, set out butter and pickles while Eleanor made salad and prepared vegetables. As a finishing touch, Chad cut out a magazine picture of a pumpkin pie and gave it the place of honor, "in memory of the pumpkin pie that isn't here."

When the potatoes were mashed, the gravy thickened just right, and the chicken and rolls taken from the oven, Ellen placed them all on the table with an air of triumph and said, "I don't care if most of it did come out of cans; it's a dinner to be proud of, and I think it calls for a real thanksgiving." She spoke lightly, but Chad answered in a serious tone.

"It does. But I can't express it with each of us sitting at an end of this great table. Let's kneel here and tell the Lord we really are thankful for all He has done for us."

So they knelt by the window seat, and Chad prayed. It was the first long prayer Eleanor had ever heard him utter, and it gave her a glimpse of the yearning in his heart for a close walk with God for both of them. There was gratitude, also, for the love that encircled them and had permitted them to live and love and do their work together; and there was a petition for help and blessing on their future road.

When Chad said, "Amen," and Eleanor echoed it softly, there were tears in the eyes of both. And while the meal was less merry than it might have been, there was real joy instead. It was a true Thanksgiving dinner.

After the dishes were all washed, they sat on the davenport before the fireplace and dreamed dreams of the life that lay ahead of them after school years were done. It was pleasant to be here with no pressing work to hold them apart, with the cold and snow outside, and inside the crackle of the logs that burned to make them cozy. Years later Eleanor looked back on that evening as symbolic of all the happiness that life can hold.

Friday and Saturday were days of rare fellowship and fun. They walked thorough the winter woods or stayed in the house, just as fancy dictated. They delved into the old books or sat again by the fire in quiet, intimate conversation. During those hours they learned to know each other better than the hours in the apartment had ever permitted them to do. Eleanor perceived that

Chad's strong spiritual nature was the result of early training by devout parents; and although she could not remember her own parents, she found herself acutely aware of her great loss. *If they had lived, it might have been easier for me to know Chad's Savior,* she thought.

Chad, on the other hand, learned to understand how years of repression and a lack of youthful companionship had affected Eleanor. He saw that her failure to meet him spiritually was due largely to early training; and his heart yearned unspeakably to help her. He longed to talk with her about the sermon of the previous Sunday night and its effect on her, but she did not seem ready to discuss it. Chad was disappointed but not discouraged. He felt assured that the time for her acceptance of Christ was near and that his duty for the present was to wait and pray.

Sunday morning was bright and warm, with the snow melting rapidly in the springlike air. It seemed just the day for a drive, so Chad suggested that they visit a church in Meadville, thirty miles away. It was late when they arrived at the church. They slipped into a back pew just as the preacher was rising to begin his sermon.

Eleanor's first thought as she saw him was *You're just too handsome to be true. I wonder if that wave in your hair is natural.* She was ashamed of this flippant thought and glanced at Chad wondering whether he had seen her smile. But he was frowning intently at the preacher, so Eleanor settled to listen.

She soon forgot the preacher's wavy hair and Grecian nose, however, as she became enthralled by his message entitled "A Bond-servant of Jesus Christ."

He described the ceremony whereby a Hebrew slave, gaining his freedom after years of bondage, and wishing to signify his desire to become a lifelong bond servant of his beloved master, had his ear pierced through with an awl so that he should thereafter be recognized as belonging to him.

This he likened to the life of the Christian. Christ has bought him with his own life on the cross of Calvary, but it remains for the Christian to yield possession of his life and his will to the Master who loves him.

"Paul was glad to call himself such a bond servant," he said. "Peter and James and John lived and died for Him. Stephen was stoned to death for Him. Hundreds of His bond servants were thrown to lions, thousands of others were burned at the stake; and who can number those who were beheaded rather than leave His service? During the intervening centuries a host of His servants have sacrificed and toiled and borne ridicule that His work might be done effectively. Whitefield, Wesley, Moody, and Finney, later stirred the crowds in His behalf, reminding them of the One they had forgotten. And can we forget what has been done on the mission field by men and women like Livingstone, Carey, Judson, Paton, Hudson Taylor, and Mary Slessor, who counted it a joy to give service unto death that His gospel might be given to all nations?

"Today the call is still going forth. Our Lord needs servants—bond servants—as never before; men and women ready to leave their old lives, their wills, their plans, and purposes to go forth for Him, to live and serve Him, in far lands and here at home. He needs men and women in every walk of life; in the pulpit, in the doctor's office, in the bank, the machine shop, the schoolroom—every place where human beings live and toil, He wants His servants to go forth on His business.

"There has never been a day so urgent as this. The forces of might are increasing faster than the forces of right; and the judgment of this world seems impending.

"Can we refuse the Master's call? 'Ye are not your own, ye are bought with a price,' says Paul the apostle. As bond servants of our Lord, we *must* answer, 'Here am I, Lord; send me.'

"Our Lord as an obedient Son said, 'Lo, I come to do thy will!' If we love God truly, can we do less? Shall we not come, saying in utter humility and sincerity, 'Not my will . . . but Thine'?"

Eleanor and Chad slipped out as soon as the benediction was over. Both were greatly moved, and the rest of the day was a quiet one. Eleanor longed to discuss the sermon but could not speak easily of it. Chad wanted to talk about it but felt it was wiser to let Eleanor bring up the subject herself. He knew she was pondering the message, and he prayed silently that the Holy Spirit would open her heart to receive the truth.

As the shadows of evening began to fall, they packed the car once more and started back to the city; but during the long drive, they were unusually silent. However, the warmth and friendliness of the snug little apartment broke the tension.

"It's been a wonderful time, Ellen. Let's do that every chance we get! The noise and dirt of the city are easier to bear if they are mixed up with a few real times like that."

Eleanor's eyes smiled in happy agreement as she replied, "It *does* liven one up to get out into the woods. We'll always have the cabin to go to since I can't sell it. (I'll tell you about that some day.) We can run away anytime we choose, but after each run-away time it will be a little harder to run back, I'm afraid. Some day, Chad, we'll take the children and go there and stay."

11

All Monday morning they were busy, Eleanor with neglected ironing, Chad with some electrical repairs. Eleanor's thoughts, however, were not on the shirts she was pressing so carefully. She kept seeing a Hebrew servant asking his master to pierce his ear; and hearing the plea for Christians today to give themselves in complete surrender as bond servants to Christ. Her heart longed to answer the call. She never had been satisfied with half-way commitments. She knew that if she yielded, she must yield completely. And the cost of doing so she dared not contemplate. But there was Chad—Chad, whose love for her pleaded constantly and silently for her to open her heart to his Savior. She knew that Chad would never be satisfied to let this issue die, and she herself could not ignore it longer. It must be settled.

On the one side there was surrender to Christ—and all its implications, which made her draw back in fear. On the other side there was a continuance of her self-will—and the fact that never again would Chad be satisfied with her. In utter despair, Eleanor dropped her head on her hands and let the tears have their way.

So it was that Chad found her later. He had never seen her cry in his way before, and he gathered her close begging her to tell him the cause. When she could not speak, he asked softly, "Is it about yesterday's sermon?"

Eleanor nodded and moved more closely into his arms.

"I thought so," he went on, "and though I don't like to see you cry, I'm glad we heard that sermon, for it said better than I ever could the things I have wanted to say to you. Oh, Ellen, you do believe that Christ died for your sins, don't you? The Scripture says, 'If we confess our sins, he [God] is faithful and just to forgive us our sins, and to cleanse us from all unrighteousness.' Just tell God everything, Ellen, and thank Him for forgiveness from all sin through Christ. Remember, He means what He says, and then just turn everything over to Him! Can't you just let go and let the Lord be your Master for all time? I do believe He is your Savior. I believe that you've accepted His sacrifice for you. Don't you want to give Him complete control now? It would be wonderful for us to serve Him together."

She was silent in his arms, then her voice came in sobs, "Oh, I wish I could!"

"You can, honey. It's not hard. Let me tell you what happened to me this summer. You know I accepted Christ as a little boy. But the last two years I've gone on my way doing much as I pleased and not giving Him His due at all. Then this summer when I was so lonely for you, I found what a friend He can be. Mom helped me a lot by her talks to me. And I know, too, that her prayers were a big help. It's hard to tell just what happened, but one night after I talked to Mom I felt such a longing for Him that I confessed my lack of love and gave myself anew to Him, for service or sacrifice as He sees fit. And another night I knelt by the bench near my dad's grave and gave *you* to Him. I do want to be completely and utterly surrendered, but my life is so bound up in yours that I can't do the thing my conscience bids me, without your cooperation. You know what I mean, dear. We can't go on as we have. We are living a lie all the time, and we'll never be really happy again until we tell the world that we are man and wife and take the consequences, whatever they be!"

"Oh, we can't!"

"You've said that so many times, but now I don't see it anymore. You may lose your job with Professor Nichols. I don't think you will. But even if you do, we'll manage somehow. We may have to give up this apartment and take just one little room. But we'd be together. And God would not forsake us, I'm sure. Come on, dear heart, let's kneel together and tell Him we will."

79

Chad stood up and tried to draw her to his side, but she burst into a wild storm of tears and drew away. Chad's face became stern, and his voice was firm as he spoke.

"Ellen, there's something more to this than I can understand. Can't you tell me?"

She clung to him in desperation and finally sobbed, "Oh, I have to tell you, but I'd rather die!"

He picked her up and laid her on the couch, then bringing some warm damp cloths, bathed her face and eyes. He brought her a glass of water and for long minutes sat by her side smoothing her hair, patting her hot trembling hands, and waiting. When she was quieter, he spoke again.

"You'll have to tell me whatever it is, dear. That's the only way we'll ever get it straight. It must be pretty bad to make you feel like this. But it can't be bad enough to shake our love, and it isn't so bad that our Lord can't make it all right. So let's get it over."

She clung to his hands, saying desperately, "Hold me tight, Chad. This is going to be *hard*."

Then she drew a deep breath and began her story. Some of it he had heard before; some was entirely new to him. She gave him all the background—Aunt Ruth's unfortunate marriage and consequent hatred of all men, the unreasonable restrictions she had placed upon Eleanor, Aunt Ruth's illness and death, and finally—reluctantly—the terms of the will.

"So, if I married before I was twenty-five," Eleanor barely whispered, "I should lose all the money. I've never cared for money except for my education and for setting me up in my chosen profession. But it *wasn't* right for Auntie to bind me that way! I didn't care till I met you, but then I couldn't stand to wait two more years because of her foolish prejudice. If I lose the principal, I can never go on with the work I had planned. And I'd planned for you, too, Chad. The money would enable us both to do big things in our field. So I thought we could keep our marriage a secret till I was twenty-five, then we could tell it and we could use the money together. But I see things differently now. Oh, I don't know what to do!"

She stopped in exhaustion and, when Chad did not answer, looked anxiously into his face. It was white and stern, and she pulled away from him in shame.

But he drew her back and only said, "Go on."

"I *can't* go on. There's no place to go. I'm just now beginning to comprehend the awful thing I've done. I didn't know human beings could get into such a mess. There isn't *any* way out that's the right way."

"Oh, yes, there is, and it's up to us to find it. It's much worse than I imagined, and any solution is going to cost something. If I had dreamed of such a thing as this you couldn't have paid me to marry you. You're more than life itself to me now, and even when I first met you I knew I couldn't live without you. But two years isn't eternity, and we could have endured it. Then we could have married openly, and together we could have made that money work for God and the world through a long life of happiness together. But it's too late to think of that. We have to find to our way out of this tangle, and I'll admit it's a puzzler."

Chad drew from her dress the chain that she always wore and turned the little wedding ring around and around in his fingers. After what seemed to Eleanor an unbearably long time, he asked,

"Can you talk about this some more without getting too much upset? Will you tell me all the facts and let me see the papers you have?"

She quietly brought a big envelope and laid the documents before him.

"I might as well save you the trouble of wading through them," she said wearily. "I know them by heart. My own parents hadn't much money at all. The lake cabin and adjoining farm belonged to Daddy and is so fixed that it can't be sold so long as there's a Stewart in direct descent to inherit it. The oldest son gets it if there is one, otherwise the oldest daughter. Just before I was born Daddy used all his money to modernize it, expecting to open a high-class summer camp there for boys. Then when he and Mother were taken, all there was left for me was the cottage and farm. The farming land is only forty acres, and the income from it just about pays for taxes and upkeep. There was some stock in a company that hadn't paid dividends in years. So Aunt Ruth had to take me. When I was about eighteen, the stock company reorganized and has been paying me a little income ever since. And when Auntie died, the will said I was to get $200 a month until the age of twenty-five, then if I wasn't married, I was to get her entire estate. It's a big one, Chad—I'm afraid to tell you how big. Her husband was very wealthy. But, according to the will, if I married under twenty-five, the entire amount is to go to Xenia Laboratories for research work. So you see what it means. Till I'm twenty-five, I get the $200 each month. Since we came into this apartment, Chad, I've not used any money except my salary and what you gave me. So there's a lot in the bank now, and no matter what happens there'll be $200 a month for another fifteen months, when I'll be twenty-five. But after that, if I acknowledge our marriage, there'll be nothing! I guess that's all,'' she finished flatly.

For the remainder of the afternoon Chad put questions to Eleanor, which she answered, until there was no detail he did not know. Eleanor did not attempt to argue or justify her course. The recital had left her too weary for any decision, and she simply awaited her husband's move.

After the supper dishes were washed Eleanor brought out her books to try to study. Chad went into the tiny dressing room and closed the door. At the end of half an hour Ellen had to admit that she had not seen one word of the text she was looking at, and, as she turned the pages back to begin again, Chad came out with his overcoat on.

"I have to go to the lab, Ellen, and I'll be late getting back. Don't wait up for me, I'm leaving this decision to you, dear. It is your problem, and you must decide. I've been praying as I never prayed before, and I hope you won't think I'm trying to dictate. It's a hard thing to give up such a sum of money as that and to surrender with it all the plans of your life. The thought of it staggers me. But we won't really suffer, Ellen, if that is the right way, for God will be with us. He'll open up other fields of service for us. So, if He tells you to do this thing we'll do it together, and I know He will bless us. But, as I said before, the decision is yours. I will never force you to do anything, and I'll stand by you whatever you do. I'm going to leave it to you and the Lord.''

After the door closed behind Chad, Eleanor tried again to study, but to no avail. At last she closed her books with a sigh and sat quietly in the big chair, turning over and over in her mind the difficult problem with which she was faced.

"If I didn't love Chad so much," she told herself, "I wouldn't care. But he wants me to tell about our marriage. I know he does—even though I lose all the money. Oh, I do want to serve Jesus Christ, since He loved me and bought me with His own blood. How nice it would be if Chad and I could dedicate ourselves together to God and live always for Him!''

"But your laboratory?" a voice whispered. "How about the wonderful work you plan to do together? It's not wrong to try to keep the money in order to serve humanity. In all your plans there isn't one selfish motive. It isn't wrong for you to love your husband, either. You work better with him. Together you and he will have a great ministry of healing. It would be absurd to give up this wonderful plan!''

Dear me! thought Eleanor. *I wonder if that minister we heard yesterday had any idea what a commotion he would stir up by his sermon. I'll never forget it. After I get the money, Chad and I will dedicate it and ourselves both to the Lord. I just can't take chances on losing it now, even though Chad wants me to. I'll tell him the price is too high. He'll be disappointed, but he said he'd stand by me in any case. Anyway, he'll be glad I have decided to give myself to God as soon as I get the money. Fifteen months isn't long. Then I'll give my whole life to God.*

12

Worn with her mental and spiritual battle, Eleanor undressed and was asleep almost as soon as her head touched the pillow. She was awakened by the sharp insistent ringing of the telephone. As she reached for her housecoat she glanced at the clock and then at the empty pillow beside her on the bed. Two o'clock and Chad not home! Sudden panic swept over her, and her hand trembled as she took up the receiver.

"Miss Stewart?"

"Yes."

"This is Memorial Hospital. Your brother has been slightly injured and is here. He is asking for you. Can you come?"

"Yes—oh, yes, I'll be there right away!"

She dialed a number and asked for a cab, then dressed with feverish haste. Her brother—Chad, of course. He would give his name and ask them to call her, and they would conclude she was his sister.

Eleanor told the driver to go as fast as he could, then huddled into a corner of the backseat and tried to pray. She could only manage to whisper through tight lips. "Oh, Chad, wait for me—I'm coming!"

Up the hospital steps she flew. She gave her name to the night clerk, and he motioned her to a room where she was met by an interne in white.

"Miss Stewart? Your brother is calling for you. We'll go right up. Be as quiet as you can."

"Is he—is it bad?"

"We can't say yet. He was brought in after having been found on the sidewalk, apparently struck by a drunken hit-and-run driver. We don't know how long he had been there, but he is suffering from exposure. We've had him in the emergency room, but we'll have to wait until morning for a more thorough examination. Perhaps your being here will quiet him now. He seems very restless and troubled."

The interne stopped before a large white door. Eleanor caught her quivering lip between her teeth, drew a long breath, and then approached the high bed behind the screen.

Chad lay there, looking as quiet and still as though he were asleep, but when he heard Eleanor's soft steps he opened his eyes and smiled tenderly.

"Ellen! I knew you'd come."

"Oh, my dear, what have they done to you?"

She leaned over and kissed him, and he closed his eyes again in happy relief.

Drawing up a hard, straight-backed chair Eleanor sat by the side of the bed and took Chad's hand in her own. It was cold and limp; so different from the strong hand that had held hers a few hours before. Choking back the tears, she sat quietly while minutes dragged past. She thought Chad was asleep, but when she changed the cramped position of her arm, he opened his eyes and in a far-away quiet voice said, "Ellen."

"Here, dear."

Will you do something for me?"

"Of course. Just tell me, Chad. I'll do everything I can."

"I think I'll be all right soon . . . I'm not feeling so bad . . . just tired. But Mother ought to know. Will you call Dean Harrison and have him call home?"

"Just as soon as morning comes."

"Call Professor Merritt, too. I won't be able to go to the lab for a few days, probably. And . . . Ellen?"

"Yes, dear heart."

"There's something else. Bob may come when the Dean calls, and maybe Mom too. They'll go to my room at Merritt's." Chad's breath was coming in short gasps. Eleanor tried to stop him, but he shook away her restraining hand. "No—let me speak. When you feel like it I want you to let folks know we're married, but not until then. If the folks come and don't find any of my things there, they'll wonder. Ellen, take my clothes and books back there, so they won't know.''

"Yes—yes, I will. Now dear, you must be quiet. I'll stay until you go to sleep.''

Ellen sat quietly stroking the dear hand until Chad's heavy breathing told her that he was really asleep. She was beginning to put her wraps on quietly when the interne came in.

"We gave him a heavy opiate,'' he said. "He will probably sleep several hours. We have a room here where you can lie down if you wish.''

"No,'' Ellen replied reluctantly. "If he will sleep I have some messages to send and some errands to attend to. I'll be back as soon as possible.''

It was with numb hands and a heart wrung with grief that Eleanor hastily packed Chad's clothes and books and a few other belongings into suitcases in order to carry them back to his old room. *Will he ever wear them again?* she wondered, looking with swimming eyes at the shirts she had ironed—was it yesterday? It seemed such a long time ago.

The taxi driver helped her move the boxes and suitcases up to the room over the garage, and then, while he waited below, she hurriedly hung the suits in the closet, laid the shirts in the drawers, piled books on the table and shelves, and even hung the laundry bag with its soiled garments on a hook in the closet.

At the hospital once more, she sat motionless by the bedside for several hours, never tiring of watching the beloved face on the pillow. At eight o'clock she called Dean Harrison and Professor Merritt, then resumed her post.

And her thoughts during these long hours of waiting? Eleanor lived again and again through the events of the preceding day, each time arriving at her final decision with a more bitter regret. She had been wrong. Deliberately. She had rejected the loving fellowship of the Master, and now He was letting her suffer. All the money in the world didn't mean anything compared with Chad. All she wanted now was to tell the whole world she was his own, his happy wife. If he would only get well again they would face the world together. Everything would be all right.

Eleanor bowed her head in her hands and prayed silently.

Oh, God, if you'll just save Chad and give him back to me, I'll give you all I have forever.

Reaching up, she unfastened the chain about her neck and slipped from it her wedding ring. For another hour she sat holding it in her hand, waiting with her heart beating hard for the moment when Chad's eyes would open.

He stirred at last and opened his eyes, to meet Ellen's smile and soft words, "Better, dear?"

"I'm fine now. I just feel light and empty. I probably need something to eat. Did you get everything taken care of?"

"All done. Don't worry about a thing."

"I won't," Chad said obediently.

Eleanor drew in a quick breath and said, "Chad—would you do something for me?"

"Of course, dear, if I can."

Eleanor opened her hand, and Chad saw the little gold ring lying in her palm. Then she held out her left hand.

"Will you put it on—where it belongs?"

A glad smile, almost unbelieving, illumined Chad's face. With unsteady fingers he picked up the ring, then looked for a long moment into her eyes and said, "Is it all right now?"

"All right," she answered tremulously.

Chad slipped the wedding ring on her finger, then pressed her hand to his lips. "Mrs. Charles Stewart, in public as well as in private," he whispered with a little of his old gaiety. Then, with a grateful smile, he added, "Oh, Ellen, Christ did solve the problem when we let Him."

All day he slept, and Eleanor did not leave him. Once the nurse care in and told her softly that a Dean Harrison and a Professor Merritt had called downstairs but had not been permitted to come up to Mr. Stewart's room. Dean Harrison had left a message that the young man's brother would arrive that evening.

But as the afternoon wore on, and Chad still slept, a heavy foreboding took possession of Eleanor's heart. When the rosy sunset light filled the white room, Chad finally opened his eyes again and smiled.

"It *is* all right, isn't it, Ellen?"

"All right, dearest."

When the nurse came in a few moments later, Eleanor was on her knees by the bedside, and Chad lay smiling peacefully. Eleanor looked up questioningly as the nurse reached for his pulse and then turned away. He had fallen asleep once more. But this time he would not wake.

13

All that night Eleanor walked around the apartment with wide, tearless eyes. From one room to the other she wandered, dwelling on every minute of the day just passed. It couldn't be true! She'd wake up in the morning and see Chad's tousled head on the pillow, and they would have a good laugh over her nightmare. God didn't let things like this happen. Hadn't she told Him that if He'd save Chad she would love and serve Him forever? Didn't He want her life in service? Maybe He thought she wasn't worthy of Chad. She hadn't been, of course, but she was trying, and with Chad helping her she could have grown into something worthwhile.

But He had rejected her. He had heard her promise and then taken Chad away. He had left her all alone, for there was nothing left. Did people go on living like this? Would the body keep moving with the heart completely dead?

She had laughed at Chad for taking out life insurance. People like him, young and strong, didn't die. Old people died. But Chad was dead, and she had never had a chance to tell a soul she was his wife. God hadn't heard her prayer. Then her promise to Him was void!

Relieved of that promise, she would go back to the life she had known before Chad entered it. In all this awful crash, one thing remained—her work. From now on she would work, work, work—and forget. Perhaps some day this painfully wonderful year would be blotted out of her memory. Surely if one practiced forgetting, practiced hard and continually, one could forget!

Chad's things were gone from the apartment, and she was glad. They would only have brought back painful memories. As soon as possible she would leave too and go somewhere in the city where no one knew her. She would go to Chad's funeral, of course, and tell him good-bye forever, and then she would set to work.

As the light of a new day began to dawn, Eleanor saw on the table Chad's Bible, which she had forgotten to carry away. Well, if she had renounced God, she certainly did not want His Book lying around. Without opening it she thrust it quickly into the back of a dresser drawer. She would send it to Chad's mother. She was the kind of person who pleased God by taking His chastenings meekly; she would have more use for the Bible. Eleanor didn't intend to read it anymore.

Suddenly she stood transfixed as her gaze rested on the narrow gold band on her left hand. A long moment she hesitated, then with a quick gesture slipped it off. Finding the blue velvet box it had come in, she replaced it in its satin bed, then snapped the cover shut.

Early that morning she telephoned Carolyn Fleet. Trying to keep her voice even, she said, ''Carolyn, remember Chad Stewart? He died last night after being struck by an automobile. I suppose the funeral will be back at his home. I want to go, but not alone. If you and Fred will make the trip with me, I will pay your expenses and for the time you lose from your teaching.''

''Oh, my dear!'' answered Carolyn. She had always wondered how things stood between Eleanor and Chad. ''I'm so sorry. Can I come and stay with you today? I can do it easily.''

''I don't want you to miss school.''

''That's quite all right. I'm coming up as soon as I can get there. What is your address now?''

Eleanor gave her the address dully, realizing that Carolyn would never guess by the appearance of the apartment that Chad had lived there until two nights before.

When Carolyn arrived, intending to comfort Eleanor as best she could, she found a difficult task confronting her. Eleanor was so poised and quiet the older woman was at a loss for words.

Although Carolyn had never suspected their true relationship, she knew that Eleanor and Chad had been deeply attached to each other; and this stony calm on Eleanor's part perplexed her.

In the afternoon they went together to the University chapel where the quiet figure was to lie for a few hours before starting the journey home. Chad looked so peaceful and happy that Carolyn found it hard to realize it was death she was looking upon. Eleanor took one or two deep breaths but otherwise showed no emotion at all. A few other students who had been in the chapel departed quietly when they saw "Stewart's girlfriend" come in, and in a short time Carolyn too slipped out unobtrusively, leaving Eleanor alone with her dead.

When Carolyn finally re-entered the chapel, Eleanor was sitting quietly in a seat, her eyes fixed on the stained glass window. She left with Carolyn without a backward glance.

Through the long hours of the night as they traveled on the jerky little train that bore them northward, Eleanor lay back against the pillow she had rented from the conductor and kept her eyes closed. Only occasional restlessness gave evidence that she was not asleep.

Fred and Carolyn in the seat across the aisle slept fitfully. Whenever they wakened they turned anxious eyes on the girl and were vaguely disturbed by her unnatural quietness.

In the early morning they alighted at the little town and rested for a few hours before going out to the country church where the service was to be held. Carolyn and Fred tried to talk, but they soon realized that Eleanor did not hear them, and, feeling that she desired it, they left her alone.

That afternoon as they drove over the gravel roads running between fields of dry stubble and through timberland, Carolyn chatted idly with Fred, who sat by the driver. If addressed, Eleanor replied politely, but the rest of the time she sat quietly. But her thoughts were busy. Remembering Chad's description of them, she identified with mixed emotions the big brick high school where Chad had studied for four years; the country road over which he had walked every day; the bridge from which he had once dived and almost lost his life; the fields where he had toiled during the summer, and finally, the church with the cemetery on the hill behind it.

As they entered the church, Carolyn became conscious that many pairs of eyes followed the "city strangers." Ellen walked as if alone, her eyes fixed on the flower-banked couch at the front; and Carolyn had to touch her arm to lead her to a seat. A young woman was playing softly on the upright piano, and the church was rapidly filling. Eleanor was beginning to wonder how long she could endure this hush, when a sober-faced little group came down the aisle and occupied the pews that had been reserved at the front.

Eleanor recognized them immediately. The white-haired woman was Chad's beloved "Mom." The tall dark young man was Bob, and the girl who resembled him, sister Connie. A pair of long, blonde braids identified Chad's "special" little sister, Mary Lou. The other girl in the pew was probably Bob's fiancée, Marilyn. Eleanor wondered what would happen if she were to walk over and seat herself at Marilyn's side—if she should tell the family and friends that she had been nearest and dearest to Chad. In order to keep her thoughts away from that quiet figure at the front, she went over and over the possibilities of this scene until she feared she would actually speak out.

Then she looked out the window, and the watchful Carolyn saw such a spasm of pain cross her face that she slipped an arm around Eleanor's shoulders. Glancing out the window, she tried to ascertain the cause of the distress, but all she saw was a small country churchyard with tombstones tipped at all degrees, and in one corner a rustic bench under a tree.

The service was not one of morbid grief. The young people grouped around the piano sang hymns of hope and assurance, and the same note was echoed in the brief message. The preacher was even joyful as he told of the spiritual experiences Chad had described to him the previous summer.

Tall youths, Chad's friends, carried him up the hill to his last resting place, while the young folk at the head of the procession sang again "Asleep in Jesus, Blessed Sleep." Eleanor would not look at the grave but stood at the edge of the crowd. Just as the minister's voice ceased, she heard a shrill childish voice cry out, "Oh, Mommy, I don't want them to do that to my Chad!"

92

Sobbing little Mary Lou was lifted into brother Bob's arms, where she buried her head against his shoulder.

As the quiet group moved away, Carolyn said, "Will you go with me to speak to Chad's mother, Eleanor?"

"No! And if anyone tries to speak to me, don't let him!" She walked swiftly to the bench in the corner, waiting for Carolyn to rejoin her. Without a glance at the flower-heaped mound, she went away.

After Fred and Carolyn had left Eleanor at her apartment, Carolyn said, "There's more to this than we know, Fred. This isn't any ordinary grief we've seen. If Eleanor doesn't relax and let herself have a good cry, her nerves will snap."

"We'll have to keep in touch with her and try to cheer her up," Fred responded.

Fred and Carolyn fully intended to keep this good resolution, but a sudden illness on the part of their son, in addition to the responsibilities of teaching school, diverted their energies, and weeks passed before they had time for her again.

14

On Friday morning to the surprise of Professor Nichols, Eleanor appeared in the laboratory as usual.

"Miss Eleanor, I am at a loss for words which would console you on the loss of your young friend," he began uncertainly. "If you would like to take a short interlude of several days before starting your work—"

"Thank you, Professor Nichols," a quiet voice replied. "The best consolation I can find is in my work. Do you mind if I stay here all day and continue last week's experiments?"

Last week! Eleanor thought. *Was that when I left this work unfinished to go off into a different world with a boy I once knew? Was last week Thanksgiving, and was Chad here?*

She resumed her work diligently, and the old gentleman began to wonder whether he had been mistaken about her having cared for the Stewart boy, since she was apparently so indifferent to his tragic death.

* * *

The proofs of the book had been returned. There was much painstaking labor ahead for both the professor and his assistant, and into it they now plunged whole-heartedly. The professor tired quickly these days, so Eleanor found herself bearing the heavy end of the burden, checking and rechecking the precious

94

pages that had to be so accurate. But hard work left little time for wandering thoughts, for which she was thankful.

On Sunday morning Eleanor cleaned the apartment in desperation. Windows, cupboards, floors, were scrubbed until they shone. As lunchtime approached, Eleanor dared not trust herself to sit down alone at the table, so she made a cheese sandwich and ate it as she walked about. In the afternoon she began to mend, although there was no further need of practicing such economy. After an hour had passed, Eleanor rose and went to a drawer to find some hose that needed darning. There lay a pair of Chad's socks.

The suddenness of finding them there broke through the armor she had forged for her soul, and as she caught them up to her cheek convulsively, the cry "Oh, Chad!" escaped her.

How she longed to sit down and give way to her grief! But that would never do. She was doing too well at controlling her emotions to give way now. So she brushed her hair, put on her wraps, and went for a long walk, a walk that left her so exhausted she could do nothing else but sleep that night.

When she awakened the next morning the sun was shining brightly through the window, and with a quick cry of "Chad! We're late!" Eleanor sat straight up in bed. But the empty pillow brought a return of memory, and it was an hour before she could assume her wonted calm. With it came a grim determination: today she would leave the apartment and never come back. All morning she worked, packing dishes and linens to send to the lake. A telephone call to the university revealed that there was a room available in one of the women's dormitories, so Eleanor sought out the landlord of the apartment, paid him an extra month's rent in lieu of the notice she should have given, and gave him shipping instructions for the packed boxes.

Handing him the keys, she walked away without a backward glance. It was too hard to look back. It was even harder to look ahead, if she let her gaze rove from the goal of hard work and success that she had set for herself. Only one thing was left in life for Eleanor Stewart—to work so hard that success would be hers, and so hard that two undesirable elements would be crowded out. One element was dreams. The other was memory.

One week before Christmas Eleanor received a letter from Carolyn Fleet. It read:

My dear Eleanor:

I am ashamed not to have written you ere this. But Jerry has been very ill and all my thought and time have been given to him. He is better now, and our hearts are full of gratitude to God. We cannot have the usual Christmas hilarity, but we plan a quiet day with our youngsters, and both Fred and I would like to have you with us. Can't you come for the week? Or if not for so long, at least for the day? If you will say yes, Fred will drive in to get you. We really want you.

Love,
Carolyn

Eleanor's answer left Carolyn troubled:

Dear Carolyn:

Thank you very much for your thoughtful kindness. A friendship like yours deserves a better object. I could not possibly prove a pleasant guest this year. And your children should have the best the day can give, especially since they were separated from you last year.

I am expecting to spent the day working, for there is real need for haste on the book if it is to get done before Professor Nichols goes to California for some lectures he has promised to give at Stanwyk University. He wants me to go along, and I may do so. It may be more beneficial to me than regular school work.

In any case, I shall be very busy. Don't worry about me, dear friend.

With love,
Eleanor

The next day another letter arrived. Over it Eleanor spent more time. It had been delayed in delivery, for the address was only "Care of the Registrar." When Eleanor saw the postmark she sat for many minutes turning it over in her hands. Finally, drawing a long, deep breath, she opened it. The color came and went in her face as she read:

Dear Miss Stewart:

In looking through Chad's books and papers which were sent home to us, your name has recurred so frequently that we believe you must have held a large place in Chad's heart. Our hearts all go out affectionately to the girl who meant so much to our boy. We knew last summer that some deeper emotion had wrought a change in him, and felt that it was not just the 'cousinly' affection he laughingly declared it, when Mary Lou asked about the frequent letters he received.

Am I presuming too much, my dear, in thinking that your sorrow is as deep as our own at this time? We all feel that anyone whom Chad loved is dear to us, and belongs with us at this Christmastide, which will be a hard one for us. Will you not come and spend it with us?

Of course, if you have dear ones of your own, we would not ask you to leave them. But if you have no other plans we would like to have you here. My other son is to be married quietly during Christmas week, and we will try to make it a time full of God's peace and joy, even though it cannot be a merry one.

We have been praying for you and want to know and love you for your own sake as well as Chad's.

> Sincerely,
> Margaret Stewart

Eleanor's first impulse was to accept. Her heart went out in a rush of longing to know these people who were Chad's own. She wanted to cuddle little Mary Lou in her arms, to help Connie with the wedding plans, to feel around her the arms that had rocked the baby Chad, and to lay her head on that shoulder where he had slept. The way she had chosen to follow was a lonely one, and the fellowship and love of the Stewart family would mean much to her.

But a memory of Chad's voice came.

"We won't go back, dear, till you can go as my wife."

Well, he had gone—without her. If she went now it would be only as his friend. Could she do that? She recalled the faces of all the family as she had seen them on the day of the funeral, and her longing at that time to take her rightful place among them. No, she was not strong enough to go through with it. She could endure anything but kindness. Their kindness would probably draw out from her the whole story, and then her ambition—the only thing left to her by the recent tragedy—would be forever frustrated. Whatever happened, she must avoid Chad's family.

Eleanor drew out her note paper and in a few moments her pen was flying over the paper.

Dear Mrs. Stewart:

It was kind of you to ask me to spend Christmas with you, but it is necessary to refuse the invitation. I am very busy with some scientific work and have neither the time nor inclination for any social contacts.

Wishing all of you the best the season has to offer, I am

Very truly yours,
Eleanor Stewart

There! she thought decisively, sealing the envelope quickly as though she were afraid she might change her mind. *Now they probably won't even write any more; and it's just as well.*

Eleanor spent Christmas working alone in the laboratory. The Professor, on having heard her holiday plans, invited her to spend the day with him and his wife, but he had learned recently that Miss Eleanor was happier when left alone, so he did not urge the invitation too strongly.

* * *

The corrected proofs of the book went to the publisher the last week in January, and the day after they were mailed Professor and Mrs. Nichols boarded a train for California. Eleanor had given them a half-promise that when she finished writing a term paper she might follow them. At one time in her life she would have grasped such an opportunity for travel and wider experience in her field; but as she turned away from the station where she had gone to see the old couple off, she realized that it mattered little to her whether she went or stayed.

To Eleanor, work was the solution of all difficulties. She now plunged recklessly into study and research, and after several weeks of labor the paper lay on her desk neatly typed and bound.

But California was out of the question. That same night she walked to the telegraph office and wrote out a telegram:

PROFESSOR L F NICHOLS
SUNNY PLAZA HOTEL
LOS ANGELES CALIFORNIA
SORRY IMPOSSIBLE FOR ME
TO COME BEST
WISHES FOR LECTURES
ELEANOR STEWART

Eleanor handed the yellow sheet to operator at the desk, then turned and walked out the door. She did not go home, however. For several hours she walked up one snowy street and down another, alone except for occasional passers-by, from whose gaze the darkness shielded her troubled face. Sometimes she tried unsuccessfully to pray, sometimes she tried to make herself believe that this was all a dream from which she would wake up secure and happy. And sometimes she merely smiled sardonically, thinking wryly that Fortune plays strange tricks on people who try to manage their lives to please themselves.

At last, noticing by a clock in a store window that it was nearly midnight, Eleanor turned her weary steps homeward. Climbing the narrow steps to her room she opened the door, and without turning on the light, flung herself face down on the cot. There was nothing left to do but face the facts.

"Oh, Chad," Eleanor whispered softly, "if you had only known!"

But Chad had died without knowing what Eleanor had now learned—that during the coming summer, his child would be born.

15

Eleanor awoke with the sun streaming into her face. She had slept all night without undressing and was now cold and stiff. She drew a blanket over herself and lay quietly, letting a full realization of her difficulties come over her again.

Did ever any girl have such troubles as I? she thought. *Or was anyone so much alone?*

Thoughts of Chad crowded in. Sweet thoughts, thoughts that heretofore Eleanor had diligently routed. The longing for him seemed unbearable. If only she could feel that even though dead, he was near her! She had heard that sometimes husbands and wives loved so deeply that the presence of the departed one lingered and kept the other from loneliness. Surely she had loved Chad as much as anyone ever had loved a husband. But he was completely gone, and the silence and emptiness were unbroken.

Perhaps if she were to go back where he used to be, she could draw him close again!

Eleanor dressed quickly and went to the library to one particular corner where Chad had preferred to sit with his books. There sprawled a fat, pimply-faced youth munching potato chips. She turned away with a shiver.

Next she tried the room at the laboratory where they had eaten their lunches. Peering in quietly at the door, she saw a new assistant busily rearranging the room. Apparently he had taken away the little table they had used to spread out their sandwiches and books.

Our apartment, thought Eleanor. *I'll go there!*

The streetcar was filled with laboring men in blue overalls just coming off their shift in the mill instead of the students Eleanor and Chad had always seen. Eleanor swayed back and forth on the strap and formulated her plan. If the apartment were still vacant, she would see the landlord and ask him if she might go in to look for a ring she had lost. And maybe she would find Chad there.

But the windows were not empty. From the street Eleanor could see a little fuzzy head over the back of a high chair, and in another window a tiny blue sweater drying on a frame. There was nothing here to help her, and she turned away disconsolately.

Suddenly a thought came to her. *The cottage!* she exclaimed almost aloud. *I must go there! I can rest there, and I do believe Chad will be there waiting for me!*

By mid-afternoon Eleanor had packed her few possessions into trunks, called the express company, turned in her room keys, and notified the registrar that she was dropping her classes. She was almost happy as she started for the railroad station.

It was growing dark when the train stopped at the flag station to let off a young lady passenger, and by the time she had walked a mile and a half through the woods to the cottage, night had fallen. But Eleanor was not afraid. This was familiar ground. As she opened the door to the big living room the chill air smote her; but as soon as she had turned on the light she felt better.

Hurrying across the floor, she stopped and touched a match to the paper under the logs and kindling that Chad had laid there weeks before. The davenport was still before the fireplace and seemed to reach out friendly, inviting arms. So Eleanor disappeared into the bedroom to come back in a moment with pillows and blankets. Then, while the fire snapped and crackled, she lay on the couch where she had sat with Chad and, for the first time since his death, allowed herself to think freely of him. As she stared at the flames, her eyes grew heavy, and finally dropped in sleep. And once more she was wandering through the autumn woods with Chad laughing beside her.

He still seemed near the next morning, and all day as Eleanor roamed the house the presence lingered. The whole cottage was to her a picture gallery, with each room and corner bringing back its remembrance.

I'll stay right here, Eleanor thought, comparing this sweet comfort with the emptiness of the past weeks. *The house is tight, and the furnace good. The farmer will bring in my groceries from town, and I needn't work anymore. I'm tired, and I'll just stay here and live with my memory pictures of Chad.*

She had no difficulty arranging matters. Sven Oleson, the young farmer, had just moved out to the farm and was eager to please. His mother-in-law lived with them and would be glad to help Eleanor with the housework.

After a few weeks, however, Hulda came to the cottage to stay. She loved to scour and sweep and to spend hours in the kitchen cooking and baking dishes that she hoped would increase the young lady's lagging appetite. She also tried to interest Eleanor in cooking and sewing, but soon found her efforts were useless.

Eleanor cared only for the picture gallery. When she worked about with old Hulda, reality pressed too closely upon her, and the pain in her breast awoke to life again. So she let Hulda do the work, and she wandered through the woods, talking to the presence at her side. Or she lay before the fire dreaming that Chad's arms were around her.

Occasionally there were bad times when the pictures faded, and Eleanor knew it was foolish to deceive herself. But the dreams were so pleasant and the reality so cruel that more and more she took refuge in her memories.

When April came, she gathered wild flowers and mosses and built the rock garden she and Chad had planned. In May the woods were full of flowers, and she made the collection they had intended to do together. Many hours were spent with her camera. Eleanor was glad she had fitted up a darkroom to develop pictures, for the presence seemed very near in the darkness.

She secured wild flower and bird slides so exquisite that she thrilled to their beauty. As she worked she would murmur softly, "We'll put these in a book someday, won't we, Chad?"

Late in June, when the strawberries were red under the green leaves, and the young robins had all learned to fly away from the nest by the porch, Eleanor told Hulda good-bye and locked the door of the cottage again.

"You'll be comin' back again after a while, won't you?" asked the old lady, with tears in her eyes, for Eleanor had grown very dear to her. "Comin' back and bringin' the little one?"

But Eleanor kissed the wrinkled hand lying on her own round arm and said absently, "I don't know Hulda. I'll let you know."

16

August. The white walls of a hospital. High beds, and blurred pictures of doctors and nurses coming and going, bright lights, and finally a thin, wailing little cry.

"You have a son, Mrs. Stewart," the doctor said.

Eleanor nodded apathetically, and the doctor wondered.

On a sunny, shimmering afternoon the nurse let her go out on the sun porch. After the nurse had taken the baby back to his basket in the nursery, Eleanor lay in the long deck chair and let her gaze wander across the valley to the far-off hills with purple shadows beneath them and white clouds above. Near at hand all she could see were the tops of the trees clustering about the hospital. As she looked down at them, the soft green appeared so restful Eleanor imagined it to be a great, cool, bed into which she could sink down, down until she found sleep and oblivion. Lying with half-closed eyes quietly gazing at that cool, green bed, Eleanor finally drifted off into the first really sound sleep she had had in weeks.

She was awakened by the sound of voices coming from the other end of the porch. The screen and some palms hid her from view, and she could not help but listen, as the voices carried clearly to her ears. She was able to identify one voice as that of her doctor; the other was unfamiliar.

"Those are the only two babies I could find," Dr. Durbin said. "I called up three different hospitals, and this one little Italian girl baby is the only one available on such short notice. The nurse said she is a beautiful child. The little fellow we have here is not so attractive, as you noticed. We thought at first he wouldn't pull through, but he is finally starting to take hold on life. He may be a fine fellow yet. That's all I can do for you. Take your choice.''

Eleanor held her breath and listened intently.

"Well, I want a nice healthy one, but certainly not an Italian,'' the other voice said. "And I have to have some baby at once. Isn't there any other source to which you could go?''

"Man, we don't have baby factories! Sane people like to keep their babies. You'd better take the little girl and be glad you got her.''

"I tell you an Italian child won't do. Tell me about the boy again.''

"Not much to tell.'' Was there contempt in Dr. Durbin's voice? "The mother says the father was killed last winter. Insists she can't care for the child and doesn't seem interested in it. I feel that she came here to this little place to get away from the notice of friends or relatives. There's one thing—she says the baby must be placed with Christian parents. Aside from that condition, she apparently wants only to forget it.''

"What if she should some day change her mind and try to claim it?''

"Not a chance. She'll never know where it is. It wouldn't be fair to the foster parents for a real parent to have any information that might make for trouble later.''

"Well—'' and a chair scraped back "—I guess it will have to be the boy, then. I wish I had more time, but I haven't. Let's go look at him again.''

Another chair scraped, then footsteps faded away down the corridor. Eleanor lay with a pale, expressionless face. Perhaps some day she would wake up and feel sorry. Just now she couldn't feel anything except an utter weariness of life. There was a great lump in her breast that left no room for joy or sorrow.

She ought to be feeling very bad now. This was her baby being given away like a kitten or a puppy—but she couldn't believe it. Once when she was a little girl she had grieved for days after seeing a little, squirming, blind ball of fur separated from the mother collie. But she was not grieving now. When this little bundle of flannel she saw five times a day was taken away, it would mean that that part of her life, of which it was the only remnant, would be forever past. She would be glad when it was over. At least she hoped she would be glad again. It was so long since she had been glad about anything.

"As soon as I can get out of here I'll go back to college," Eleanor told herself with a firm set to her lips. "I'll work harder than ever. I'll fill the days with study and work, and I'll have my dreams to help me through the nights. I'll manage to live. Strange how I keep on living with only a hard, cold lump instead of a heart. I suppose I'll get used to it. I may even find happiness in my work—a real kind of happiness that will fill my time and give me peace."

Happiness! Once she had been happy in a different way, she reflected. But she didn't want to be happy that way again. It hurt too much. This dead feeling was better. She didn't feel dead like this at night anyway, when she could go back into the memory gallery to gather courage and strength for the next day's ordeal. Somehow she would show the world yet.

The next afternoon Dr. Durbin and a lawyer came to Eleanor with a sheaf of papers to sign. They were surprised that she asked no questions but seemed eager to sign her name and have them go away. She wrote "Eleanor Stewart" firmly across the bottom of each document, then turned her head away and closed her eyes. It was done. The baby was no longer hers. Her last bridge was burned behind her, and her work lay ahead.

* * *

In October, when classes resumed at the university, Eleanor registered for work once more. The leaves were red and brown and golden on the big old campus trees, but she could see only her books. She paid no attention to the clear, blue days when the smoke from burning leaves give the air an acrid tang. She never noticed the sparkling, frosty nights. She studied, studied. It would take work to make up what she had missed last spring if she were to graduate with her class. But she could do it, and then—next year—graduate medical school!

But in a few weeks Eleanor realized that something was wrong. Her mind seemed strangely loath to take up the burden again, and the old trick of easy memorizing had slipped from her. Worst of all, the dreams did not return so easily at night.

"I have my mind on too many things," Eleanor rationalized. "After I get caught up with my classes and get everything under control again, I'll relax and dream."

November brought gray days and dull skies, and while the campus resounded with gaily shouted plans for the Thanksgiving holidays, Eleanor's voice was not heard. She was working. The nights were becoming things of such loneliness that she made them as short as possible by working late and getting up early. So tired was she when she finally did lie down, that sleep eluded her completely. Hour after hour she lay looking at the dark ceiling, going over the day's lectures or trying to quiet herself enough to let the dreams come again. Try as she might, she could not quite capture the mood of dreams—and she was heartsick for them.

"I'm working too hard," she would say, pulling her pillow restlessly into another angle. "I'll take a day or two to rest and relax, and then I'll find the picture gallery again. I'll take four days at Thanksgiving and do nothing but dream. I'll have Chad with me again then."

Relaxation does not come at call. When Thanksgiving came and Eleanor lay down to find her dreams, she was sorely disappointed. Hour by hour she could reconstruct the events of the year before, those beautiful days at the lake, but when she tried to relive them, to make Chad's presence real again, everything faded. Sometimes she could catch a glimpse of his figure, but if she drew near and tried to see his face it vanished.

Then she would lie and try with all her powers to picture Chad's face. How the hair lay back from his forehead in a golden wave. How his eyes twinkled in laughter and his lips curved in an ever-ready smile . . .

"It's no use!" her lips trembled. "Even his face is gone from me now!"

Swiftly she sat up and turned on the light, then began to hunt through her desk for a picture of Chad. Surely she had one!

Of course most of her pictures were at the lake with her cameras, but there must be some little snapshot here.

But there was none.

The next day she went up to the library and asked for a copy of the yearbook of two years previous. Swiftly she turned over the shiny pages until she found a picture of Professor Merritt's laboratory, showing the professor and his three assistants at work. One of them must be Chad, but the picture was not clear, and Eleanor felt no recognition as she looked at it. That wasn't her Chad . . .

When the Thanksgiving holiday was over, Eleanor was glad to go back to school. She studied harder than ever, hoping to get tired and to sleep, and in that sleep to find her dreams again. She did get tired. But she did not sleep.

One night as she lay staring into the darkness trying vainly to bring Chad's face back out of the shadows, she began to grow resentful. "Life could have been so beautiful and useful if circumstances had been different. What right did anyone have to try to control me in that way? If Chad and I could have had the money with no strings attached, we could have lived fruitfully through years and years of service. From the beginning our marriage was clouded by the shadow of that money.

"Or if Chad hadn't gone home that summer we still might have worked everything out. It was his visit home that stirred him up and made him dissatisfied. His mother and her prayers changed Chad—made him want to tell of our marriage—and that caused the discussion which made him leave that night. If he hadn't been so troubled and absent-minded he might have seen the car before it hit him . . ."

Eleanor now had a new line of thought. Her tortured brain began, during the long sleepless nights, to build up resentment —not against Aunt Ruth, for she was gone—but against Chad's family, especially his mother. The resentment became a poison in her soul.

A few days before Christmas, another note came from the farm up north—not an invitation this time, but just a message of hope and cheer, a wish that the year ahead might be filled with God's blessing. Accompanying the note was a box of home-made cookies wrapped in green tissue, tied with a red ribbon, and trimmed with a fragrant cedar spray.

Her lips set in determination, Eleanor tore the note in two, tossed it into the wastebasket, and after a moment's hesitation, threw the box after it.

That night Eleanor slept, and she dreamed of Chad. But he had his back to her, and every time she drew near he ran away. He had something in his arms that cried out as he ran, and then she knew he was holding a baby—their baby! Chad had it and wouldn't let her see it!

Perspiration was standing out on Eleanor's forehead when she awoke in terror. Switching on the light, she looked at the clock. Half-past two. There would be no more sleep for her that night, she knew, so she took out her books and began to study.

Later that morning Eleanor walked into the drugstore near the campus and asked for a drug she remembered buying for Aunt Ruth when the pain became too severe to be borne. A sleeping powder would insure her getting a few hours of sleep when she became too weary at night to study any longer.

That night Elanor took her first dose, and was so gratified with the results that she repeated the experiment the next night, and the next. Soon the habit of taking a powder before going to bed was well established, and Eleanor now slept regularly—but was not rested. As the quarter drew to a close, she knew that her grades would be far below any she had ever before received, because even though she was doing her best, that best was not very good.

Loneliness began to overwhelm her in the daytime, too. She drew away from her classmates, afraid that in a moment of weakness she would tell the whole wretched story to a sympathetic listener.

Then a new presence began to haunt her. It was the face of her baby.

Sometimes when she tried to study, the little face would come between her eyes and the book. When she walked the streets in desperation, trying to evade it, it followed. There was only one place where the baby's face did not come, and that was into Eleanor's drugged sleep; so she began going to bed earlier and taking larger doses of the sedative. She would awaken heavy-eyed and pale in the early morning and try once more to study. But her mind refused to obey orders anymore, and when Eleanor finally wrote her quarterly examinations, she was afraid to re-read what she had written. But at last examinations were at an end.

Eleanor was idly thumbing over back numbers of magazines, looking at pictures of babies, when a message was delivered to her. Mrs. Martin, the dean of women, wished to see Miss Eleanor Stewart in her office. In trepidation Eleanor set out.

The dean was very kind. Surely Miss Stewart knew that her work was not up to its previous standard. Was something wrong? She did not look well. She looked tired. Since she apparently needed a rest, why not take a vacation . . . enter a sanitarium . . . travel, if possible. . . . At any rate, it was advisable for Miss Stewart to leave school and finish later, for her own good.

Snow was flying through the cold, sharp air when Eleanor came out of the administration building. Her thoughts in a turmoil, she turned her steps toward the lake hardly feeling the chill wind. She, Eleanor Stewart, had been advised to leave school! She who had been the brilliant scholar, the promising bacteriologist, the benefactor of mankind, advised not to finish college!

Along the lakeshore the wind was so strong that Eleanor could hardly hold her course; but she kept on walking until she reached a place where huge blocks of stone were piled to hold back the ceaselessly pounding breakers. Oblivious to the cold, Eleanor perched on a great slab and looked out over the gray lake. For the first time in her life, she admitted utter defeat. She had consoled herself for every loss with the thought of an all-engrossing profession in which she could excel and make the world take notice—and now that, her last solace in life, was gone.

Why has all this happened to me? she asked herself, bitterly. *Is there any possible way to find peace? I don't even ask happiness anymore—just peace enough to live on.* Her eyes swept the gray expanse, cheerlessly. Did she want to live? It would be so easy to go to sleep once for all in the great gray bed. Not a soul in the would care, and at last she would find peace.

Or would she? Yes, if death were only an eternal sleep. But then that would mean Chad was asleep. And he wasn't. Somewhere he must surely be alive and waiting for her. Dying would mean meeting him, and she wasn't ready. She must get ready. A sudden thought brought a glimmer of hope. Maybe if she were to do the things she should, God would let her die and go to Chad!

A new chain of reasoning quickly formed itself in Eleanor's mind. Perhaps the reason she had lost Chad was that she had turned her back on God, and then God took Chad from her to punish her. If she went back and undid all the wrong, perhaps God would forgive her and let her be happy again. Of course Chad was gone, and the baby was gone, but if she could just find Chad's face and smile in her gallery of memory, if she could just hear his voice in her dreams once more, everything would be all right.

Eleanor's eyes sparkled hopefully as she got down from the great slab and began walking back to the campus, laying her plans as she went. First she would go to see the lawyer and tell him about her marriage. Then she would go to Chad's mother and tell her. Next—what next? Oh, yes—she would find a little baby whose mother didn't want it, and she would work to support it. Ruefully Eleanor realized she would *have* to work, as Aunt Ruth's money would be gone. But if she could have Chad's smile back, she would be happy scrubbing floors, if need be.

Eleanor arrived back at her room shaking with cold, but she did not rest. She worked diligently until once more all her possessions were packed, ready to be taken away. This was the second time she had left the university suddenly. The last time she had left in despair. This time things were going to be better!

17

John R. Hastings, Attorney-at-Law,'' the gold letters on the door said. Eleanor pushed the door open with some trepidation, now that the moment for revealing her marriage was actually at hand.

Mr. Hastings's secretary, who also acted as his receptionist, looked curiously at the girl standing before her. *She must be young, but she looks old,* she thought. *The circles under her eyes! Her clothes are nice, but it looks like she wouldn't even care if she got them on inside out. Those gloves don't match. She sure is nervous . . .*

But she merely said, "Do you have an appointment?"

"Well, no—that is, Mr. Hastings knows me, and I'm sure he'll see me. Just tell him Miss Eleanor Stewart is here."

Mentally the secretary retorted, as she rose to enter the inner office, *And you'll stay a "Miss" as long as you look like that, girlie. Why don't you get some rest?*

In a few moments she returned. "Mr. Hastings will see you now."

The white-haired old lawyer rose to greet Eleanor with an outstretched hand. "Miss Stewart! I had planned to write you this very week relative to the settlement of the estate, and now you have saved me the trouble. There will be just a few formalities for you to attend to, then the money will be yours."

A shadow lingered in the doorway. "That will be all for now, Miss Cox," Mr. Hastings said, and the door closed impatiently. It would have been interesting to know what this big-eyed, pale-faced girl had to do with an estate and money. But the typewriter keys began to rattle again.

Eleanor's heart pounded against her side as she drew in her breath to begin. It would be hard, of course, but that was part of the atonement she was making.

"Mr. Hastings, I came up to tell you I'm not going to get any money."

"You what?"

"The money isn't rightfully mine. I came to tell you I'm not entitled to it. I—I—I've been married." There! It was out.

Dismay and consternation spread over the old gentleman's face. "Tell me about it," he said gently.

In a few words Eleanor laid before him the whole story. As she talked, he shook his head occasionally but did not speak. "Is that all?" he asked.

At length she paused. "That's all."

"You know what this means?" he asked, regretfully.

"Yes, I know."

"I am very sorry—I never had any idea—" he stammered, at a loss for words.

"If you feel sorry for me because I am losing the money," Eleanor said quietly, "don't bother. I don't care about it at all. Other things are much more important. If I have to sign any papers or anything, I'll do it now."

Mr. Hastings arose and went slowly into the inmost room, while Eleanor waited listlessly. Her head ached, and her hands were cold and numb. She wished all this were over so she could go to bed and rest, rest until she wasn't tired anymore.

Carrying a bundle of papers, the old man returned. "This is the entire file of papers," he said. "I will have Miss Cox prepare them, and if you care to wait you can sign them after lunch. Completion of the formalities, however, will necessarily await your birthday, ten days from now."

Mr. Hastings leafed through the documents again, then started at the sight of an envelope that had slipped into the folds of a larger paper.

"The sealed envelope!" he exclaimed.

"What is it?" asked Eleanor curiously.

"Here," he said, handing her the envelope, "is something your aunt gave me a week before her death. She instructed me not to open it but to keep it for you in case you had reason to claim it. I had forgotten about its existence until just now."

Eleanor glanced with some interest at the envelope, which bore in a dear, familiar handwriting the words "To My Niece Eleanor Stewart, In Case She Marries Before Her Twenty-fifth Birthday."

Wonderingly Eleanor tore open the missive, while Mr. Hastings looked on with interest. Eleanor read in a low voice:

My Dear Eleanor:

I have always been fond of surprising you and am taking one more opportunity of doing so. You will not receive this unless you are courageous enough to marry before you are twenty-five, in spite of the fact that, so far as you know, it will have cost you your entire fortune. Yours must be real love, not a foolish whim such as ruined my life. May God bless you, my dear. I want you to have my property regardless. Enclosed in this envelope is a new will, which will void the one that will be read after my funeral. Even Mr. Hastings does not know of this arrangement. May the money bring you and your husband, whom I wish I could know, only happiness.

Love,
Aunt Ruth

Eleanor had become deadly pale. She handed all the papers back to the old gentleman saying unsteadily, "I don't understand."

"I do," he said with a smile. "You are to be congratulated. Mrs. Edwards has surprised both of us. Instead of forfeiting the inheritance through your earlier marriage, this letter will give you all the property, with your Aunt's blessing."

"I—could—have—had—the—money—anyway," Eleanor said slowly to herself, as the enormity of the situation dawned upon her.

"It's yours—every penny of it!" said Mr. Hastings.

"But I don't want it!"

Mr. Hastings looked amazed. "Don't want it?" he repeated uncomprehendingly.

"I never want to hear of it again!"

"Well, I can understand that you are reluctant to profit from any grief so great as that of the death of your aunt, but I believe that in time you will realize that it will be the wisest course for you to take the money and put it to good use in education, travel, and so on."

"Mr. Hastings," said Eleanor, her fingers gripping the edge of his desk, "please understand me. My husband is dead. His death was brought about by a misunderstanding concerning this inheritance. The money has brought nothing but a curse into my life. I won't have a penny of it. I won't!"

"Miss Stewart!" Mr. Hastings exclaimed in alarm. Eleanor's voice was rising hysterically, and she was trembling from head to foot.

"I tell you I won't take it! Take it away! Take it away!"

Calmly, soothingly, Mr. Hastings spoke. "please sit down, Miss Stewart. We won't discuss it any further now. We can wait until after your birthday to settle everything."

"But if I don't want it I don't have to—"

Miss Cox tapped lightly on the door, then opened it. "Mr. Hastings, the man from Hurley's is here. He can't wait and wants to know whether you can spare him just five minutes immediately."

"I'll see him. Will you excuse me, please, Miss Stewart?"

Mr. Hastings disappeared into the outer office. The new will still lay on the desk, and as Eleanor glanced at it, a quick resolution took shape in her mind. Reaching across the desk, she seized it, then glanced at the closed door through which Mr. Hastings would be returning soon.

Hurriedly she picked up her purse and stepped through another door which she thought must lead directly into the hall. It did, and when a few minutes later Mr. Hastings returned to his office, he found it empty and the will gone.

"Miss Cox!" he called. "Did you see Miss Stewart leave?"

"No, I didn't." Miss Cox came into the office with alacrity. "Is she gone?"

"Disappeared, taking with her a most important paper. I wonder if I should try to follow her."

"If I were you," Miss Cox remarked gravely, "I'd leave her alone. She looks as though she could go crazy any minute."

"Yes, poor child, she does," replied the old gentleman. He stepped out into the hall and looked anxiously about. He heard the elevator door closing several floors below and realized that already Eleanor would be mingling with the crowds on the street. He turned back to his office and seated himself at his desk with a troubled air. "Well, well, I'll just wait and see if she will communicate with me in a few days. I'll save this letter that her aunt wrote. It may be useful if she should lose that will."

The next morning's mail brought a note from Eleanor. It read—

Mr. Hastings:

I refuse to take the money. I tore up the new will and threw it in the river. Now you can't force the money on me. It will do more good and less harm if given to the Xenia Laboratories as the old will specified. For my part, I will only try to forget all the pain it has given me.

Thank you for your kindness.

Sincerely,
Eleanor Stewart

18

It was dark when the big bus stopped in front of the farmhouse. "Here's your stop, ma'am," said the driver, then went back to help Eleanor with her bag.

As the bus drove away, Eleanor took a long look at the house that was her destination, before she started up the path. Lights from the windows shone cheerily out across the new-fallen snow, and Eleanor thought, *This is how it looked to Chad when he used to come home from school in the winter.*

Picking up her suitcase, she started picking her way along the snowy path leading to the front door. *This isn't the way we planned it!* she thought bitterly. *We were going to come home together, but now—*

Climbing the porch steps wearily, Eleanor set her suitcase down and pushed the doorbell. Hearing footsteps approaching, she steeled herself as if for a blow. This would be hard, but she must atone somehow.

The door opened, and there stood Connie, Chad's dark haired, pretty sister.

"I'm—" Eleanor began but was interrupted.

"Why, we thought you weren't coming! Do come in out of the snow, and I'll call Mother."

Connie led the way into a warm, comfortable-looking room and said, "It's so cold out that you must be chilled through. Sit there by the radiator and get warm." As she spoke she slipped Eleanor's coat from her shoulders and propelled her toward a big

117

armchair. Then she excused herself and went out, returning shortly with Chad's mother.

"Miss Elder, I'm sorry we weren't looking for you," said the latter, extending her hand cordially. "When you didn't come on the noon train we thought you would wait until tomorrow. But your room is all ready."

Eleanor's head was beginning to reel with exhaustion, and she longed to be taken to a room—anyone's room—where she could lie down. But this mistake must be cleared up

"Oh, you've made a mistake," she gasped. "I'm not Miss Elder. You weren't expecting me! I'm—I'm—"

She faltered, then glanced from the mother's perplexed face to Connie's, her eyes finally resting on a third person who had just entered the doorway—grave-faced little Mary Lou.

Mary Lou's blue eyes opened wide. Her face lit up with a sudden smile, and she came slowly forward, saying, "Oh, I know you, I do! Mother, don't you know her? She's Chad's Ellen!"

At the sound of the beloved name which she had not heard for many weary months, Eleanor's control began to leave her. The lump in her breast began to break up, and for a moment she feared she would cry.

But Mrs. Stewart came toward her and said with a sob in her voice, "Mary Lou is right. It *is* Chad's little friend. Oh, my dear, you don't know how glad we are to see you!"

She put her arms around the trembling girl and drew her close. Eleanor drew a long shuddering breath at the kind touch and the loving tenderness in Mrs. Stewart's face and let herself relax momentarily. Then, remembering her errand here she stiffened again. Mrs. Stewart let her go and looked keenly into her face.

"Why, you're a sick child! Now you're going to lie down while I fix you something to eat. You haven't eaten, have you?" she said, as she saw protest rising in Eleanor's face.

"No—oh, no, don't please! I can't. I just want to talk to you, and then I must go!"

"You may talk to me, but you may not go away," corrected the older woman gently. "You are ill, I can see that. You're not fit to travel."

"But I can't stay, and after I've talked with you, you won't want me to. Please let me tell you—"

"Now, now, we won't talk just yet. You're going to lie down and then eat. Girls, take Ellen's bag into Chad's room."

Mrs. Stewart led Eleanor through a hall, into a typical boy's room. She removed her little coat, then drew up a small rocking chair as she said, "Since supper is almost ready, perhaps it would be better for you to eat first and rest afterward. But sit here and relax a bit while I go see to things. We are celebrating tonight. Marilyn, my daughter-in-law, is coming to the table for her first meal since her baby was born, and we are making a party of it. If you would like to wash, there is a bathroom just next to this room."

She started out the door, then returned and, stooping, kissed the pale forehead, saying softly, "This was Chad's room, my dear, and it has been waiting for you for a long time."

Left alone, Eleanor looked around the little room with misty eyes. On every side were keepsakes that had belonged to Chad. Oh, she was so tired—why not let go and rest here in this room where Chad had lived before. Perhaps he would come back if she slept here.

But determination struggled to get the uppermost place in her mind. No, she must not! She would not sleep again until she had told these kind people her story. Then they would hate her. Perhaps God would accept that as part of her punishment and forgive her someday.

"I'll tell them now!" With difficulty Eleanor dragged her aching body from the rocking chair. Stepping into the hall, she saw a light at the end of the passage. *That must be the kitchen,* she thought and started in that direction.

Pausing to steady herself before she entered, Eleanor took a long look at the occupants of the kitchen. Connie and Mary Lou were hurrying about helping to prepare the meal. Marilyn, looking weak but happy, was sitting in a big chair with Bob perched on the arm, his arm around her shoulder. The mother was standing at the stove with her back to the door. Just as Eleanor was about to enter the kitchen to make them all listen to her story, Mrs. Stewart spoke with a shaking voice, and her words caused her unseen listener to stand electrified.

"Children, I know how you feel. It's true, all that you say of her. But remember, Chad loved her! I've prayed for her every day since he—left us, and now God has sent her to us. I can see that she needs us, and we are going to receive her as one of our own. She is our own. It will break my heart if any one of you fails to do for her all that you'd do for Chad if he were here!"

Connie and Mary Lou threw their arms about her, assuring her of co-operation, while Marilyn wiped her eyes and Bob said huskily, "All right, Mother, if you say so. After all, if Chad loved her, she could not be anything but all right."

"Thank you, my dears," smiled the mother, tears running down her cheeks. "Now I'm going to—"

Eleanor waited to hear no more. She turned and fled to her room. She couldn't face them now. If they would get angry with her she could tell the story, but kindness would kill her.

In the drawer of the night table she found a pencil and some paper and wrote hastily:

Mrs. Stewart:
You wouldn't let me tell you what I came for. I heard what you said just now, and I can't stay. Don't love me or pray for me anymore, for I'm too wicked, and I'm sure God wouldn't want you to.

Chad and I were married two years ago, and I wouldn't let him tell because I wanted my aunt's money. So God took him away from me. Then last August when our baby came, I gave him away because I didn't want him.

I didn't mean to hurt Chad. He was so dear, but I can't find his face anymore, so I know God is angry. The rest of you must forget me, too.

Eleanor Stewart

Eleanor drew on her hat and coat, picked up her bag, and in a moment had slipped quietly out the front door.

Once on the highway, she ran until she was breathless, walked a while, then ran again. The wind tore at her skirt and almost drove her off the road more than once. Her feet were like lead, but she must not stop here in the bright moonlight.

Past the little schoolhouse, over the long bridge, over what seemed like miles of highway until finally Eleanor recognized the corner leading up to the little church. Here she stopped, spent, and crept behind a big tree to lean against it and rest her pounding heart.

Up over the hill came the headlights of an automobile. She cowered further back into the shadows until it passed, then started on again. Down the hollow, up the other hill past the dark church, and on into the silent yard behind it.

She knew just where to go. There were two tall pines keeping watch over the long mound she was seeking, and there in the moonlight she knelt and traced his name on the gray stone with her cold fingers. With all her heart she wished her name were on it too, that she were lying down there beside him, rested and quiet.

Loneliness and trouble, perplexity and sorrow, rolled over Eleanor in such a flood that the world began to reel around her. Clutching the stone desperately, she cried, "Oh, Chad, I can't go on!" Then she slipped down into a heap on the snow-covered mound.

* * *

Back in the farmhouse, Bob and Marilyn had gone into the front bedroom and stood looking down into the basket where tiny Patty lay.

"Poor little baby." Bob laughed. "She's going to look like her daddy."

"She's a lovely baby," said Marilyn loyally, "and I'm glad she's dark. If her hair curls like yours, I'll be perfectly happy."

"If she has your disposition, Lyn, *I'll* be perfectly happy," Bob returned. "You're such an easy person to love!"

He turned her face toward his and with a kiss said softly, "I liked you at seven, I loved you at seventeen, and I'll still love you at seventy!"

Marilyn thanked him with shining eyes, then turned to tuck the covers more warmly about the little one. In the hall they could hear Mother knocking at the door of Chad's room to announce supper. At first she knocked lightly, then more loudly. Finally she called in an anxious voice.

"I'm going to go see what's up," Bob told Marilyn and started down the hall. He entered Chad's room just in time to hear his mother cry out in anguish. With a white face she turned and reached out her arms to Bob, who caught her.

"She's gone!" exclaimed Mrs. Stewart, brokenly. "Oh, my Chad's little baby!"

Connie snatched the note and read it aloud, while the others stood in shocked silence and Mrs. Stewart sat and wept for the little grandchild she would never see. Loving arms stole around her to comfort her, and at length she wiped her eyes and said, "Forgive me, dears, for my weakness. This is a greater grief than death, but it isn't beyond the help of our heavenly Father. We'll have to let Him take this burden, as He has all others."

In a puzzled tone Mary Lou spoke. "But I don't know what she meant. Where did Eleanor go?"

Mrs. Stewart sat up sharply. "Oh, how thoughtless we've been! Where *did* she go, indeed? It's a bad night to be out, and there's no bus at this hour."

Bob was already getting into his coat, and as the mother went for her own, she directed the girls. "Marilyn, into bed at once, child. Connie, have a hot bath and plenty of blankets ready. Mary Lou, keep the soup warm and get the hot water bags ready. The poor girl was ill when she came!"

Hurriedly Bob and Mrs. Stewart climbed into the car and drove off, praying for guidance about the road to take. They kept the headlights dim, that they might see more clearly into the shadows on both sides of the road, and neither spoke for a while. Finally Bob burst out, still keeping a sharp watch on his side of the road.

"Mom, I can't get it at all. Chad was so straightforward and hated anything that wasn't fair and square. How could he ever have fallen in love with a little—" he sought momentarily for an adjective "—*snip* like she is! Why, the way she wrote back after Chad left was abominable!"

"Son, let's not judge her," came the reply in broken tones. "Chad's death was a shock to us all, and how much more to her! If her baby was born in August, Chad couldn't even have known it was coming! I believe that grief and shock have unbalanced her."

"Well, that was a bad break, Mom," Bob conceded. "Think of Marilyn's having to face that. But," he argued, "why didn't she tell us and let us help her?"

"That I can't answer, Bob. The mention she made of money throws some light on the situation, but it's not clear yet. I'm trying to realize that they were married when Chad was at home that last summer. I knew there was something on his mind, but he wouldn't talk, and I put it in the Lord's hands to work out. He did do a wonderful work in Chad's heart that year."

"Yes, there *was* a change," admitted Bob. "All his carelessness and recklessness seemed gone, but I thought he was just worried over the farm work and my leg."

"I was sure it had to do with this girl. He showed us her picture once and asked me how I'd like her for a daughter. She looked sweet and good, and I can't think Chad misjudged her. Remember how he spoke of her in that last letter?"

"Yes, I do. But it doesn't tie up with what she says. And giving away Chad's baby!"

Mrs. Stewart sobbed for a few moments before answering.

"That's hardest of all. It's like a knife thrust through my heart. But if I'm suffering, how is she feeling? I'm frightened, Bob! We've come four miles and haven't found her. Where is she?"

"Perhaps someone else picked her up and gave her a ride," Bob suggested.

"Not another car has passed, and we haven't seen anyone. We were only a few minutes behind her!"

They had reached the crossroad, and now Bob backed the car and turned. Slowly they drove back, with hearts growing more anxious. Twice Bob thought he saw someone, but when he got out to investigate, he found only a snow-covered stump or a pile of brush. Finally they came to the big white gate leading from the main road to the cemetery. As always, Mrs. Stewart's eyes turned sadly to the two mounds under the pines. Then she clutched Bob's arm.

"Stop, oh stop! There, Bob, by the stone. Oh, we should have known she would come here!"

Bob was already running up the slope toward the pines.

19

Eleanor was lost. If she could only find her way home, Chad would be there with a tiny baby in his arms. But in every direction she turned, she ran into an impenetrable thicket that beat her back with icy blows and tore at her body with sharp, thorny branches. She was sore and cold and her chest hurt when she breathed. But she had to get home to Chad and the baby! She struggled to her feet in another attempt but fell again. Once more she arose to go on, but strong hands held her back. In fear she cried out, striking at the hands, but slipped back into the blackness. Fighting out of it, she beat at the encircling arms bearing her away, then heard Chad say, "Quiet, little sister, it's all right now. Mom, you'll have to drive. You're not man enough to hold this little wildcat down."

Chad wouldn't call her a wildcat! She *must* get away. Desperately she struggled, but the strong arms held her tight, and now the blackness was getting thicker and thicker. She was tired. It would be easier to let go and sink into it than to fight anymore. Now the waves were pounding on the stone slabs on Lake Shore Drive. This time she would let go and sleep in the lake forever. Let go . . . let go . . .

Connie and Mary Lou were standing in the door waiting as Bob came up the steps with his unconscious burden. Her eyes wide with fear and sympathy, Connie led Bob directly into the bedroom where she had prepared a bed. As soon as he could get away, Bob tiptoed softly into Marilyn's room to tell her what had happened. Kneeling with his arms about her, he concluded, "I'm afraid for her, darling, but I did my best for Chad's sake. All we can do now is pray."

That was a busy night. While working over Eleanor, Mother Stewart said once, "Thank God for that warm coat. She'd have frozen without it. As it is, I fear this is a bad night's work. Mary Lou, tell Bob to call Dr. Leigh."

Dr. Leigh arrived as rapidly as he could and heard the story with a grave face.

"Fever, pneumonia, and one or two other things are all we have to fight, I judge," he snorted. "I wonder if the fool girls of this day are worth the trouble they cause!"

But he was working as he talked, and he stayed all night. Mrs. Stewart sent the girls to bed, then took up her place in the bedroom beside the doctor, laboring with him to fan the little spark of life and keep it from being extinguished.

As they worked, Mrs. Stewart told the doctor such parts of Eleanor's story as she knew, and together they tried to picture the happenings of the past two years that had culminated in this night's tragedy.

When morning came Eleanor still lay breathing hoarsely, but sleeping. At first she had stirred and moaned in pain, but as the hours passed she sank into a deep slumber.

Connie came the next day to take her mother's place at the bedside. But before Mrs. Stewart lay down to rest, she made a long distance call to the university and asked for the dean of women. Then the two troubled women, actually hundreds of miles apart but yet united by their concern for Eleanor, tried to piece together facts that might be of assistance in helping her.

"She insisted she had no relatives, Mrs, Stewart. Are you an aunt?"

"No, I am no kin. But she was a—dear friend of my son who was killed there over a year ago."

"Oh, I remember. Well, Eleanor has apparently been near a break for some time. She was formerly a brilliant student, but last quarter her work disintegrated and I was much concerned after I talked with her several days ago. I feared just such a crash as this but had no chance to warn her, as she wouldn't talk and seemed anxious to leave as soon as possible. Then I called at her room yesterday morning and found it empty.''

"Has she no friends who should be notified?'' asked Mrs. Stewart.

"None that I know of,'' came the answer. "Inquiries that I made yesterday disclosed the fact that all last quarter Eleanor was decidedly reserved and unfriendly. She worked with Professor Nichols up until a year ago, and he valued her work highly. However, he is in California and quite ill himself. I know of no other friends.''

Mother Stewart walked back to the bedside and looked down at the flushed face on the pillow.

"Poor little wanderer!'' she exclaimed. "We may never know what brought her to this. Watch her carefully, Connie dear, and if you need me don't hesitate to call. I shall lie down, for I'll be busy again tonight, I can see.''

As the day passed the fever mounted, and with it came delirium. That night the endurance of both Dr. Leigh and Mrs. Stewart was tested, and the next time the doctor returned, he brought a nurse.

For days Eleanor lay tossing in delirium, talking in broken sentences, which helped the watchers to learn more of her story. Sometimes her voice was pleading: "Auntie, please let me go with the others. I'll be good, truly I will.'' Sometimes it was sullen and angry. "You're cheating, Aunt Ruth, and I can beat you at that game.'' Again there was happy, carefree laughter which startled them, it seemed so normal: "Chad, look at that! Oh, bring the camera, quick!'' or, "Chad, we'll come back here and build a laboratory in the woods and show the whole world what a team we are!'' The tones became businesslike as Eleanor said, "Professor Nichols, the last slides weren't good enough. I'll get what you want if I have to stay up all night.''

Then there were hours when the battle in her soul over the money was laid bare—when they heard her pleading with Chad to be patient until she was twenty-five—when over and again she prayed, "Oh, God, save Chad for me, and I'll give up the money and love and serve You forever.''

Other hours there were when she talked of her picture gallery of memory, and the listeners were almost able to tread it with her. Then when the pictures faded and she begged piteously for a recollection of Chad's face, the listeners felt the tears run down their cheeks, though hers were hot and dry. Once she said to Marilyn and Bob as they sat by her, "Carolyn, you and Fred understand, don't you? I daren't let myself cry, for I could never stop."

So often did the name Carolyn occur that Connie searched Eleanor's bags and purse for some clue to its owner. And when she found Carolyn's address, she wrote telling her of Eleanor's illness. Carolyn, her tender heart reproaching her for her failure to contact Eleanor, took several days' leave from her schoolroom and came to help with the arduous task of nursing. Mrs. Stewart learned from her many new things about Eleanor, and Carolyn wept when she was shown the pitiful little note of confession.

"It is hard for me to forgive myself for not helping her more after Chad died. I had no idea that they were married, but I had always thought that they were suited to each other and expected they would marry eventually. I wonder why Eleanor didn't tell me."

"It all seems to hinge on a large sum of money she was to inherit," said Mrs. Stewart, perplexedly. "Apparently Chad didn't know about the money at first, for she constantly pleads for his forgiveness. Last night she said, 'Chad, if you'll live and go on loving me, we'll work together for your Lord.'"

After a few minutes of silence Mrs. Stewart spoke again.

"Are you a Christian, Mrs. Fleet?"

"Yes, I am, though I confess I have been a rather careless one. But I have prayed for Eleanor ever since Chad's death, even though I haven't contacted her as I should have. When I think of what she must have endured before the baby came, my heart aches."

"Mrs. Fleet," said Mrs. Stewart, tears coming into her tired eyes. "I am trying to learn to trust my Lord in this matter as in others. But the thought that I may never know Chad's baby is the hardest cross I have ever had to bear."

Carolyn tried to console her. "Perhaps when Eleanor is better we can find out where the baby is and get it again. Is it a boy or girl?" she added.

"We don't know even that. The note tells us all that we know except what we have learned from her delirium."

For many sleepless days and nights nothing availed to give the sufferer any relief from her delirious fever, and the doctor grew increasingly troubled. In spite of all that could be done, the battle seemed to be a losing one.

One night the flame of life burned lower than ever, and both Carolyn and Mrs. Stewart watched all night, apprehensively. Over and over their own hearts were wrung by her cries.

"Oh, please bring back my baby. It's not a puppy! It's my own little baby!"

Mrs. Stewart hid her face in her hands while Carolyn tried to quiet the troubled girl.

"No, don't try to hold me! If you don't bring the baby back, I'll have to go after it. I can't go to heaven to see Chad without the baby!"

"Yes, yes," said Carolyn soothingly. "Just go to sleep dear, and we'll see about the baby later."

"No, I want it now. You haven't any right to hide it from me. He's my own little son—my little Chad!"

Mrs. Stewart hurried from the room, sobbing. Bob and Marilyn, wakened from their sleep in the adjoining room, came to the door to see if they could help. The pleadings became even more frantic. Eleanor could scarcely be held in bed. At last, in her ravings, Eleanor's eyes lighted on Marilyn's face, and reaching out both arms to her, she implored, "Oh, won't *you* get my baby?"

"Yes—oh, yes," faltered Marilyn, and before the others could stop her, she ran into the other room and came back with baby Patty in her arms. With white face and eyes brimming with tears, she laid the tiny flannel bundle on the pillow by Eleanor, and said, "Here it is, dear. Now won't you go to sleep?"

A peaceful look came over the agitated face. With a long sobbing breath, Eleanor lay back and said, "Yes—I will go to sleep now."

And she did. Hour after hour she slept, her pulse growing fainter all the while. Baby Patty, having unconsciously prolonged a life, was put back to sleep in her bassinet, and Carolyn was prevailed upon to take a few hours of needed rest. Mrs. Stewart watched alone.

About four o'clock she telephoned hurriedly for Dr. Leigh, then knelt by the bed in agonizing prayer pleading for the life of this one who had wronged her, that she be allowed to live in order to learn of God's love to even His erring children.

Mrs. Stewart never knew how long she knelt there, but as she remained waiting for the Lord to speak to her she felt a hand on her shoulder. Looking up, she saw that it was Eleanor's. She had awakened.

"Chad's mother?" Her lips formed the words.

"Yes. And your mother, dear."

The brown eyes filled with tears, and the lips quivered. "I'm afraid," came the weak tones. "Can you hold me?"

With a prayer for strength, Mother Stewart gathered the sick girl into her arms, and Eleanor laid her head on the shoulder that had once pillowed her husband's head. Kneeling there by the bed, with Eleanor in her arms like a tired baby, Mrs. Stewart started to sing. The restless form grew quiet again as the mother sang softly the hymns of faith and assurance that had often stilled her own soul. She grew cramped and cold but dared not move. One song seemed to soothe more than any other, and over and over she sang it:

> "Oh, what wonderful, wonderful rest,
> Trusting completely in Jesus I'm blest;
> Sweetly He comforts and shields from alarms,
> Holding me safe in His mighty arms."

Dr. Leigh had come and stood watching in the shadows. Once he carried in a chair and placed it at Mrs. Stewart's back, then resumed his post at the foot of the bed, where his keen eyes could study the sleeper. After another half hour had passed, he reached for one limp hand and began to count the pulse. A satisfied sigh escaped his lips. He straightened the pillow and lifted Eleanor back on it, then stooped to raise Mrs. Stewart. Placing her reverently in the easy chair, he said, "When I left yesterday I wouldn't have given two cents for her life. Now she's on the uphill road. And you did it, Margaret Stewart!"

Eleanor rested and slept for a week. Carolyn took her leave, promising to come again when school was out. Tenderly those who remained did everything possible to help Eleanor regain her strength and rejoiced to see her response to their care.

Mary Lou appointed herself Eleanor's personal attendant, feeding her, looking out for her every need. This relieved Mother Stewart, who was needed, now that the crisis was over, to look after two new patients in the rooms upstairs. However, several times each day she came in with cheery greetings, and every night she slept on the cot in the corner. As soon as Eleanor was able, she remonstrated at this arrangement, feeling sure that it was uncomfortable to Mrs. Stewart. But that good lady only replied, patting the thin hand, "You are more dear to me than you know, Eleanor Stewart, and I'm taking no chance on any more trouble. If I sleep poorly in your room, I wouldn't sleep at all out of it. So you may as well resign yourself to my company until you're strong enough to put me out!"

"I'd never do that," Eleanor said. "I can't understand why you love me or do so much for me. But I'm just weak enough to enjoy it, so I lie here and am thankful for all of you. I wish I had known you years ago, Mother. It would have made such a difference."

Softly Mrs. Stewart replied, "While we are being thankful, let us not forget who brought us together and thank Him for all He has done."

"I do," said Eleanor shyly, "but I still don't understand how you can be so nice to me. If you just knew how wicked I've been. I must tell you—"

A hand came over her lips. "Not another word now. Of course you want to tell me the whole story, and some day you shall, when you are stronger. Then we will bury the bad things and the sad things forever and sort out the glad things to keep in our hearts. But you're not ready for that yet, so just rest and know we all love you."

Eleanor needed no verbal reminder of that love, for all day little acts of kindness showed her what a place she had already been given in the affections of the family. And to the lonely girl who had never known family life before, this was a sweet new experience.

Mary Lou considered Eleanor her own peculiar possession. "You were Chad's, you know," she said, gravely, "And I was Chad's special sister. I think God sent you to me to cure the lonesomeness."

"I'm sure He sent you to me, precious sister," Eleanor said quickly. "I never had a little sister before, and I didn't know how much I needed one."

"I 'spect we need each other. Do you mind if I talk about Chad, Eleanor?" she continued, respectfully.

"I'd love it, dear. It seems to bring him nearer. Someday when I get well I'm going to the cottage at the lake where we used to go together and see if I can find a good picture of him. I want one so badly!"

"Chad loved you awful much. I know he did," averred Mary Lou, stoutly. Then a sudden thought occurred to her, and she questioned, "Say, didn't he have a nickname he called you? Have you got a name not so proper as Eleanor? Didn't he call you Ellen?"

A look of pain passed over the pale face. "Yes, that was his pet name for me, Mary Lou, but I don't think I could quite stand it if anyone else used it. In high school my friends called me Len. Do you like that?"

"Yes, I do" replied Mary Lou, her eyes shining. "It sounds more 'folksy,' as Mrs. Hunt, our kitchen lady, says. Now I have to go help Mother fix the trays for upstairs. Good-bye, Len."

Connie was more reserved than Mary Lou, but Eleanor soon grew to admire and love her dearly. She had a quick mind, a ready wit, and a love for all things beautiful. Every unoccupied minute of the day found her at the piano, sometimes practicing scales and arpeggios but more often losing her soul in a flood of beautiful music. Had Eleanor suspected that Connie played to help while away the tedious hours of convalescence, she would have been correct.

Often in the evening Bob and Marilyn would sing with Connie, and it was with a sweet pain that Eleanor heard once more the choruses that she had first heard from Chad at the lake. Sometimes Mrs. Stewart sang too, and on those occasions her rich voice led all the others. Mary Lou liked to join the group, and on hearing her uncertain renditions of the tunes, Eleanor smiled to remember Chad's remark "When Mary Lou and I want to sing, we go to the woods to do it." None of the family ever even smiled at her erratic warblings, however, and always welcomed her into the group around the piano.

Eleanor's heart ached when she saw the companionable happiness of Bob and Marilyn, but she hid her pain, determined to bring no further shadow into the home of these dear ones who had done so much for her. Bob was inclined to be restrained in her presence, although he seemed to want to be friendly. As their acquaintance ripened, Eleanor saw in Bob many traits that reminded her of Chad, although the brothers were vastly different in appearance. Marilyn was, as Chad had once said, "jolly and comfortable." Her laugh came quickly and brightened the household with its contagion. Eleanor reflected often on what a comfort Marilyn must have been to Chad's family during this last sad year.

This was a happy, busy, household, with each one taking part in the work. The boarders in the little sanitarium upstairs were not really ill, but rather folk who needed rest and quiet. The tonic of cheerful courage that emanated from Mrs. Stewart seemed to do them more good than any doctor's prescription.

As Eleanor lay in her room listening to the cheerful bustle of the household outside her door, she longed to regain strength enough to take some part in it. The most desirable thing in life she could think of just now was to be able to work and rest in this contented house, made especially dear to her because every room in it had been visited by Chad's spirit and had echoed to his boyish voice.

I wonder if I'll ever want to go back to school, she thought one day, lying wanly on her pillows. *I don't seem to care about anything anymore. I haven't any ambition. I suppose the time is coming when I'll have to start some kind of lifework again, but just now it's so nice to lie here and rest."*

Eleanor's mind, once so keen and analytical, seemed to partake of the lethargy of her body and was occupied with no thoughts more weighty than Mary Lou's chatter of the little chicks in the brooder house, or the question of what color hat Connie should buy to wear with her new suit, or—most interesting of all—Marilyn's day-by-day accounts of her care of baby Patty.

Mrs. Stewart's companionship and love were especially treasured by Eleanor, whose whole love-hungry nature went out to her in a passionate devotion. And the mother heart, still aching over the loss of her firstborn, found consolation in caring for this one who had been so dear to him. Both Eleanor and the older woman looked forward to the time for opening up the past with its "bad things, its sad things, and its glad things." Eleanor felt she would not really begin life again until that was done.

She had one other uneasiness about which she never confided.

20

It was a bright April morning. When Eleanor awoke there was a cardinal singing in the bare tree outside her window, and the fresh scent of spring was in the air. Mary Lou brought in her breakfast tray, then announced importantly, "Connie and I are going to drive to Woodstock today. It's over thirty miles, and it's a real large city. Mother is letting me miss school to go."

"How nice! What are you going to do over there?"

"Buy things!" Mary Lou rose up on her tiptoes with pent-up excitement. "Connie's going to get her new hat, and Marilyn needs some house dresses, and we're going to pick them out, and we're going to get some socks and shirts for Bob, and Mom needs some sheets and towels—and I have eighty-three cents to spend!" She paused breathless. "Oh, and Connie and I are both going to get new shoes."

Eleanor laughed at her exuberance. "You're surely going to have a grand day. I wish I could go along."

"Oh, I wish you could go too," said Mary Lou with longing in her voice. "I've never been to Woodstock since I can remember. Will the stores be much larger than they are in Benton?"

"Oh, yes," Eleanor assured her. "It will be wonderful for you." Then a sudden thought struck her. Laying down her toast, she said confidentially, "Mary Lou, if I give you some money will you and Connie do some shopping for me?"

"Oh, we'd love to!"

"Well, I'll be working on a list, and before you go you ask Connie to come in and see me."

An hour later Connie and Mary Lou came in all ready for the drive, Connie looking fresh and lovely in the new blue suit and Mary Lou walking primly behind her in a pretty dark blue coat that had been freshly sponged and pressed.

"You look like two princesses!" exclaimed Eleanor admiringly. "Oh, Connie, be sure to get a red hat. With that blue suit and white blouse, it would be lovely."

"Do you think so?" asked Connie. "My purse and gloves are blue, you know."

"So much the better," Eleanor assured her. "You mustn't match everything. It spoils the effect."

"Where is your purse, Mary Lou?" asked Eleanor, turning to that effervescent little person. "I want to put this list in it."

"I haven't any good one," said Mary Lou, reluctantly. "Just a teeny one I got when I was six, and it looks silly now. So Connie has my money. I thought I'd buy a purse today, but eighty-three cents won't buy me a purse and the other things I want, too."

"I'm so glad it won't," said Eleanor, with a smile. "I've been lying here trying to think up something I could buy to show you how dear my new sisters are to me, but I didn't know what you needed. Connie, I want you to get a nice red purse and gloves to change off with. You're going to look positively stunning in that suit with red accessories! And Mary Lou must pick out a purse and gloves for herself, too."

"Gloves—for me!" squealed Mary Lou. "I never had any just-for-looks gloves. They were always to keep warm in. Oh, I'm 'most afraid to think of it."

Eleanor and Connie laughed, then Eleanor asked, "Connie, what does Mother need? Has she a nice purse?"

"It's not very nice," said Mary Lou before Connie could answer. "She always stuffs it so full of things."

"What kind of things?" laughed Eleanor.

"Oh, books and papers and things to carry to Sunday school," answered Connie. "You see, she teaches the primary class, and she almost needs a suitcase to carry her things in."

"Well, we can fix that. You girls pick out a nice zipper case with several pockets and have her initial put on it. No, don't object," she said, as Connie's face took on a protesting frown. "I have to get a little fun out of these long days. Oh, and I want you to get Patty a bonnet, a pink satin one if you can find it, like the one Marilyn was admiring in the catalog. Then buy a big, big, box of chocolates for Bob and Marilyn, and go to an ice cream parlor and get yourselves the nicest treats you can."

As she concluded, Mary Lou jumped and squealed again in joyous anticipation, but Connie leaned over the bed and kissed Eleanor, saying softly, "I'll do it because I know it will make you happy. Isn't there anything you want for yourself?"

Eleanor laughed. "Oh, I forgot about me. Yes, I want a box of letter paper and five three-cent stamps. That's truly all I want just now."

A few minutes after Mary Lou and Connie left, Marilyn and Bob came in carrying baby Patty, dressed to go out. "She's come to tell Auntie bye-bye," said Marilyn. "She's going to visit her other grandma. Connie and Mary Lou will drop us off there this morning and pick up Bob again tonight to bring him back. Patty and I shall stay a week."

Eleanor reached out her arms for the rosy-cheeked baby and held her close for a minute before handing her back to her mother. "Take good care of her," she said gently.

"Yes, and you keep on getting better," returned Marilyn. "When I come home I'll expect to see you out driving a team of horses."

"I wish I could." Eleanor laughed. "It won't be long now."

A few minutes later she heard the car go down the drive, as Mrs. Stewart called a cheery good-bye from the porch. Then the house was strangely quiet, and Eleanor returned to her thoughts.

This was the first time she had ever held baby Patty, though she had often longed to cradle her in her arms. Now her arms seemed so empty that she almost cried out with pain. Burying her head in her arms on the pillow, Eleanor wept and prayed. Her thoughts were once more with her own little lost baby. She realized that soon she must again face the tangled issues of life.

But now she knew she did not have to go through life alone. Her Savior would take her by the hand and lead her. The Stewarts said so.

Eleanor went over again in her mind the story of her loving Savior; how He had come to earth as the divine Son of God, had died for her—*for her*—on Calvary's cross, and had risen again, the victor over death, in order that she, Eleanor Stewart, might be enabled to live a right life and serve Him forever. And some day, perhaps soon, He was coming again to take His own back to glory with Him to live there forever, joyous and glad.

To all of this Eleanor had once given intellectual assent but had kept back her will from surrendering to this wonderful Savior. Now all her selfishness had been seared away. Christ had won her completely for Himself.

"Oh, Father," Eleanor prayed, glad tears running down her cheeks, "I'm Thine, and I am so glad. Jesus, I love Thee, and I thank Thee for this wonderful peace. Father, not my will but Thine be done, for the rest of my life and forever."

God had answered Chad's prayer.

From this day on, she was His. A phrase she had heard Chad use came to her mind: "Christ's—for service or sacrifice." If He wanted her to live and work for Him, she would do it with all her strength and talent. If He wanted her to suffer for Him, she could do that, too. She knew her life would always have its share of sorrow, for no happiness could ever be great enough to overcome her grief for her baby. But God could use even that to His glory. Eleanor wanted to rest in His hands, unresisting as a piece of soft clay, His to use just as He willed.

She prayed again: "Dear Lord, forgive the failures and terrible mistakes that came because I was so wilful—and take me now to use just as Thou wilt. Show me the way, and help me to walk in it. Teach me to trust Thee in everything. Thou canst care for my baby. Help me to trust even in that. And if it be Thy will, let me live to show the world what Thou canst do with even the poorest material Thou hast. Amen."

Eleanor had sought peace in work, in love in self-abnegation, but now she had found it forever in Jesus Christ, her Savior.

In the middle of the morning Mrs. Stewart came in. "Why, what a happy face you have this morning," she exclaimed, setting down a big glass of milk. "Is there something special that makes it beam so?"

"Something very special, Mother," Eleanor responded, in a glad voice. "I have just completed the transaction of turning over what is left of this life of mine to the One who bought and paid for it. He has accepted me, and—oh, Mother, I'm so happy!" Eleanor's voice broke.

Mrs. Stewart's face was transformed with joy. Kissing Eleanor she said, "My dear, there is joy even in heaven over this. Surely there is joy here, for we have all been praying for you. How glad Chad would be!"

"Chad doesn't seem so far away now," said Eleanor thoughtfully, "for he is with the Lord, and the Lord is right here, isn't He?"

"Yes, dear, with us always. Chad and my own dear husband aren't really far from us, Len. They've just gone on a little while before, and we must walk together here and help each other bear the loneliness."

"Oh, we will!"

"You're going to be a big blessing to me, Len," said Mother Stewart, "because you have known sorrow yourself and can understand mine."

"I'll do anything to show you how grateful I am!" exclaimed Eleanor, happily.

"Well, right now, little lady, you will please me by drinking that nice glass of milk I brought you? Then you and I are going to plan a picnic."

"A picnic?" said Eleanor curiously, sipping away at the milk.

"Yes, ma'am! Doctor Leigh says you are to get up today! What do you think of that? So you're going to dress and take a long trip to—the living room, where you can sit in a big chair or lie on the couch when you feel like it, while I do the family mending. We'll have lunch brought in to us like real ladies of leisure. This afternoon you must rest a while, but tonight, if you are not too tired, you may eat with us at the table."

"How grand!" Eleanor's eyes sparkled. "It will feel so good to be dressed again. I wonder if my clothes will fit," she remarked, glancing at the thin hand that held the glass of milk.

"If they don't now, they soon will," said Mother Stewart, cheerily. "Good milk and eggs and country air do wonders for all my patents."

Then Mother Stewart combed the brown curls and tied them up with a blue ribbon. Eleanor looked with a mixture of emotions as out of the closet came the blue jersey dress she had worn the night she came. How much her world had changed since she had last worn it! Now she still had sorrow, but she had a great joy also, and instead of longing for death she wanted to live and serve.

21

The sunshine was streaming through the windows in the living room, and to Eleanor, who had lain so long in the little bedroom, the world looked gay and bright. Mother Stewart settled her carefully on the davenport, drew a shawl over her, then carried in a bag bulging with darning and sat down in the big chair opposite Eleanor.

"This isn't one week's accumulation." She laughed, threading a needle. "I haven't mended a pair of socks since you came. My family are about to go barefoot."

"I don't think Mary Lou would mind," smiled Eleanor. "She would probably welcome the opportunity."

They sat in silence for a moment, Eleanor drinking in the sunshine, Mother Stewart rocking and industriously weaving her needle in and out. Then the older woman leaned forward and said encouragingly, "I don't wish to urge matters unduly, my dear, but don't you think that today, while we are alone, would be a good day for you to tell me the story you have been saving up? Let's get it over with once for all."

"Yes, let's do," said Eleanor, "although it isn't a bit easy to tell. I couldn't do it if I weren't so eager to clear Chad of any blame in the matter. He was so fine and straight, Mother. It was my crooked thinking that twisted up both our lives so badly."

"Suppose you just tell me the facts and let me form my own opinion," said Mother Stewart, gently. "But tell me all of it, because if you are going to put this thing behind you forever, you mustn't leave any little bits of it hanging around in your memory.''

This was the first time Eleanor had been able to talk to anyone of Chad, and at first her voice trembled as she told of the Christmas house party and the night on the moonlit crest of the hill. As she progressed, however, she grew more sure of herself and was able to talk quietly and even happily of their love for each other and their longing for marriage. But Eleanor's face grew downcast as she confessed her scheme for the marriage.

''You can't understand that, Mother, because you never knew my aunt,'' Eleanor tried to explain. ''She meant well, but actually she helped me lay the foundation for all this trouble.''

With mingled desire and reluctance Eleanor described their marriage and the weekends they had spent at the cottage, the days in school when they barely saw each other, and the summer when they were torn apart by the circumstances they themselves had created.

''That must have been harder on Chad than me,'' Eleanor mused. ''I was pleasing myself about keeping the secret, while Chad was only keeping quiet because I said he must. Mother, Chad hated that secrecy. It hurts me so to think how I must have hurt him. I was just determined to have my own way. He was so loyal to me that he never criticized. That must have been a hard summer for him!''

''I believe it was, dear,'' relied Mother Stewart, rocking quietly, ''although he never spoke of the sacrifice he was making. He did the farm work and teased the girls and spent his evenings with Bob, so that none of us would guess his feelings. But since then I have remembered many times when he would be gone all of Sunday afternoon and none of us would see him. He must have been taking long walks in the woods, alone with his heavenly Father. He and I had some conversations together that told me he was growing closer to the Lord. So although I sensed, as mothers do, that he was troubled over something, I knew the matter could be left in God's hands.''

Eleanor reached out impulsively and smoothed the work-worn hand that had paused momentarily from its work.

''No wonder Chad was so good, with a mother like you!'' she exclaimed.

"Chad was much more like his father than like me, Eleanor,"
was the reply. "Both Chad and Mary Lou inherited appearance
and temperament from my husband."

After a few moments' quietness, Eleanor spoke again. She
described their last autumn together, the little apartment, the
happy hours of study and work, the attendance at the shabby little church—and always the growing realization that their duty
was to confess their marriage and face the consequences together.

"Then came that Thanksgiving, Mother. It's hard to talk of
that even to you, for it was four days of heaven. I *can't* be altogether sorry about anything that gave us so much happiness. My
only regret is that we didn't come out with the truth when we
should have. Perhaps we might have had a lifetime together instead of—this." Her voice dropped almost to a whisper, and her
lips trembled.

Then came the story of the trip to church on the Sunday after Thanksgiving. "I haven't any idea who that preacher was,"
Eleanor declared. "But I'm sure God sent us there that day, for I
never had a minute's peace from then on until I told Chad everything. But that was after we came home. It must have been a
shock to him, but he didn't scold me. He did try to show me the
right way, and I know he was praying all the time that I'd decide
to tell the truth and trust God for the future. That last night—oh,
Mother, how can I tell it?—he kissed me good-bye and went to
the lab. I know now that he went there to pray. And even while
he was probably on his knees in prayer, I decided against the
right way. I determined to keep the secret and get Aunt Ruth's
money. That was the night that—oh, it hurts so, Mother—he—
never came back!"

The mother dropped her sewing from her lap and gathered
the weeping girl close. For the first time that she could remember, Eleanor knew the comfort of a mother's arms, and from that
haven she sobbed out the rest of the story.

"I did make him glad at the last, for I put on his ring and
told him we'd tell everyone at once. But when he—went—I
thought God had turned His back on me. So I changed my mind
and put the ring away. The day of the funeral I couldn't even
look at you, for fear I'd collapse and tell the whole story."

Fumbling for a handkerchief, Eleanor wiped her eyes, drew a long breath, and resumed her tale.

"Even when I knew the baby was coming, I wouldn't give in. I can't tell you much about that time, for I don't remember. There's a sort of haze over it all. I went to the cottage and hired a dear Swedish woman to live with me, and it seemed as though Chad were there too. I still remember how close he seemed, and how I could even talk to him. I wasn't unhappy at all. It's hard to believe it was just a year ago."

Noticing that Mother Stewart's eyes were growing misty, Eleanor hesitated for a moment, but at the quiet words "Go on, dear" she obediently continued.

"This—oh, this is the hardest of all, Mother. I know that Chad is with the Lord, and even though I blame myself for his death, I can't grieve too much knowing how happy he is. But oh, Mother—how can I go on without my baby? How could I ever have done such a thing? I ask myself those questions over and over and realize I must have been absolutely out of my mind!"

"Why *did* you do it, dear?"

"I don't remember very well. I remember thinking he would burden me and keep me from going on with my work. It wasn't money, for I had all I needed. I could have placed him in some home until I finished school, but my mind was so unsettled I couldn't think at all. Oh, if I could do it over again!"

Her voice was broken, and her hands were twisting the already wet handkerchief into knots. Mrs. Stewart feared the effect that this emotional outburst would have on her, yet knew Eleanor would not be at ease mentally until she had poured out this great heartful of trouble she had kept to herself so long. Praying for wisdom, the older woman continued.

"Tell me about him, dear. What did he look like? How large was he?"

"I don't know much. I wouldn't look at him. The nurse said he weighed ten pounds, so he must have been quite large for a baby, though he seemed tiny. I don't remember ever really looking at his face," she repeated, dismally. "He wasn't strong, you know. The doctor was worried about him at first, but by the time the man—took him away, the doctor said he was all right."

"How did you arrange the adoption?" Mother Stewart asked in forced tones. Her heart ached for the girl, but her own grief was about to overwhelm her.

"The doctor did it. I only made one requirement—that the parents must be Christians. I must have thought I was making a concession to Chad—I don't know. I wanted to get it all over with and get back to school. They took him away, and I never kissed him once!"

For some time they sat in silence. Then, thinking the story concluded, Mother Stewart began to speak, but Eleanor interrupted.

"Let me go on. There's only a little more. I want to be done with it. When I did go back to school, I was tormented with trying to remember Chad's face. The harder I tried, the more hazy it became. Then I got to thinking of the baby, and finally I couldn't study or concentrate on anything. I think the dean has told you how my schoolwork went to pieces. I began to blame Aunt Ruth and you for it all. I blamed Auntie for making my marriage difficult, and you because your influence made Chad feel as he did about it. At last things were so bad I thought I would go crazy if I couldn't feel near to Chad and see his face again. I thought if I confessed to my lawyer and you, that God would do something for me—perhaps give back Chad's memory."

On hearing about the trip to the lawyer's office and the discovery of the second will, Mrs. Stewart sympathized with Eleanor.

"I think something gave way in my brain when he read that," Eleanor said. "I was sure I was out of my mind. I felt driven by demons. I destroyed that will, then I came here, and you know the rest. Mother, *why* did you care for me, and how *can* you be so good to me, knowing all I've done?"

Mrs. Stewart drew a long breath, then took one of the thin, trembling hands in her own as she said, "I did it because I loved you. We all love you. I've prayed for you every day since Chad's funeral. Your face that day told me you needed prayer. And as I've prayed, I've grown to love you until you are now as one of my own, and I never intend to let you go."

"But I did such awful things," Eleanor protested.

"God has forgiven you," Mrs. Stewart pointed out soberly. "Am I to judge when He forgives? The things you did were wrong, certainly, but not too great for Him to pardon. And your own sorrow has been too great for me to add to it by censure. But I want to say one thing, dear, and then we will close the subject forever. Don't blame yourself too much. You didn't really know what you were doing when you gave the dear baby away. If you only had had a mother or sister with you, she would have kept you from doing that heartbreaking thing. But God comforted me when I learned about the baby that night you came here, and He will comfort you. Though we cannot be with and care for your little son, He can. You and I will be in constant prayer that he will grow to be a good man, one who will serve and honor the Lord all his life. So even though separated, we can do much to shape his life."

"Mother," exclaimed Eleanor, her face brightening, "that helps me so much."

The only sounds in the room were the music of a bluebird on the bough outside the window and the clatter of pans from the kitchen where Mrs. Hunt bustled about.

Mrs. Stewart placed her hand over the thin one that was lying on her knee and said, "Len, every sorrow or pain that comes to us can be used for God's glory. If we grow bitter or rebellious, the suffering has been in vain. But if we learn from it sympathy and forbearance, it can become a blessing that will bear fruit for Him. You have given your life to Him to use as He sees fit. Let Him take all these things also and bless you through them. You have a long life ahead of you, dear, if God wills, and in spite of the sad past it can be a happy one."

"You believe strongly in prayer, don't you, Mother?" asked Eleanor, running her finger over the pattern in the sofa.

"Indeed I do! You yourself are a proof that God hears and answers. I asked Him to send you, and He did."

"If I ask Him to give back my baby, do you think He will do it?" There was a note of hope in Eleanor's voice, and Mother Stewart hesitated before replying.

"I can't say, dear. He will if it is best. But perhaps the baby is in a place where he will be cared for better than we could do it.

Perhaps it isn't God's will to bring him back. Those other parents love him too, you know. I can't say what God will do, Eleanor, except that He will do what is best for everyone concerned. We will just pray that His will may be done.

"Now you're going to rest while I help Mrs. Hunt get the trays ready for the folks upstairs. Then you and I will eat at the little table in the south window."

When Mrs. Stewart left the room, Eleanor arose and walked slowly about, happy to be on her feet again. On the piano she found a picture of Chad's father. For some minutes she stood looking into the tired, kind eyes, then said softly, "You're like my Chad. I'm glad you were there when he got Home."

By its side was a photograph of Chad, which Eleanor decided must have been taken at the time he graduated from high school. This young boy, however, bore such little resemblance to the man who had been her husband that Eleanor turned away with a sigh.

As soon as I can, I'll go to the cottage and find a picture I like, she thought.

Eleanor's eyes fell on the piano keyboard, and, as though motivated by a sudden remembrance, she seated herself and began to feel out a tune uncertainly. When Mrs. Stewart returned she broke off playing and asked, "Mother, what is this tune? Do you know it? I can't remember where I have heard it before, but all the time I've been getting better it has been running through my head."

"My dear," said Mrs. Stewart, "I sang that tune to you for about two hours the night we were afraid you wouldn't live. That was the only thing that would quiet you."

"Oh, won't you sing it again now?" Eleanor begged. "I'll play for you."

The rich tones went direct to Eleanor's heart once more, with their message of peace and trust.

"Oh, what wonderful, wonderful rest,
    Trusting completely in Jesus I'm blest;
    Sweetly He comforts and shields from alarms,
    Holding me safe in His mighty arms."

As they ate the tempting lunch Mrs. Hunt brought in, they talked of many things. Little incidents Mother Stewart related told Eleanor much of Chad's happy background. She heard, too, of the night when the Doctor Dad left them and Mary Lou was born.

"We never realized how bad my husband's heart was," commented Mrs. Stewart, "although I knew he worked too hard. Dr. Leigh kept advising him to stop and take a long rest, but he felt he was needed, and wouldn't. Then came that evening. He went out on a call and got caught in a snowstorm. Before he could get home the car stalled, and he walked about two miles through the deep drifts to get home to me—knowing that Mary Lou was expected at any time.

"As soon as I saw his face I knew he was ill. It was a terrible night. The telephone went out of commission. So I sent Bob and Connie together to the next farm to get help. Chad stayed with me. The neighbor's wife put her children to bed and came with her husband as fast as she could. But they were too late. The baby was born soon after, but Daddy was—gone.

"Chad told me once that it was that experience that made him decide definitely to be a doctor. He had thought of it before, but after that night he knew he could do nothing else." Tears were in Eleanor's eyes as she finished.

"At first I thought I would die, too," continued Mother Stewart, "but I had to live for the children. The road has been hard and lonesome, but God has given me grace for each day, and He has given much of happiness, too. He never makes the burden too heavy, and He has taught me the meaning of real joy. It is something that goes deep into the heart and has nothing to do with outside circumstances."

"I hope the Lord will find me as ready to learn as you have been," said Eleanor, humbly. "He has given me a big advantage to start with, by placing me here where you can teach me. Will you let me stay until I learn how to go on alone ?"

"Let you stay!" exclaimed Mother Stewart in surprise. "Why, you are my own daughter now, and this is your home. You are to stay until you want to leave—and I hope you won't ever want to do that."

After lunch Eleanor tried to help clear away the dishes, but found her hands too weak to be trusted. So she lay on the couch again. When Mrs. Stewart returned from the kitchen, Eleanor said, "There's one thing we've forgotten to talk about. Even though I am your daughter—I'm going to pay my expenses here. Please, Mother, don't object, or I shan't feel that I belong. I know that doctors and nurses and medicine all take money, and if you'll tell me what it has cost you, I'll write a check. I can't pay for the love and care you've given me, nor for the kindness of the girls and Bob, but I can pay the other bills, and I must."

"Can you afford it, Eleanor?" Mother Stewart asked in surprise. "Remember, you will have no money from your aunt's estate."

"I know that. But since Auntie died I've seldom spent all the monthly income she left me. I was paid for working with Professor Nichols at the University, and I never had time to be extravagant. Then my father and mother left some stock that pays me about twenty-five dollars a month, and Chad had life insurance that pays fifty dollars."

"Chad had life insurance for you?" exclaimed his mother in surprise.

"Yes, he took it out just as soon as he got back that fall. He said he had sold his colt to get the money."

"God surely led him there," mused the mother. "We wondered what became of the money he wanted more than his precious colt."

"I have the cottage and farm, too," Eleanor added, "but they just about pay for taxes and upkeep. If I really need money, I can rent the cottage. It is a lovely place."

"Don't worry about it now," instructed Mrs. Stewart. "Just rest and grow strong. You may pay your bills and help here as you see fit. You are a part of the family, and we all work together. What we want most now is for you to feel that you belong."

"I do already," returned Eleanor, gratefully. "No one could want to run away from such a place. I'll write to the University tomorrow and have them send my trunk."

"It is here now." Mrs. Stewart smiled.

"Really!" exclaimed Eleanor, in amazement. "When did you send for it ?"

"When you were sick. It is in the back hall. Bob will move it into your room for you anytime you want it."

"Oh, I'm so glad! Maybe he can move it tonight. Chad's Bible is in it, and I want it."

"Now," said Mrs. Stewart, rising and going to her desk, "there is a letter here I want you to read, but I am going to help you back to your room first and leave you alone while you read it. You need to rest before the girls get home, for Mary Lou will probably be so full of her trip that she will be all over the house talking to everyone at once."

Back in her own room, Eleanor lay with the letter in her hand. It was addressed in Chad's writing to his mother and was postmarked 11:30 on that last night he was alive. He must have mailed it just before he was struck.

Dear Mom: [she read]

I'm writing just a note tonight for I need your help—I mean your prayer help. It will mean a lot to me to know you are with me in this. I want you to pray for Eleanor. I told you about her last summer, and you must have guessed how much she means to me. I wish you could know her. Some day you shall. The day I bring her to you as a daughter will be the happiest day of my life. I can't tell you much about her, for I haven't the words. She's good and fine and brave, and so sweet that it makes my breath come fast when I think of her. But she has a terrific problem in her life just now and needs help. It isn't her fault entirely, but she has to make the decision. The problem is such a big one and the consequences of a decision are so great they stagger me. But it has to be done. Some day I'll tell you about it. But I must go to her now. Pray for us both, Mother, that she may be true to the Lord in her decision and that I may love Him better because I love her so much.

Give my love to Bob and the girls. I'll write a real letter in a couple of days. Lots of love to my Mom,

Chad

Eleanor read it through twice, then lay with the letter under her cheek while she rested. As she drifted off to sleep, she whispered, "God does answer prayer, doesn't He, Chad?"

22

The sound of a door slamming and a rush of feet along the hall awakened Eleanor from her doze. She heard Mary Lou call, "Mom, oh, Mom, where are you?" Then she heard Mrs. Stewart's cautiously whispered answer, "Sh! darling, Eleanor is asleep. Not quite so wild!"

Feeling rested after her nap and eager to see what the girls had bought, Eleanor threw off the blanket and slipped into her pumps. Voices came from the kitchen, and as she turned down the hall in that direction she was gratified to notice that she felt stronger and surer of step than when she had arisen that morning. She was really getting well!

As she paused in the kitchen door, Mary Lou looked up from the armful of bundles she was putting on the table, and cried, "Oh, it's Len! And she's up! Oh, you're so pretty! Can I kiss you?" It was fortunate that the doorframe was there, or both of them would have gone down in the wild rush Mary Lou made. Mother Stewart caught her and pulled her back.

"Careful, little Indian!" she cautioned. "Eleanor is a bit unsteady yet. Now, if you want to kiss her, do it quietly."

Eleanor opened her arms, and the little girl snuggled close and lifted her face. "Oh, I love you so much. It's like a Christmas present to have you here."

Eleanor returned the caress and whispered softly, "You're a dear little sister."

Then the parcels were opened. Connie's hat and the new purses, gloves, and shoes had to be admired, and the zipper case presented to Mother.

"Why, bless your heart," she exclaimed. "I've wanted one of these for years, but I thought only bankers and stockbrokers could afford them. What made you do this for me, Len ?"

"Oh, it's such a little compared with what you have done for me," she replied, "I wanted to do something for the folks who have been so good to me these long weeks. I lost a birthday while I was sick, so I wanted to celebrate today, and that's the only way I knew."

"Did you really lose a birthday?" asked Mary Lou anxiously. That was a major catastrophe!

"I think I must have." Eleanor smiled. "I was twenty-four when I came, and the calendar says I'm twenty-five now. I don't remember seeing a birthday lying around, so I must have lost it."

Chuckling, Mary Lou began to jump about and up and down as if animated by a hidden spring, as once more she looked over her treasures. Finally Mother Stewart bade her go with Connie to put away their purchases and change their dresses. She kept running back, however, to recount some exploit of the day, and at last Mrs. Stewart sighed. "We may as well listen to it and get it over with. Mary Lou, you take Eleanor into the living room and tell her about your trip while Connie and I help Mrs. Hunt with supper."

So off they went to the davenport, where Mary Lou settled Eleanor on the cushions, then sat cross-legged on the floor beside her and chattered away like a little magpie. She described the stores, the beautiful windows, a flat tire that two men had to fix, a little room called a "nelevator" that went up and down, the ten-cent store where she wanted so badly to stay, the banana split at the ice cream parlor, and a dozen other things. In the midst of the recital she made several trips to the kitchen, from each of which she returned with smiles and shining eyes.

"Do you ever sit still?" asked Eleanor, watching the restless little feet that were now pushing the big rocker back and forth vigorously.

"Not 'less I have to. I do sit still at school 'cause I should. It would shame Mom very badly if I was naughty at school. Do you like school, Len?"

"Yes, I do. I have always thought it was fun to learn things."

"Well, I don't. But I'm going to keep on and study hard and some day be a doctor."

"A doctor!" exclaimed Eleanor in surprise.

"Yes," and Mary Lou nodded emphatically. "I truly am. There's always been a Dr. Stewart, and Bob and Connie don't want to be doctors. So it has to be me. There are lady doctors, aren't there ?"

"Oh, yes," Eleanor assured her. "I once planned to be one myself."

"Oh, Len!" Mary Lou's face lighted up. "I have the nicest idea. You go on and be one, and you and I can have a doctor's office together."

"I don't know," replied Eleanor musingly. "Perhaps I will some day. When I get better we'll see."

"I'd like that almost as well as doctoring with Chad," continued Mary Lou. "Were you and Chad going to be doctors together, Len?"

"Yes, we were, dear—but God had something better for Chad," Eleanor replied softly.

"If that was God's way, then it's better for you, too. That's what Mom told me when he went away, and it made me feel not so bad anymore."

It surprised Eleanor that she could talk of Chad so easily now. She had thought she never could speak his name again, but here she was almost enjoying the conversation about him. He seemed so near now.

"Supper!" called Connie from the dining room.

"Oh, let me lead you out," begged Mary Lou of Eleanor. So she gave the little girl her hand, and Mary Lou proudly led the way to the dining room and placed Eleanor in a seat next to herself.

Bob sat at the head of the table and reverently asked God's blessing on the food and those who partook of it. Then Mary Lou undertook the duty of seeing that Eleanor was supplied with bread and vegetables, salad and milk.

"Gracious, little sister!" exclaimed Eleanor. "You must want to fatten me up for the market."

"I want you to get well," whispered Mary Lou in a low voice, "so we can begin doctoring."

When the table had been cleared in readiness for the dessert, Mary Lou left the room and shortly reappeared carrying a huge apple pie decorated with lighted candles. Before Eleanor had done more than open her mouth in surprise, Connie started to sing, and they all joined in.

"Happy birthday to you,
Happy birthday to you,
Happy birthday, dear Eleanor,
Happy birthday to you."

"We didn't have a cake," explained Mary Lou, "but pie tastes better anyway. And here's a birthday present for you. We didn't know you had had a birthday, or we would have brought you something really nice."

She laid a white box on Eleanor's plate. When the string was untied, it proved to be an assortment of salted nuts, and Eleanor exclaimed, "How did anyone guess that I'm very fond of these?"

Mary Lou laughed delightedly.

"It wasn't a guess. I *knew*. That summer Chad was home, he and I went to Benton one day, and he bought nuts to send to his best girl who was a regular squirrel over them, he said. I *know* that was you."

Mrs. Stewart glanced anxiously at Eleanor as Mary Lou burst forth in this way. How would she take this casual mention of Chad? Then as Eleanor laughed gaily and answered, "That was a joke with us, and I love you for remembering it," the mother drew a breath of thankful relief. She knew that the healing for which she had prayed was a blessed fact.

After the dishes were washed, the family gathered in the living room, and Connie brought out a new book of choruses. Tired but happy, Eleanor sat and listened as the voices blended in one song of praise after another. It was good to be part of this loving family. She was beginning to realize how much she had missed by holding aloof from them. She had staggered and fallen carrying her heavy burden alone, when all the time these stronger ones could have upheld and strengthened her.

"Now let us sing 'Blest Be the Tie That Binds,'" said Mother Stewart, "and then at least two of my chicks must be in bed," and she smiled at Eleanor and Mary Lou. Connie struck a few chords, and the grand old words rang out.

After the hymn, Bob, looking a little awkward, approached Eleanor and laid a flat package in her lap, saying as he did so, "I didn't know that this was to be a birthday celebration tonight, but here is something Marilyn and I have been expecting for a week. It came today and carries our best wishes."

Wonderingly Eleanor tore the package open, then drew in a breath of astonishment.

"Bob! Where did you get it? Oh, how can I thank you? It's —oh, it's so good! Mother—girls—look!"

They all gathered around. There in Eleanor's lap lay a framed picture of herself and Chad.

Hand in hand, they were coming over the brow of a hill, heads back, hair blowing in the breeze, while joy and hope and youth in love glowed from their faces.

"Oh—it's so wonderful to see his face again," Eleanor murmured, tears gathering in her eyes. "No, please let me cry. I'm not sad, I'm just happy. I remember when we took that. Chad was trying out a new time control on my camera. It was taken on that last day at the lake, just before we started home. Bob, *how* and *where* did you get it?"

"The undeveloped film was in Chad's suit that was sent home afterwards," replied Bob, looking pleased that his surprise had been such a success. "I just recently found it again and decided to have it developed, although I feared it was too old to be good. But the pictures were fine. Isn't that great of the dear old chap?" he concluded with a husky voice, trying to be casual.

Mother Stewart and each of the girls had to take a turn at studying the picture. Seeing the longing in their eyes, Bob promised that he would have a print made for each of them to keep. This enlargement, slightly tinted, placed in a simple silver frame, was for Eleanor alone, to remind her of those last beautiful days together.

"Bob," said Eleanor, when the picture was returned to her. "I can't tell you how much I thank you. If you only knew how I've tried to remember Chad's face. This brings it back, just the way I want to remember him. Oh, I am so grateful to the Lord for bringing me here!" she concluded, looking from one dear face to the other. "You're the nicest folks I know!"

23

April days sped past, and May followed in swift succession. Eleanor was so well and energetic by the time June arrived that it was hard to realize she had ever been ill. Mother Stewart's nursing had been triumphantly successful.

As soon as she felt able, Eleanor had written Mr. Hastings, informing him of her illness and her present circumstances. The lawyer's reply arrived by return mail, and together with sincere wishes for her improved health he stated his desire to confer with her about her inheritance.

Oh, dear! thought Eleanor impatiently. *That money again!*

But it seemed that this was the end of it all. Mr. Hastings had written the trustees of the laboratories informing them of Eleanor's desire to give them the full estate. Knowing the circumstances of the will, they were loath to accept the full sum and suggested an early conference in which some compromise solution could be reached.

"Mother, I wish you'd read this letter and tell me what you think" she said, entering the kitchen where Mother Stewart was cutting out cookies. That busy lady wiped the flour from her hands and took the letter, reading rapidly to herself while Eleanor sat on a stool and munched a cooky with a preoccupied air.

"Tell me first what you want to do about it," replied Mrs. Stewart, looking from the paper when she had finished.

"It makes me so tired. I want to let the old will stand and be through with the whole matter once for all."

"Since you asked my opinion," said Mrs. Stewart, resuming her occupation, "it seems to me that a much better plan would be for you to meet with Mr. Hastings and one of the trustees of the laboratory and listen to what they wish to suggest."

"I really don't want that money—any of it," said Eleanor wearily. "Why should I have to take it?"

"The fact that they want to divide the sum with you may be the Lord's leading, my dear," was the gentle reply. "You are trying to follow Him now, are you not? He may have some use for that money."

"But what could I do with it?" continued Eleanor. "I don't want to pour it out thoughtlessly on the first worthy cause I can think of, and I can't bear to think of handling it myself. It caused so much trouble once that I guess I'm afraid of it!"

"Ah, but you don't have to worry over it," was the reassuring reply. "Pray over it, then leave it in God's hands. The laboratory is a most worthy project, but it isn't definitely the Lord's work. If the money or any part of it is to be yours, you have an obligation as His steward to spend it as He would have you. There are many places in His work where the need is very great."

"Well, in that case, I am willing to talk to Mr. Hastings or anyone else," said Eleanor thoughtfully. "If it seems the right thing to do, I will take a part of the money to use for the Lord's work, but I'm quite sure that none of it shall ever be kept for my own use. God has provided for me otherwise, and I'm young and strong and can work for my living anyway."

So matters were arranged, and in a few days Mr. Hastings arrived with two gentlemen from the laboratory.

It was finally agreed by all that the laboratory should keep half the money, and that the other half should be Eleanor's. Mr. Hastings promised to take care of the legal formalities, and the conference was over.

"Now, what shall I do with it, Mother?" asked Eleanor, when the money had been deposited in the bank in her name.

"That is a matter for us to pray over and talk about, dear," replied Mrs. Stewart. "I have some suggestions, but we will want to see where the Spirit leads."

It was finally decided that one third of the sum should be given to a leper hospital that an old schoolmate of Mrs. Stewart's had founded in China. Another third should go to a settlement house, and the remainder should endow a scholarship in Bethel College in the city where Eleanor and Chad had lived and been so happy. So three checks were written and mailed, and Eleanor drew a breath of relief for she was tired of money. The load was gone.

Farm life was new to Eleanor and very interesting. She entered zestfully into every phase of it and quickly learned to help in the kitchen, garden, orchard, and even the field.

The rooms upstairs filled one by one as summer came. Here, too, Eleanor found that she could be useful, for her years of waiting on Aunt Ruth had made her adept at nursing. Mother Stewart soon came to rely much on Eleanor's help in the little sanitarium, whereby easing the load that she herself carried.

Canning season brought a new venture. Eleanor, Connie, and Marilyn opened a small canning factory in the huge shed in the backyard. There they cleaned and prepared fruits and vegetables, washed the jars, and operated the pressure canner. They made jams and jellies in open kettles and concocted many batches of pickles. This was fascinating work to Eleanor. Her long hours of meticulous labor in the science laboratory stood her in good stead now, and she quickly adapted herself to the careful detail needed for successful canning.

Canning was new and fascinating to Eleanor, but it was an old and somewhat tiresome story to Connie. So more and more the responsibility shifted. As the shelves in the basement storeroom filled, Eleanor grew correspondingly proud of her handiwork.

On Mondays the laundry was a busy place. The washing machine was so large that Eleanor smiled, comparing it mentally with the little one she had used in the city apartment. Mrs. Stewart always supervised the laundry herself and sang as she worked. Perhaps her occupation influenced her thoughts, for as she rinsed the clothes her favorite hymn seemed to be

"Whiter than the snow,
Yes, whiter than the snow,
Wash me in blood of the Lamb
And I shall be whiter than the snow!"

Hanging the glistening white sheets out in the sunshine, she was sometimes heard repeating to herself, "His clothes were white as no fuller on earth could white them," or, "Christ loved the church and gave Himself for it, that He might sanctify and cleanse it with the washing of water through the Word."

Tuesday was ironing day. One of the girls would do the flatwork on an electric ironer, and another would work with the hand iron on dresses and shirts and aprons.

One day as Eleanor operated the ironer and Marilyn was busy ironing a heap of baby Patty's dresses, Marilyn told some of the story of how this model farm came to be.

"When Doctor Dad was alive they rented out the farmland, for of course he could not tend it himself. My father farmed it for him, and we lived in the little cottage on the other side of the orchard. It was my mother and father who came here the night that Doctor Dad died. I was a rather small girl then, but I can remember when he went. Afterward my mother came over and helped Mother Stewart quite a lot, for you know Mary Lou was a tiny baby and Mother Stewart wasn't well.

"She had to discover some way of supporting the family, so Chad and Bob undertook to run the farm. I can remember how small Bob looked as he worked in the fields. Doctor Dad had left some insurance, and Mother Stewart decided to take it and fix up this big house for a convalescent home. Dad's doctor friends said they would help by sending patients to her. So she had a furnace put in and three bathrooms. The upstairs used to be four big rooms before it was made into six small ones with two bathrooms. Then Mother Stewart had two more rooms built on downstairs so that the whole family could be together and so that she might preserve as much of their home life as possible.

"There already was electricity in the house, so Mother bought all the labor saving devices she could afford. It has been a paying proposition from the start."

"She's the most wonderful person I ever met, Marilyn," replied Eleanor, looking up from her work. "It's almost worth having been sick to have have her care for me."

"She's brave, too," Marilyn added. "Why, if Bob were taken away, I couldn't carry on as she has. The only thing she hasn't done that she and the doctor planned is build a fireplace. They had intended to have one in the end of the living room, but she wouldn't do it. Said she couldn't quite stand that."

"I know how she feels," replied Eleanor with a catch in her voice. "You can go on living, but there are a few doors of memory you daren't open any more.

"You're another brave one, Eleanor," Marilyn continued. "You never complain, and yet sometimes I feel almost ashamed of the happiness that Bob and I have when I know you can't help but feel lonesome."

"I am lonesome, Marilyn, and I can't deny it," was the frank reply. "But I am much happier than I was last winter, for I was all alone then. Now this home and family are part mine, and I feel so near to Chad that I can almost see him at times. He is with Christ, and since I am learning to abide in Him, Chad is bound to be near."

"Well, your coming here has been a blessing to the family too," said Marilyn. "You have helped to soothe the hurt in Mother's heart over Chad's death. She loves to have the one he loved here in the home."

For a long minute Eleanor did not reply, then said with an effort, "I truly don't grieve for Chad anymore, Marilyn. He was the best and most beautiful thing that life could ever give. But he is with God now, and, although I am lonely at times, the old heartache and bitterness have gone, and God has given me a real peace about his death. But there's one pain that *never* goes. Oh, Marilyn, I want my baby!"

Marilyn turned from the ironing board and put her arms about Eleanor's shoulders, smoothing the brown head that had drooped in sudden sorrow.

"I know you do, dear. I don't see how you stand it. But God can help that pain too. Bob and I pray every day for you and him. And—do you know what?" Marilyn's voice dropped to a confiding whisper. "I am praying now that you will get your baby back."

Eleanor looked up in surprise.

"Yes, I am," said the young wife, confidently. "At first I didn't have faith to ask that. But one day I decided I would unless God gave me a sign that I shouldn't. That night when I read my Bible the chapter I read was in James, and one of the verses was, 'Ye have not because ye ask not.' So it came to me that it was wrong not to ask God for things we long for."

"But what if it isn't His will?" argued Eleanor. "How could He want me to have him again when I gave him away? All I can pray is that God will take care of him and make him be kind of man Chad was. I haven't any right to ask for him back."

Marilyn's tender heart was wrung by Eleanor's dejection. "Why, none of us get what we deserve," she continued hopefully. "We deserved death, and yet God gave Jesus to save us. I didn't deserve anything at all, but God gave me Bob and Patty. I just don't believe that God has any pets!"

"But I was so wicked!" cried Eleanor in anguish. "Mother tries to make me feel better by saying I wasn't responsible. But I was! It's all my fault!"

Marilyn tried to think of something else comforting. "Well, remember David," she said finally. "He was much more wicked than you. But because he repented, he came to be called 'a man after God's own heart.' None of us are what we should be, and who's to judge which of us is most wicked? Only God can do that, and when He does I don't believe it will be you. Come on, honey, dry your eyes, and let's finish this ironing. We're all praying for little Chad, (that's what Bob and I call him), and if God doesn't send him back to us, He will give us peace about him. I know that!"

* * *

With the advancing summer, the work in the fields became very heavy. Bob and Uncle John and Tom Page, the hired man, were kept so busy that the girls had to help with the chores.

Then there came a day in August when Uncle John got overheated in the field and had to lie down with an ice pack on his head. The air was hot and sultry, and off in the west a gray-green cloud betokened a coming storm. But the alfalfa hay was just right for storing in the mow.

So Connie and Eleanor donned overalls and raced out. Connie and Bob and Tom wielded pitchforks while Eleanor drove the team. Quickly, silently they worked while the big cloud drew nearer. It was a race, but the farmers won, and at half past five, when the rain came accompanied by a high wind and lurid flashes of lightning, the last load of hay was safely under cover.

Through all these experiences and days of healthful labor and exercise, Eleanor felt as if she really belonged to the family. After that lonesome year she had spent, the love and gayity of this home seemed like a foretaste of heaven. Having come at last to a haven of rest after a stormy voyage, she thought she would never want to leave this safe port again.

One of the first Sundays after she was able to be about, Eleanor went to church and Sunday school with the family. She thought the folk at the church exhibited an undue curiosity about her. Underneath it all lay kindliness and good will, but Eleanor had yet to learn the ways of country people. When she realized that she was the subject of gossip and some conjecture, she was embarrassed and preferred to remain at home rather than face their whispers and glances again. Also she disliked to cause pain to the Stewarts. Therefore she hesitated to go with them.

Divining through motherly intuition the reason for Eleanor's reluctance to appear again in church, Mrs. Stewart asked for the marriage certificate and had it framed. This she hung with her copy of the picture of Chad and Eleanor, side by side in the living room. There it hung when the Ladies' Aid Society met a week later.

As the weeks passed and the neighbors saw how Eleanor fitted into the family and how they accepted her as one of themselves, talk soon died down. Having lived in the community for a quarter of a century, the Stewarts were loved and respected by all, and when the first burst of curiosity and wonder had subsided, the neighbors were ready to open their hearts to the girl whom Chad had loved.

Mother Stewart told the story of the baby to several close friends, and their prayers joined hers for the welfare of the little lost one.

Gradually Eleanor attended church more regularly and learned to love it. One Sunday when Mother Stewart was kept at home by an ailing patient, Eleanor taught the primary class with enjoyment. But she drew back from the young people's social affairs. She was always willing and eager to keep baby Patty while Bob and Marilyn went out, glad for an opportunity to pour out on that little person all her frustrated mother love. But when they urged her to attend young people's parties, they received only one answer, a firm no.

On one project, however, Eleanor did work with the young people and thereby won their friendship and admiration. At the back of the church the hillside rose abruptly and made a barren setting for the cemetery beyond. Log steps, which had been in place for many years, formed the only break in the rocky hillside. One day Connie and some friends expressed a desire to improve the appearance of the ugly hillside by making at least a presentable stairway along its slope.

Eleanor listened in silence for some moments, then spoke hesitantly.

"I have a plan for a rock garden," she said, "which would be lovely on that hillside. There are plenty of rocks, and, if the boys will help, I think it can be made."

The idea appealed to all of them. They began work on the project almost immediately, boys and girls both using all the time they could spare from farm work to contribute to beautifying the hillside. Under Eleanor's direction, the boys placed the rocks and made terraces and steps. The girls searched the woods for the right kinds of ferns and other plants. Flower catalogs were consulted for suggestions, and special rock garden plants were ordered from a nursery. By mid-August the barren hillside had become a place of real beauty, covered with delicate ferns, velvety moss, and trailing vines. Next year there would be flowers ready to bloom.

The Sunday following completion of the project found the young people out under the trees at sunset, holding a dedicatory service for their labor of love. Hymns and choruses were sung, then the president of the group led in prayer. After the prayer, the pastor spoke, thanking the young workers in behalf of the church for their service, which had added so greatly to the beauty of the property. Then turning toward Eleanor, he said, "I think one person deserves special thanks. I understand that Eleanor Stewart designed this garden and supervised its execution. I wonder if she will say a word to us about it."

Eleanor's face flushed, then paled. She had never in her life said a word in a Christian service. Her heart beat fast at the impossible suggestion.

But her eyes fell on Mother Stewart's confident face, and the smile that she saw there, expressing love and pride in her, gave the assurance she needed. Rising to her feet, she faced the group, and, though her lips trembled at first, they steadied before long.

"The garden plan," she began, "was one that Chad and I made together for a hillside near which we hoped to live when we had finished school. That hill was so much like this one that I realized the same plans could be used here. At first I hesitated to use our plan, but I knew Chad would have said, 'Go on.' So I did. I hope that it will be a place of beauty and blessing for many years to come. And I hope you'll all think of it as a gift from Chad."

She sat down quickly, and Mary Lou leaned over to squeeze her hand, while Mother Stewart wiped her eyes furtively.

On the way home, walking across the fields that lay between the house and the church, Mrs. Stewart said, "That was a big thing you did, Eleanor, my dear, and you've made me ashamed of myself this day."

"Ashamed? You?" said Eleanor in surprise. "Oh, Mother, of what?"

But Mrs. Stewart did not reply. It was many weeks before Eleanor learned the answer to her question.

* * *

So the summer had passed, with its work and play, its sunshine, its occasional storms. It was not always clear sailing for the girl who was learning to let the Pilot navigate her ship through "life's tempestuous sea." For days at a time, she worked and sang, studied her Bible, and prayed, finding life full and good. Then would come sleepless nights and days when the lamp of faith turned low.

When any soul is really fighting to achieve and grow for the Lord, Satan uses all his devices to cause trouble. So it was with Eleanor. There were bouts with fear and doubt and loneliness and weakness, and there were times when the battle seemed a losing one. But she had learned to go to the Source of life for help and strength, and when things were blackest she prayed hardest. And gradually she was growing. Help and encouragement she still needed, but she now knew that the day was coming when she could face the world again to take up whatever work God had chosen for her.

One day Eleanor and Mrs. Stewart were seated on the porch, shelling peas.

"Eleanor," said the older woman, "don't you think you ought to go back to school?"

"Go back to school!" echoed Eleanor, in surprise.

"Hadn't you thought of it?" Mrs. Stewart continued.

"Yes," the girl admitted, "but not favorably. Mother, I know I just couldn't bear to go back to the University again."

"You need not. There are other schools."

"But—but—I thought you wanted me to stay here with you."

Mother Stewart reached out and squeezed Eleanor's hand.

"My dear child," she said, "if I were to be selfish about this I should like nothing better than for you to stay here and help me on the farm. I love to have you here. But I mustn't be selfish. Your training thus far has been too valuable for you to throw away. Perhaps you might want to teach later or enter some other field of work where a college degree would be required. Even if you don't know now what you would like to do, you can finish your college work and then decide as the Lord leads you."

"I suppose you are right," said Eleanor thoughtfully. "But where could I go to school besides the university?"

"Bethel College," suggested Mrs. Stewart quietly.

Eleanor spread her hands in dismay. "I couldn't afford it," she demurred. "Don't forget I've given away my money."

"Eleanor Stewart!" said the mother in mock reproof. "I believe you are simply making excuses now. Have you forgotten that you have endowed a scholarship there and that you are to name the recipient?"

"Yes," said Eleanor, with a laugh, "I honestly had forgotten. But why can't Connie have that? That's what I had in mind. She wants to go to college."

"Connie can wait. She would like one more year of music with Mr. Mueller in Benton before she goes, and I need her here this year. Won't you go on and finish, Eleanor, and then if the Lord wills you can stay with me while Connie goes? Perhaps for that purpose you came here to us."

Eleanor drew a long breath and said, "I think you are right. So, if you will promise to back me up with your most powerful prayers, I'll try."

"Of course I'll pray for you, dear, and the Lord will lead every step of the way."

And so it was settled, and Eleanor began to look forward to the opening of school.

But the summer had yet one more momentous experience in store for her.

Mary Lou had definitely and trustfully accepted Christ as her Savior and was preparing to follow Him in baptism. One Saturday evening Eleanor sat on the front porch and could not help overhearing Mother Stewart and the little girl talking seriously in the living room. In simple terms, the mother explained the meaning and symbolism of baptism and its necessity for the obedient Christian believer. She answered Mary Lou's questions with Scripture verses and showed the little girl the duties and obligations that were entailed by the privilege of church membership, describing the church to her as the Body of Christ, in which each member must contribute his part.

As Eleanor sat in the twilight and overheard the conversation, she began to consider her own part in that sacred Body. The words that Mother Stewart had said about baptism had made a deep impression on her. Finally she arose and went to her room, where she sat down and opened her Bible, seeking the references Mother Stewart had used.

"We are buried with Him by baptism into death, that like as Christ was raised up from the dead by the glory of the Father, even so we also should walk in newness of life."

Next morning at the close of his sermon, the pastor extended the usual invitation. As the congregation began singing the invitation hymn, Mary Lou stepped from her mother's side and walked shyly down the aisle. A moment later Eleanor followed.

Mary Lou, upon questioning by the pastor, gave a clear statement of faith that left no doubt in his mind as to the validity of her Christian experience. Then Eleanor gave her testimony —just as direct, just as simple. There were tears in many eyes when the two had finished.

That evening Mary Lou and Eleanor entered the baptismal waters together. As she came up out of the water, "to walk in newness of life," Eleanor turned her gaze for a moment thru the window to the two tall pines that stood on the hill. To the ones who were watching her, her face seemed to glow with an inner light.

24

Dear Mother:

(This is the first time in my life that I have ever written those dear words!)

Well, I'm here, and much more frightened than I was four years ago when I entered the University. Then I knew everything and was going to tell the world so. Now all I know is that of the three hundred students on this campus, I feel the most ignorant and as strange as if I'd been reared in Timbuktu. Among the other students I feel as old as Uncle John.

I didn't have a bit of trouble getting my transcripts from the University. Mrs. Martin and I had a lovely half hour together. I see now that I could have been spared many hours of lonely agonizing if I had tried to meet her halfway last winter. How silly I was! Yet, I'm not sorry about anything now, for it all led me to you and the farm.

After I left her I decided to run up to the lab for a few minutes and ask about my dear old Professor Nichols. But as I left the office, I met Professor Merritt, for whom Chad worked so long. When he saw me he grabbed both my hands and we stood there in the street, neither of us able to say a word. Finally he gulped and choked and managed to say, "You gave us a bad scare last spring, young lady."

I couldn't answer, for the sight of him had brought back too many memories. He saw I couldn't talk, so went on, "What a pair of children you were! And to think you were married! I suspected as much, but when you took his death so calmly, I decided I'd been mistaken. And all the time you weren't calm at all, but just a little bottled-up volcano!''

I was so surprised that I found my voice again and said, ''How did you ever guess we were married?''

''Well, Chad just wasn't a good dissembler. And I'm not so old and absent-minded as Professor Nichols! I just had an intuition. But when Chad died, you certainly put up a good act.''

''To everyone but myself,'' I said. Then (we had been walking along) we reached the door of his building, and I felt suddenly led by the Spirit to witness for the Lord who had done so much for me.

''It's a queer story,'' I said, ''and my part of it isn't very credi-table. But it has been worthwhile, for through all these experiences I've learned to know the Lord that Chad loved and served. And I've found my place in Chad's dear home. So I can go on. The life that is left to me shall be spent in service to that Lord.''

He looked embarrassed but finally managed to bring forth a re-ply. ''Chad had the real thing, I believe,'' he said.

''You can have it, too.'' I answered. That frightened him, I guess, for he wished me well and said a hurried goodbye.

By that time I hadn't the courage to open any more closed pages. So I took the car for Bethel. It is hard to realize that these two institutions are only an hour's ride apart in this big city

The dean of women at Bethel is a motherly soul whose hus-band was formerly a teacher here. She looked me over, asked a few questions, and evidently decided that my age and experience fitted me for a position of grave responsibility, for she gave me a big room with two freshmen. Apparently I'm to mother them! One is a very large, placid-looking girl named Angela. She doesn't look ex-citing. The other is a tiny, red-headed cherub with the face of an an-gel and the loveliest brown eyes. Her name is Wilhelmina. She looks pathetically lonesome and homesick, and I anticipate having to rock her to sleep tonight. She is just the kind of child one could cuddle.

Time to go to supper. I'll write more tomorrow or over the weekend. Don't forget to pray often for your absent child. She real-izes as she steps out from the shelter of your care that the battle isn't over—not by a whole lot! Give all the family my love, and kiss baby Patty for me. I miss her very much. And lots of love to the dearest mother on earth.

Len

P.S. Help! Help! Someone tell me by return mail who Philip King is. I started to ask Angela, and she was so shocked that I had to let her think I was joking. Where have I been all my life that I've never heard of him before? And why is the fact that he is back (from where?) the biggest thrill of the campus? If you can help me in this way, you may save my career from shipwreck at the outset.

The Farm—September 24

Dear Len:

Just a note as we're getting two new boarders today and are busy. Mom will write tonight and tell you any news. But for the sake of your reputation, I'll tell you about Philip King. He has been teacher of Christian education and practical work at Bethel for about five years. In the summer he speaks at youth camps and assemblies and is, without a doubt, the most popular youth worker in these parts. His wife goes with him and specializes in flannelgraph work and music. They're a great team! I never saw them, but Marilyn was at camp two years ago, and she doesn't like him. She says he's too self-satisfied. But Marilyn doesn't see any man but Bob and never did. Everyone else likes P. K.

As to where he's been—a year ago last summer he was hurt very badly in an auto accident and was in the hospital for months. He didn't teach all year. I hadn't heard that he was back in circulation. Hope this bit of information will enable you to act knowingly enough to avoid disgrace.

It's lonely here without you. But we're all remembering to pray.

Con

Bethel, October 8

Dear Folks at Home:

I promised myself I'd write you a real letter before I did one bit of studying or even washed out the clothes that have been accumulating in my laundry bag. I've been so rushed that my letters have been dashed off between classes or in any odd moment I could find. Today I got homesick for you all and vowed I'd treat you better. Your letters mean so much to me that I want you to keep them coming.

You asked me about my roommates. I have to laugh at the way I described them to you. As a judge of character, I'd make a fine scrubwoman. Angela, the "placid" one, is as temperamental as an April day and in my humble opinion is a spoiled baby. She's an

170

only child of wealthy parents, and at first I couldn't figure out why she ever came to Bethel. Certainly not from any deep desire to learn! But it didn't take long to find the answer to that one! She's infatuated with Philip King.

When he walks into chapel she gets a soulful look in her eyes and never takes her glance off him. I'm not in her Christian ed. class, but I've been hearing reports of her attitude there. P.K.—with all his conceit—is getting a bit embarrassed. Most of the tales I hear come from my other roommate, Wilhelmina—she of the angelic countenance. She's just another example of my gullibility. Instead of being a cuddly innocent, she's a little "hellion." She says a neighbor called her that when she was six and she has been trying to live up—or down—to it ever since. She is called Billy, and of all the undisciplined little hoydens you could imagine, she takes the lead. She thinks laws were made to be broken, and she doesn't care in the least about her lessons. She was sent here as a disciplinary measure. (I am becoming aware of the fact that a lot of families use Bethel as a reform school!)

Angela and Billy agree just like the gingham dog and the calico cat. And most of the time I'm in between them. In spite of her naughtiness, I like Billy, and when she starts out to "nail Angela's hide to the fence," as she daintily expresses it, I find myself smiling in spite of myself. The other night Angela should have been studying psychology but instead was raving about the charms of P.K. It seems that in his absence he has added a new charm—a lock of white hair amid the brown waves. It is picturesque, no denying it. And the sight of it wrings Angela's soul anew every day. She says it speaks to her of the great suffering he underwent last year. "But," she adds soulfully, "he wears it just like a banner."

"Banner, my eye!" snorts Billy. "He wears it like a medal. Banners stand for a cause—but medals mean personal achievements. He feels he earned that picturesque adornment. Anyway" —oh, heartless Billy!— "that's not from his injury. He had a boil there. Our doctor lanced it, and he told me."

That shook Angela's tender soul so deeply she couldn't continue the argument, so she retired in mournful silence into her books. That's the kind of thing I live with. Do you wonder that I do my studying in the library and spend my free hour in the afternoon in the park?

That hour, by the way, is the happiest of my day. This lovely fall weather the park is full of mothers and babies, and I have great fun watching them—the babies. Most of them are chubby, well-washed-and-combed little busybodies that toddle around and fall in the grass or reach out from their strollers to pull another's hair or poke inquisitive fingers into his eyes or mouth. I sit on the bench and smile at them and pray for my little baby, that he too may be well and happy. No, Mother, don't worry, for I won't be morbid. But I can't keep my baby out of my mind, and I have decided that every time a thought of him comes, it is God's signal to pray for him. So wherever I am when the urge comes, I pray, and it does help.

Last winter when I was so desperate and was determined to work out my atonement, one of the things I wanted to do was find a baby to care for. That desire, I must confess, has never left me even though I know now that my forgiveness doesn't depend on my own works. Surely somewhere there is one little baby who isn't wanted or who needs help. Just this week I have found an opening that may lead somewhere.

You know that each member of the Christian ed. classes has to do some practical work in a church or settlement house or other agency. I have been assigned to the Anna Henderson Institute. You know all about it undoubtedly, as it is one of our denominational projects. I've only been down once but am encouraged to believe that somewhere in that horrible neighborhood, full of ragged, unkempt children, I can find one baby who needs mothering—said mothering to be done by me!

Before I close, please tell Marilyn that I share her views about P.K. His persuasiveness and teaching ability are wonderful, and at first I was thrilled by his lectures. But two weeks of them have convinced me that he is as much aware of his charms as anyone else, and I can't stand that.

He puzzles me, though. He looks so familiar. I'm sure I've seen him before, but where?

My dearest love to you all. I'm going to write more regularly now that I'm settled. Must stop now and arbitrate a dispute between Angela and Billy as to which of them will wear my plaid jacket. It fits neither.

Len

Bethel, November 8

Dear Mother:

Before Thanksgiving comes any nearer, I am sorry to have to tell you that I can't get home for the festivities. I don't feel that I can afford the expense of the trip for such a short stay, so I'll save my money to come for the Christmas holidays. Just think—two whole weeks then! For Thanksgiving Fred and Carolyn insist on my visiting them.

Angela and Billy will both go home for four days. They live here in the city, so it's no problem for them. In fact they live only a few blocks apart. I have discovered that they attended rival high schools, which gives them another topic for warfare. I anticipate that long weekend with the keenest delight. The silence in our room will be balm to my soul.

That soul needs some kind of balm tonight. For the first time in my life I have been laughed at, and I didn't like it. I admit the incident was funny, but Dr. King needn't have rubbed it in.

(Yes, I call him Dr. all the time now, because I get so tired of hearing Angela and his other devotees calling him Philip.)

Last night we had a party in the gym to help the students get better acquainted with each other. The youngsters' chatter didn't interest me, so I decided to hunt up some lonesome-looking youths and maids to see if I could help them. I had just settled comfortably in a corner to talk to a bashful-looking lad named Dick Dunlap, who needs to have his self-confidence built up, when someone started a game of Bible baseball.

I agreed to take part though I had qualms about my batting abilities, Bible study having been added to my life so recently.

At first all went well, and as I happened to have questions "pitched" at me which reminded me of the book of Bible stories in Aunt Ruth's library, I found myself in the position of star player on my team. Dr. King was the pitcher for the other team, but even against him I was going strong. Suddenly he threw a wicked curve ball at me, so to speak. "Who was Ahab's wife?" he asked.

Quick as a wink I answered, "Beelzebub!"

Horrors, how they laughed! It was funny, I admit. I laughed too. But I don't think Dr. King had to be *quite* so amused. He acted as though it was the first joke he had heard in a year.

Then today in class (I take Old Testament history under him) he asked me if I didn't want to teach the class. Everyone laughed again. Now that wasn't kind. However, I'm trying not to let it bother me. It's just that being laughed at is a new experience, and I haven't learned to like it yet.

Angela and Billy continue to wrangle. Did I tell you that I have discovered that both their fathers are on the Board of Trustees at Bethel? There's a difference, though. Billy's father is just a mem-

173

ber. Angela's father is chairman and is *thinking* of giving a new library building.

Every time I go, I enjoy the work at the institute more. I wanted to work in the kindergarten but was assigned to the high school girls and am teaching handcrafts and conducting a Bible class on Friday night. Dr. King preaches at the institute twice on Sundays and is director of all the work there. He is more likeable when he is there than he is in the classroom. He really has a genius for that kind of work. The other day he said, "If my wife were stronger I'd like to give up teaching and live at the institute and just see what work for the Lord could be done in such a place." I don't know what ails his wife. Apparently she doesn't go out much, for I haven't ever seen either her or the baby, which I am told is now over a year old.

Still no luck in finding a baby I could help mother. I thought surely I could find one easily in the institute neighborhood. But those poor folk down there seem to be rich in love, at least. No matter how ragged and hungry and cold they are, or how many babies they already have, they hang tenaciously onto their newest offspring and seem to love it as much as they loved their first. I find myself spending every spare penny buying little things to help them. But I can't ask any of them to give me a baby!

I'll be thinking of you all on Thanksgiving day and am already looking forward to Christmas. Am going now to practice in one of the music rooms with Dick Dunlap (the bashful boy I wrote you about talking to at the party). He says he sings a little but hasn't practiced since he came. He's the nicest youngster I've met here. He is in the seminary, comes from Arizona, and is pretty homesick. He is afraid of most of the girls but evidently thinks I'm a motherly soul and quite safe.

Tell Mary Lou I haven't had a letter from her since I came. Give my love to all, even the calves.

Len

The Farm—November 12

Dear Len:

I am not a very good writing person. It gets me very tired. But I am lonesome today and cross at my family. Not at Mother. She is always all right. But sometimes Bob and Connie are a trial to me. And Marilyn is always sympathetic with Bob. So I feel quite alone.

It all started at breakfast. Mother wasn't down because she had a headache, and I asked if I could lead in the breakfast prayer. Then, when I started, I forgot that I wasn't alone, and I prayed just as if only God could hear me. And I prayed for my husband. Bob and Connie laughed right out. Do you think that was nice? I don't. I bet you wouldn't have laughed. Every girl expects to be married some day and getting the right kind of man isn't so easy. So I thought I'd start praying early to keep from making some awful mistake and marrying someone like Pete Novak down the road. Maybe it did sound funny to Bob and Connie, but they needn't have laughed so hard. I know now how you feel toward P.K.

Mother got up after a while, and she told me it was all right and for me to keep on praying for my husband and my children too. So I felt better.

There are four new calfs since you left. And Scotty had three little puppies. And a cow stepped on a hen and broke her leg, and Bob wanted to kill her, and I took her and bandaged her leg and put a stick on it for a splint and hid her in the barn, and she got all right, and Bob said I was a good doctor. He is an all right brother sometimes.

I must quit. I think I smell popcorn. Perhaps I should go out and forgive Bob and Connie.

Hugs and kisses,
Mary Lou

Bethel, November 15

Dear Folks:

I am quite the most humble person on the campus tonight, and the Lord has given me such a happy experience that I feel ashamed of my unworthiness. I can't write of anything else till I tell you about it. I really should have been ashamed to let Dr. King's teasing bother me, but it did. I guess I got so used to Professor Nichols calling me his star pupil, etc., that I thought the place was mine for keeps. And when Dr. King kept teasing me about Beelzebub, I resented it. Every time he got a chance he spoke of it, until I began to dread meeting him.

Then day before yesterday, a group of us were standing in the big hall outside the dining room waiting for the dinner bell. On the table near the door was a beautiful plant that some kind friend had sent in, and we were all admiring it. Angela was by my side, and suddenly, in the sweet high tone she uses when Dr. King is near, she asked, "Isn't it just divine? What gives it so many different shades of green?" I was just ready to answer her and say "God," (for it wouldn't have done a bit of good to explain nature's secret coloring processes to Angela) when Dr. King's voice, cool and assured, cut in. "That's simple. You see, each cell of the middle part of the leaves contains in its chloroplasm small green bodies called cytoplasts, which are responsible for the green color of the leaves."

Now if I had stopped for one second to collect my thoughts, I'd never have spoken, because no one else noticed that he had twisted those words. And it really didn't make a *bit* of difference. But the old spirit of setting things right rose up in me, and before I thought I burst forth with this:

"Oh, no! Each cell contains in its cytoplasm the chloroplasts which make the color."

I was sorry at once, and the silence which came over the group was so profound that it fairly smote my ears. Then it was shattered by Dr. King's voice, laughing and insolent.

"Professor Nichols would be glad to hear your explanation, I am sure, Mrs. Stewart. He will probably change his textbook if you'll correct him. I didn't know you knew your biology as well as you do your Old Testament."

That last was really a mean dig, and for a moment my "almost-red-headed temper," as Chad used to say, threatened to get out of control. But I am learning slowly to trust my Lord for even such little things, and He gave me grace to smile and let it pass. But ever since then I have been ashamed of feeling so annoyed.

Then, this morning as I was leaving chapel, I was given a notice to call at the office at once. Immediately fearful that something was wrong with you dear ones at home, I hurried down. There sat the impeccably handsome Dr. King, waiting for me.

"Won't you come in here, Mrs. Stewart?" he asked, indicating an empty conference room. I walked in, and he came in and closed the door. I couldn't imagine what on earth was up. We both sat down.

"Mrs. Stewart, first of all I must apologize to you," he said, with so much diffidence and humility that I could hardly believe it was really happening.

"What for?" I asked, although I had a good idea.

"For my inexcusable rudeness the other day. I was ashamed of myself at once, even when I still thought you wrong, but since I found out who you are, I have been eating humble pie in great quantities."

My mouth dropped open.

"How—what—why—" I began.

"I'll begin at the beginning, not to keep you in suspense. Professor Spencer, who teaches botany, is ill—with measles, of all things. Can you figure out why an old man should take such a disease? Anyway, he will be gone for at least two weeks. Well, we didn't have anyone to take his classes. So this morning I called the University asking them if they could send someone here to substitute for two weeks. I wonder if you could guess whom they recommended?''

My brain just didn't function. I sat and looked stupid.

"Their answer was that they didn't have anyone to send, but that Miss Eleanor Stewart, who collaborated with Professor Nichols on the textbook we use at Bethel, was now attending Bethel College and could undoubtedly fill the vacancy satisfactorily.''

"Oh, my!'' I managed to gasp.

"Feeling quite small,'' P.K. continued, "I crept away from the phone and went to find one of those textbooks. Of course I discovered that you were right and I was completely wrong. Then I read Professor Nichols's foreword containing the tribute to your work and was reduced one or two more sizes. I felt as small as even you could desire.''

"But, really—'' I began.

He waved me quiet.

"Please say that you will forgive me for having been so rude. Then come over and let me introduce you to the botany class. Will you teach it?''

"Oh, yes!'' I think my delight must have been written all over my face. "But what about my regular class work?''

"You are excused from your other classes for the necessary time.''

I never knew P.K. could be so humble. I was ashamed of having been so pettish. In a chastened mood, I walked across the campus with him, and he gave me a good introduction to the class. So I am now teaching at Bethel. And Dr. King has promised to see that no one *ever* says Beelzebub to me again!

This is already a long letter, but I have one more thing to tell. I've written you about enjoying the babies in the park. I have become acquainted with some of the mothers, and they let me play with their babies. One young mother, especially, has attracted me from a distance because of her unusual beauty. She has seemed very reserved, however, so I never approached her. I thought she must have a tiny baby, as its head never came popping out of the carriage.

But one day last week I noticed her sitting alone on a bench, and then as I drew near I heard the baby screaming and saw her wipe her eyes. She looked so tired and upset I had to stop.

"What's the matter with this young fellow?" I asked. (I could tell it was a boy because no girl would bellow like that!)

She looked up and smiled such a weary, teary smile and said, "He wants me to wheel him some more, and I'm too tired!"

There was my chance. I said, "Oh, can't I do it for you?"

She looked as if she thought I might want to kidnap that howling bundle, so I hastened to introduce myself as a Bethel student and showed her my library card for corroboration.

"Oh, I know you—or at least my husband does," she exclaimed, looking at the card. "I am Mrs. Philip King."

I turned to the baby, who was still howling his little head off. Oh, Mother. it almost broke my heart to look at him! He is over a year old but *so* thin and sick-looking. And such a tantrum as he was having! Poor Mrs. King looked ready to drop. So I left my books with her, and I walked that young man for an hour until he fell asleep. When I got back, little Mrs. King was curled up on that park bench with her head on my books, sound asleep herself. Poor thing! She had probably been up all night with him.

We walked back to the school together, and she told me all about the baby. He has never been well, and she herself is far from strong. The baby is so fussy that she is the only one who can care for him, and she is almost exhausted. I asked if Dr. King couldn't relieve her at night, but she cried, "Oh, no!" so quickly that I knew I had touched on a delicate subject. Then she hastened to say, "You see, my husband was hurt just before the baby came, and it was months before he was able to be about again. Even now he must be careful."

I thought to myself that he looked a great deal better able to lose a little sleep than she did, but of course I didn't say so. An idea had come to me. I was almost afraid to offer it, but I finally did. Of course you know what the idea was—to help her care for that fussy baby.

To my joy, she accepted. She had seen me in the park every day, so knew I meant it when I said I loved babies. When I told her about having been separated from my own little one, she agreed to let me borrow hers for an hour or so every afternoon. Isn't that great? She is going to stay at home and rest, and I'm going to "walk" the poor little boy. That isn't exactly the kind of vicarious motherhood I had planned, but it's better than none.

Must close now and get some sleep. If I keep on writing, I'll have to send my letter by express.

Love to all,
Len

Thanksgiving night at Bethel

Dear Folks:

Had a lovely day with Fred and Carolyn and the children. Helped Carolyn with dinner and then the dishes afterward, and later we had some jolly games. Things were so lively that I didn't have one minute during she day to "think backwards." They brought me home about nine, for I wanted to get to bed early and get a real rest. But as I crossed the campus I met Charlie, the night watchman, and he told me that the doctor had just gone into Kings' and he feared someone was ill. Then, as I passed the King apartment, I heard their baby crying. If I had stopped to think, my courage would have failed, but I just walked in, found the door unlatched, and ran up the stairs.

A distracted-looking Philip King opened the door to let me in. I found the baby screaming in his room, and Dr. Ferris, our school medic, in the dining room. Without even standing on ceremony I said, "Is there anything I can do to help?"

"Can you manage a spoiled baby?"

"I think I can," I said. "Will you let me try?"

"Go right ahead," he said abruptly. "Mrs. King has had a bad heart attack, and the baby is worrying her."

So I followed the uproar and found the baby. He was frightened and angry, and for a while I made no impression on him whatsoever. But then some of my experience with baby Patty came back to me, and I remembered that she was best quieted by a quiet person. So I sat in a chair and rocked and prayed, and finally the poor little chap went off to sleep.

I laid him in his bed and returned to the living room, where Dr. Ferris and Dr. King were talking. Mrs. King was sleeping but had to be kept quiet and watched closely. Dr. Ferris said he would send a nurse in the morning, but Dr. King would have to care for her until then.

When I heard that, I spurred up my courage and asked if I could have the baby for the night. I think they were both relieved at the suggestion, and Dr. Ferris helped me transfer the baby's paraphernalia to my own room.

So here I am with a baby on my hands. I pushed two beds against the wall and put him on the inner one to sleep, while I'm sitting on the side of the other, keeping guard. I shall lie down presently but doubt if I shall sleep. The presence of a sleeping baby boy does things to me, but don't worry about me as I really am enjoying this.

More later—Len

Monday night, Bethel

Dearest of Mothers:

Well, my baby went back home yesterday afternoon. Dr. King got a girl to care for him, and I spent an hour telling her how to do everything. Then I had to kiss him good-bye and leave him. It was wonderful while it lasted. Except for a few flare-ups, we got along nicely. Of course, I couldn't have managed it if Billy and Angela had been around—one spoiled child is enough—but Mrs. Sperry, the housemother, helped out, and we really had fun. I believe the baby is beginning to like me. He has smiled at me several times, but he's such a puny little fellow, and his smile was so pathetic that I almost cried. Mrs. Sperry told me some things that shed light on the King situation.

The Kings had been married five years before the baby came. They were overjoyed at the thought of being parents. But just two weeks before it was born, Philip was hurt in an accident. Then when the baby came it wasn't well, and I guess the care and worry made Mrs. King sick.

The queer part of it is that Dr. King doesn't seem much interested in the baby. He had been so enthusiastic about being a parent, too. Perhaps it's because the baby is so frail and unattractive. It could be, too, that he resents the little boy's having ruined his wife's health. It is very obvious that he worships the ground Lorraine (his wife) walks on.

I'm planning some big Christmas doings at the institute before I leave for home. Billy is working down there with me now and is a real help. Underneath all her faults she has a kind heart, and her little head is full of sensible ideas. Angela has asked for an assignment at the institute also—so she can bask in the sunlight of P.K.'s smile, I suspect. She moons over him all the time. If I were he I'd fail her and send her home. But I presume one can't do that to the chairman's daughter.

Dr. Hale (president of the College, in case you've forgotten) isn't at all well. He had some sort of attack last week and hasn't been in the office since. Dr. Cortland, the dean of men, is doing the headwork in his absence, and Dr. King is doing the footwork. At least he seems to be chasing hither and yon all the time. He reminds me of a boy who played in our high school orchestra and kept seven or eleven instruments going all the time. Dr. Cortland is my favorite of all the teachers. I have him for New Testament: He would make a wonderful grandfather. He's very sympathetic, and sometimes when my morale has wavered a little he has had just the right word to steady me again.

Next week I start my Christmas shopping! You have me all excited about the big surprise you have planned. I can't imagine what it can be. Four more weeks to wait!

Love,
Len

Bethel, December 18

Dear Ones at Home:

Only six more days! If they weren't so full, I couldn't stand it! I haven't finished my shopping yet, and tomorrow is the last chance I'll have. Do you know this is the first time in my life I ever bought presents for children? And now suddenly I have 78 on my list! Of course I can't afford electric trains and French dolls for that many. (Wish I could, though.) But Billy and I determined that every one of the youngsters at the institute should have a nice Christmas this year. Now listen to what she has done.

Her father gave her money for a new coat recently, and that dear child is spending every penny of it on the institute children instead. We have been shopping twice, and when we get into the toy departments we forget to come home. Our closet is full of games and books and toy automobiles, and here are 32 dolls under my bed! Billy's father is going to send a truck over to take us, the tree, and the gifts down. We will trim the tree Saturday night—my class of high school girls will do that. On Monday evening we have the big party at seven o'clock. And Tuesday noon—oh, joy!—I start for home. I am more homesick right now than I've been all fall.

I know you are anxious to know how the King baby is. He is one of my greatest joys. His mother is much better but can't carry him around, and the poor little chap can't walk. I still take him out every afternoon, and recently I have been feeding him his supper afterward, for he will eat better for me than for anyone else.

Yesterday he twisted the spoon out of my hand and then threw it on the floor. When it hit the floor, he laughed aloud. I was so sur-

181

prised I almost fell off my chair. Such tricks may not be unusual for most sixteen-month-old youngsters, but it was a decidedly new venture for that solemn little judge, and we both felt quite shaken by it.

You asked what his name is. Believe it or not, he hasn't any! The students all call him the Crown Prince, but I think that annoys Dr. King. Mrs. King jokingly says they will let him name himself when he gets older. They just call him "the little chap" and let it go at that. Queer way to treat a baby, I say.

Time for bed. I'll be with you next Tuesday in time for supper. Tell Mrs. Hunt I want hot biscuits and some of my very own raspberry jam!

Love,
Len

Bethel, December 20

Dear Connie:

Your note came just now, so I am answering right away. It's just like you, and all the rest of the wonderful family I am now a member of, to suggest that I bring some lonesome student home with me for the holidays.

I'm going to do just that! I can promise one without even stopping to think. But, if it's all right with you, I'll bring a lonesome boy instead of a girl. Remember Dick Dunlap? He is so homesick he can hardly attend to his work. And he can't afford to go home for Christmas. Having lived in Arizona all his life, he has no idea of the joys of a white Christmas. I haven't talked to him yet, but I'm sure he will come.

Once I bring him up into the pine and birch woods, so he can see the forest wrapped in its white mantle, I think the wonder of it will thrill him so much that he'll forget his homesickness.

We have had snow here for a week, but snow in a city and snow in the north woods are two entirely different things.

If it isn't all right, call me collect. If I don't hear from you, I'll invite him.

In haste—love,
Len

25

Christmas Eve, and the snow falling in great feathery wisps. All afternoon as the train traveled northward, Eleanor's heart and mind had raced far ahead. It was good to be going home for Christmas, back to that dear place where she had found joy and peace. It would be good to be a part of the family circle again, to feel once more around her those arms that had held her in the first "mother clasp" she had ever known.

At her side sat Dick Dunlap. He, too, had fallen into a reverie, and they rode in silence except for an occasional exclamation of pleasure at the beauty of the snow-clad landscape.

As the train approached their destination, however, Dick said with an embarrassed laugh, "It was fine of you to ask me to come, Eleanor, but I'm beginning to be nervous about barging in on a family party like this. Maybe they'll think I'm in the way and will wish I hadn't come."

"Listen, you," Eleanor reproved, "I have already told you ten times that the folks all said I *must* bring you. And after you once meet them, you'll know they meant it. Some time, Dick, when you know them all better, I'll tell you the story of how *I* barged in on them, as you say. That's a real story. It's a story so full of my wilfulness and their big-heartedness and God's goodness that I can't think of it yet without feeling overwhelmed by it all. After I had insulted them and wronged them, they took me in and cared for me and loved me and made a place in their home for me. They taught me what it means to live daily in close fellowship with God. And they made heaven seem so near and real that all the hurt and sting of my husband's death turned into a quiet peace that nothing can disturb. Oh, they are a wonderful family.''

"After such a build-up, I'm almost afraid I'm not good enough to meet them,'' Dick said soberly.

"You needn't be afraid,'' Eleanor assured him. "They aren't long-faced. Billy would call them a 'jolly bunch.' And I predict that your visit will be a lively one. Oh, here we are, and the train is stopping! I didn't realize! Dick, I'm so excited to be getting home again. Let's hurry!''

They slipped into their coats, and Eleanor started for the door, both arms full of bundles. Dick followed with two big suitcases. When the train stopped, they were the first to come down the steps, and Eleanor looked around eagerly for the familiar gray car. She failed to see it, and her face fell.

"Eleanor!'' called a voice from the far end of the platform, and a small figure in snowsuit and high boots came flying toward the returning girl.

"Len, oh, Len, is it really you? Oh, I'm so glad!''

"I'm glad too, little sister, but I can't hug you until we get to the car and I put these packages down.

Mary Lou began to laugh.

"There isn't any car. Come and see.''

She led the way to the rear of the station, Eleanor and Dick following in amused curiosity. There a novel sight awaited them. At the curb stood the familiar farm team hitched to an old fashioned bobsled. Bob was sitting in the driver's seat, and Connie and Marilyn were curled up on the floor of the big wagon box.

Introductions were properly made, then Dick helped Eleanor and Mary Lou in with the other girls, tucked the blankets all around, and climbed up in front with Bob. The bells on the horses jingled a gay, silvery tune as they started for home.

"I suppose you are used to sleigh rides,'' said Eleanor gaily, "but this is quite a novelty to me.''

"No,'' said Connie, "we've had very few in our lifetime. The snow plows come along and clear the roads almost as soon as it stops snowing, as a rule. But listen. Bob's telling Dick how this happened.''

"We keep these old bobs in the shed," Bob was explaining, "for on a dairy farm where the milk has to go to market every day, we have to be prepared for anything. This morning when we got up, there was a regular blizzard on, and the road was too deep for the car to tackle. So I got out the old sleds and put this box on them. The snow has kept up all day, so the plow hasn't got through yet. And when it came time to start for the train, all the girls wanted to come along for the ride."

"I don't wonder," returned Dick. "I've heard of sleigh rides all my life, but I never even saw snow until two weeks ago in the city. It was beautiful there for a few minutes but soon turned to a nasty muck that almost drove me back to Arizona."

Eleanor spoke up. "Yes, when I found him the other morning to invite him to come home with me, he was seriously considering giving up his ministerial career and departing for the Southwest by the first train."

"It wasn't quite that bad," Dick remarked, a little embarrassed at being the center of attention. "But I was plenty homesick. If I hadn't been, I would never have had the nerve to descend on you folks like this."

"Say, fellow," said Bob earnestly, "you can't know how glad I am to have another man in the crowd. There are four females in the back of this sleigh and two more at home. I'm the worst hen-pecked man in the county, and I surely welcome a little reinforcement."

"That's one way of looking at it," came Connie's voice from the back. "Really the whole household waits on him, and he's the worst-spoiled man in the county!"

"That's true," said Marilyn. "When we got ready to come to the train, I even had to put his boots on for him."

"I think you girls are teasing Bob," came the grave tones of Mary Lou. "He really isn't *badly* spoiled. And he couldn't put his boots on because he had so many clothes on he couldn't stoop over. And he had just eaten three pieces of pie."

Much to Mary Lou's bewilderment, everyone shouted with laughter. Then Bob said, "Thanks, honey, but next time just let 'em tease me. It's easier to take."

For a moment there was silence. Then the sleigh rounded a curve in the road, and they were suddenly confronted by a beautiful picture—the moon just peeping over the white-clad pines and birches.

Softly Eleanor quoted:

> "The moon above the eastern wood
> Shone at its full; the hill range stood
> Transfigured in the silver flood."

Silence reigned again, only broken by Bob's urging the horses to a swifter pace. As they obeyed, the bells began a livelier tune, and then Connie's sweet voice was heard.

> "Jingle bells, jingle bells,
> Jingle all the way."

All the others joined merrily in the song, even Dick.

"Where did you learn to sing that?" asked Eleanor, when the song was finished. "I thought you never were in any snow."

"That's right," Dick responded. "But we sing 'Jingle Bells' in Arizona anyway, just for the fun of it. It's a nice song even if it doesn't fit the climate."

As the sleigh turned into the drive, its occupants could see a white head watching from inside the front door, and the door opened as soon as the sleigh stopped. In a moment Eleanor was flying up the walk and into the arms that welcomed her.

"It's so good to be here!" she cried. Then, lowering her voice to a quick whisper, she questioned, "It was all right for me to bring Dick, wasn't it? I'll sleep on the cot in your room, and he can have my bed."

"Not a bit of it," Mother objected. "There's an empty room upstairs. I knew you would want to be back in your own nest. I'm delighted that you brought him, my dear."

Then the others swarmed up the walk and into the house, where a hot supper was waiting.

The wide doors to the living room were closed, and Eleanor guessed that the Christmas tree, of whose marvelous quantity and quality she had already been forewarned in Mary Lou's letters, was waiting behind the doors. All through the meal Mary Lou's impatience was noticeable, and when all had finished eating she began to carry off the dishes with a speed that threatened to be disastrous. The older girls rallied to the aid of the chinaware, and while Bob and Dick went on a tour of inspection to see that the chores were properly done and the precious herd was safely bedded for the night, the girls washed the dishes and put the kitchen in shining order.

When the family reassembled in the dining room, Connie was missing. But soon, from the living room, came the sound of the piano. Mary Lou drew open the doors, and there before the eyes of all stood the great tree, shimmering with many-colored lights and ornaments.

Connie began to sing and they all joined in.

> "Oh, Christmas tree!
> Oh, Christmas tree!
> How lovely are thy branches!
> In summer sun or winter snow,
> A dress of green you always show.
> Oh, Christmas tree!
> Oh, Christmas tree!
> How lovely are thy branches!"

Glorious as the Christmas tree was, it was not that which held Eleanor's attention. Her eyes were riveted on a great fireplace that had been built into the end of the room opposite the door.

Under cover of the song, she whispered to Marilyn, "The fireplace? When?"

"Just finished. Keep still, and Mother will tell about it later."

So Eleanor's curiosity had to wait. She turned to Mother Stewart and said, "Do you distribute the gifts this evening? Mine are still in my room." "No," was the reply. "We just enjoy the tree and have music and the Christmas story on Christmas Eve. Then after the lights are out, we each slip back and put our gifts at the foot of the tree. Tomorrow morning we will open them as soon as we get up."

"We get up *early* on Christmas," added Mary Lou, and everyone laughed.

"Indeed we do," corroborated Connie. "Last year that little lady woke me up at half-past two and insisted it was morning."

"Well, it was," argued Mary Lou. "Our teacher says morning begins at one minute after twelve. And it seems very foolish not to get up when you're so wide awakeful.

"Well, I'm giving you a sleeping powder tonight," laughed Connie. "Anyone who gets up before six o'clock tomorrow has to do the breakfast dishes all alone!"

Mary Lou looked so distressed that Eleanor hastened to promise her help in case of that dread event. Then Connie began to play again, an old Bohemian Christmas carol, but only Bob and Marilyn sang, while the others listened with pleasure.

"Mother," said Mary Lou suddenly, "Eleanor's been wanting to know about the fireplace. Can't you tell her now?"

"Yes, I will. The dedication of this fireplace must be a part of our Christmas Eve program. And I want Eleanor to know that she is responsible for the building of the fireplace."

"I?" questioned Eleanor, amazed. "Why, I didn't do a thing—I didn't even know about it."

"Nevertheless, you brought it about," said the mother. "Come here, my dear, and sit by me while I tell all the story. Even my own dear children, who have helped to carry out the building plans, don't know why it was done. It's a rather long story, but I want you all to hear it. Dick, you'll pardon a little family reminiscing, won't you?"

Dick, who was sitting cross-legged on the floor in front of the fireplace watching the firelight flicker on Connie's curls, nodded his consent.

"Dad and I," continued Mother, "bought this farm when Chad was a small baby. The house was old and run down with no modern conveniences at all. We worked hard to pay for it, and we spent many happy hours planning how we would remodel 'our dream house' as we called it. Then Bobby came to us, and two years later, Connie. We were happy with our three little ones, and our plans for a lovely home.

"Dad was especially interested in having a fireplace in this room. He said he and his brothers and sisters had grown up around a coal heater, and he wanted his children to have memories of a cozy family fireplace. So he drew diagrams of all the improvements we planned, centering everything about the fireplace he longed for.

"Then, one night—the very night that God brought our little Mary Lou to us—Daddy went home to be with the Lord. No one except the dear Savior himself can ever know how hard it was for me to go on without him."

Mother Stewart paused for a moment to steady her voice, then continued, briskly, "But the children needed me so I had to live and work for them. They were brave little soldiers, and we struggled on together. Using what was left of Dad's insurance money, I remodeled the house and made the little hospital he had planned. In fact, every detail of the plans was carried out—except the fireplace. I couldn't do that. The other improvements seemed necessary, but the fireplace was our lovely dream which we had shared together.

"Then Chad left us too, but in our loneliness his wife, Eleanor, came to us. And last summer she gave the rock garden which she and Chad had dreamed together, in order to beautify our little churchyard. The day we dedicated that rock garden, I realized how selfish I had been. That day I resolved that this fireplace should be built. And here it is.

"That's the story of my fireplace. Tonight I want to dedicate it to our Lord. May its light and warmth be a blessing to all who gather about it."

All were quiet as the story concluded. Then Mary Lou put her arms about her mother and said, "I'll always love the fireplace 'specially because my daddy wanted me to have it."

"Let's have the Christmas story now," suggested Bob.

The well-worn Bible was taken from the table, and Mother read the stories of the shepherds and the wise men and the wonderful gift from heaven, the little Baby in the manger. Then they all knelt together for a circle of prayer.

Once more Connie took her seat at the piano, and the little group began to sing "Silent Night," "Away in a Manger," and all the well-loved Christmas hymns. Dick was on familiar ground and sang out lustily.

Eleanor and Mary Lou soon dropped out from the singing and just sat by the fireside listening, Mary Lou elated at having

Eleanor home again, Eleanor happy to be in the dear parlor once more.

Mother Stewart's voice was next to become silent, as she sat gazing at the flames, deep in reverie, thinking of other Christmases when the Doctor Dad had been with the family.

When the fire had burned low, and Mary Lou was asleep with her head in Eleanor's lap, Eleanor suddenly said, "Before we go to bed, I'd like to hear Connie and Dick sing a duet. Won't you try 'O Holy Night'?"

Obligingly Connie opened the book again, while Dick seated himself on the piano bench beside her. They sang softly but with feeling, and suddenly each member of the little group realized that here were two perfectly blended voices, Connie's a rich contralto and Dick's a clear tenor.

"That's a good way to end the evening," said Mother Stewart, when the song was finished, and she stooped to waken Mary Lou. "As Tiny Tim says, 'God bless us, every one'—and good night, my dears."

As the family separated, Dick was left alone with Eleanor for a moment. "What an evening!" he exclaimed. "No wonder you couldn't describe this family to me. I tremble to think that I almost didn't come!"

26

In the heavy dark that comes before the dawn, Eleanor was awakened by a small figure slipping into her bed beside her.

"What is it, honey bun?" she asked. "Are you cold, or did you get lonesome?"

"I just couldn't go back to sleep," said the small person earnestly. "Connie told me that if I woke Mother up, she'd spank me (Connie, I mean). I don't *think* she means it, but I'd better not try it. I can't lie still—my legs are all wiggly. I thought maybe you'd be patienter than Connie."

"Bless your heart, I couldn't ever be impatient with you," replied Eleanor, snuggling the little girl closer. "You're such a sweet little sister."

"You're such a nice big sister. Last Christmas I was so lonesome for Chad I felt sort of sick all day. But this year, because you are here, the achy, sick feeling isn't here! It seems so all right now!"

"It is all right, dear," whispered Eleanor. "God is wonderfully good to take away the pain and give peace in its place."

"Yes, He is."

For a few minutes they lay silently, and Eleanor was dozing again when Mary Lou whispered, "Eleanor, isn't it almost morning? Mother said we could get up at six."

Eleanor turned on the light to look at her watch.

"Only five-thirty, dear. Won't you try to take another nap?"

Mary Lou sighed. "All the sleepy is ab-so-lute-ly gone out of me. But I'll try."

She tried with such good effect that both girls had to be awakened when Bob came back from stirring up the fire at half past six.

Eleanor had never had a Christmas in a family group before, and to her the early morning gathering around the tree was unforgettable. Vaguely she remembered Christmas as a time when Aunt Ruth bought her a big tree and many beautiful presents and gave them to her in a dignified way after dinner on Christmas Eve. Her formal Christmases had lacked the Christmas spirit, without which all else is worthless. She had never known anything like this Stewart assemblage.

In robes and slippers everyone sat around the tree, while Santa's little helper Pigtails, fairly bristling with excitement, distributed the gifts. Dick and Eleanor sat on the davenport and laughed at Mary Lou's obvious attempts to be everywhere at once.

The gifts were not costly, but simple things that were needed, such as a new dress for Mother from Bob and Marilyn, a snowsuit for Mary Lou, little dresses for baby Patty—who was industriously playing horsie with the Christmas tree trimmings—a suede jacket for Connie, a few books, some family games. For Eleanor there was a remembrance from each one, and as she received the packages her heart overflowed with love for these folk who had so completely taken her to their hearts. There were even gifts for Dick—a new book of choruses, some candy, and a necktie. He and Eleanor had unloaded their suitcases the night before and contributed a generous share to the pile of sparkling packages under the tree. There was a joyous confusion in the room as paper wrappings were torn off and cries of "Just what I wanted!" and "Oh, thank you!" were heard on all sides. Baby Patty crept joyously from one intriguing box to another, taking advantage of the confusion to sample forbidden sweets and caress with sticky fingers the bright new jackets on the Christmas books.

When things had quieted somewhat, Mother Stewart handed Bob a long envelope, saying softly, "I want this to be thought of as a gift from your father and me, Bob, to a good son who has carried a heavy burden bravely and well. May God bless you and Marilyn and give you many happy years together in your new home.''

Bob opened the envelope with interest and glanced quickly over the paper that it contained. His face flushed, then paled. He handed the paper to Marilyn saying huskily as he did so, ''A deed to the upper forty.''

With a gulp of deep emotion, he kissed Mother, saying, ''I can't say what I feel, Mom. But I'll try to show you how we both appreciate this.''

And Marilyn, with shining eyes, added her kiss with lips that could not speak.

As soon as breakfast was over, Bob and Dick went to the barn, then off again in the big sled to take the milk to market. While they were gone, the girls did the morning's work. Eleanor had to go all over the house, from the little sanitarium upstairs, where she helped Mother distribute Christmas cheer to the patients, to the basement, where she inspected her rows of fruits and vegetables with the pride of a craftsman.

Bob and Dick returned with the announcement that the long hill in the back pasture was in perfect condition for coasting. Mary Lou squealed with delight at the prospect, and the three girls hurried off to get into snowsuits.

''Aren't you coming, Len?'' called Connie, as Eleanor lingered behind, making no move to dress for the outdoors.

''Not this time,'' was the reply. ''Mother and I haven't had our visit yet. There'll be plenty of snow before I leave.''

She remained firm in spite of their entreaties, so finally the group set off without her, Dick making many jokes about his ''borrowed plumes.'' He had Uncle John's heavy boots and mackinaw, and an old wool cap of Bob's. Eleanor rejoiced to see how completely Dick seemed to be enjoying himself. She had not known he could be so lively. Her impression of him as a quiet homesick boy was definitely out of place now.

''But I'm glad he's having such a good time,'' she murmured, watching out the window as the party trudged down the lane and out of sight. Then she turned to the fire. Mother was upstairs with her patients, Mrs. Hunt was busy in the kitchen, and the house was quiet.

193

Eleanor lay on the sofa watching the flames and thinking back over the years. It was just three years ago, on another Christmas Day, that she and Chad had been spellbound in the first joys of their love, sitting around the fire with the merry group at the Jake cottage. Three years! Into those three years Eleanor had crowded a lifetime's experiences . . . love . . . marriage . . . happiness . . . sorrow . . . parting . . . motherhood . . . despair . . . bitterness . . . restoration . . . consecration . . . dedication . . . work . . . healing . . . and now at last almost happiness again. Just one thing was lacking. One yearning pain in Eleanor's heart never quite left her, but she had learned to go to her Refuge, and even now she closed her eyes and whispered softly, "Oh, Father, wherever my baby is today, be with him and keep him safe—and give him a merry Christmas."

Mother Stewart descended the stairs slowly and started as Eleanor sat up on the sofa.

"Why, I thought you had gone with the others!" she exclaimed.

"No." Eleanor smiled. "I preferred to stay behind and visit with you. So I told Marilyn I would listen while Patty takes her mid-morning nap, so that she could go. There's been such commotion since I came, you and I really haven't had a visit."

Mother Stewart looked dubious. "Didn't you want to go, dear? I could have minded Patty."

"Really, I'd rather stay."

"I should order you out," said Mother Stewart, laughing, "but it's too pleasant to have you here again. You need to be out playing after working so hard at school."

Eleanor sighed. "I'm not morbid, Mother, but the fact is that I just haven't the heart for things like that. I feel fifty years old."

"Oh, my dear!" remonstrated the older woman. "You mustn't feel so. And won't Dick feel badly at your staying at home?"

"Not a bit," came the prompt assurance. "He's nothing special to me, really. Dick is one of the nicest boys I know, but my interest in him is sort of maternal. He has been homesick, and since my own life has contained so much unhappiness, I can sympathize with others. That's all.''

"Have you tried to interest yourself in the other young folk?'' Mother asked, taking up her darning basket and sitting down by the window. Even on Christmas Day her hands refused to be idle.

"Yes, I have tried, but I don't fit well into just-fun gatherings,'' replied Eleanor soberly. "I'm afraid it's no use, Mother. That part of me is dead. I enjoy studying. I get a real thrill from working with my girls at Henderson Institute. But the part of me that could play—really play—died—'' her voice dwindled to almost a whisper "—when Chad died.''

"I wish you could fall in love again,'' remarked Mother unexpectedly.

Eleanor looked amazed. Then she laughed lightly.

"I am in love, Mother—with the naughtiest, spunkiest, most fascinating chap I ever knew. But he's only a year and a half old.''

"You mean the King baby, I presume,'' returned Mother Stewart, looking disappointed.

"Yes, Mother, he's the *dearest* thing. I wish you could have seen him, though, as he was when I first knew him. He was thin and pitiful and so *mad*. I've been taking care of him afternoons for two months now, and—believe it or not—he has begun to put on weight again. I'm so proud! I give him his supper and then put him to bed, and lately he's been sleeping twelve hours every night without waking once. He used to awaken every two or three hours and cry.''

Mother Stewart made a little sympathetic clucking noise and remarked, "How terrible! What was the trouble with him?''

"Mostly mismanagement,'' responded Eleanor, smiling confidingly. "Mrs. King was very ill when he came, and Dr. King was in the hospital too (he stayed there until the baby was six months old). It was an unfortunate time for a baby to descend on their household, and I understand he never had much of a schedule. Then Mrs. King is so gentle she hasn't any idea how to discipline him. His tantrums frighten her, so she lets him do as he pleases. She idolizes him, and worries over him all the time.

Until I took him over she had had no relief at all. For some peculiar reason, however, he will take discipline from me—and he's getting it!''

"He doesn't sound very attractive," commented Mother Stewart.

"I know it," Eleanor agreed. "But he definitely is. Billy met us in the park one day and said afterward that the baby has the 'makin's' of a handsome child if he ever gets strong. He has lovely golden curls and big blue eyes and the sweetest smile.''

"Every baby is sweet," remarked the mother, "But Len, dear, I'm a little concerned about you and the King baby, for I wonder if you are not getting too fond of him? Might you not be preparing more sorrow for yourself?''

"I've thought of that," returned Eleanor seriously. "I do love him, but I think it's just because my heart is aching and empty for a baby boy. When I have to come away and leave him when school is out, undoubtedly I'll be sad. But it seems to alleviate my pain just now to help care for him, and I believe the Lord wants me to do it. So please don't try to dissuade me, Mother. I'm enjoying it so much that I wish the Kings would take me on full time.''

"I won't say another word," came the promise. "When you and the Lord agree, that's all the reassurance I need.''

Eleanor looked relieved.

"By the way, how do you like Dr. King by this time?'' asked Mother Stewart. "Not at all—and a great deal.'' Eleanor laughed enigmatically. "He exasperates me beyond expression, yet I admire him greatly! Half the time in his class I sit on the edge of the seat spellbound—and the other half of the time I yearn to throw a book at him. He has been unusually endowed by the Lord with natural gifts—good looks, brains, talent, personality, and so on. 'He has everything,' Angela croons to herself, and one must agree. And when I see how adoringly he treats his wife at home, I like him for that, even though it makes my heart ache with loneliness. But when I see him with the little chap—I thoroughly dislike him!''

"What do you mean?'' asked Mother Stewart in surprise.

"Why, he doesn't care a bit for that baby!'' exclaimed Eleanor vehemently. "He doesn't abuse him, and dutifully performs all the tasks he has read that fathers ought to do—but, Mother, he doesn't *love* the baby. And to make the situation more heart-rending, the little chap loves him with all the ardor of his little soul. He reaches out his arms in glee and calls 'Daddee' the minute he sees Dr. King, and then when the high and mighty doctor does deign to pick him up, his joy is really pitiful. Then I heartily, thoroughly, absolutely dislike the Reverend Doctor!''

"I am sure that situation will right itself in time," responded the mother. "Dr. King may feel that the baby is responsible for his wife's lost health—but no father can withhold his affection from his son for long."

Eleanor looked dubious. "I think it goes deeper than that. Dr. Philip King is a thoroughly self-centered gentleman, and he just hasn't taken the little chap into his life at all. Yet he seems to like other children. He goes to the kindergarten at the institute and fondles the little ones there."

After a thoughtful pause, Eleanor went on: "There are two Philip Kings, Mother. The one I like is a kind lover and husband, a zealous worker among the city's poor, and an inspiration to the young people in the institute church. The other one (the one I abhor) is self-centered, ambitious, clever, and cynical, almost an evil influence among the Bethel students."

"An evil influence!" exclaimed Mother Stewart, shocked.

"Those are strong words, but I really think so, Mother," replied Eleanor. "The reason is that Dr. King is wilfully determined to accomplish things—all in his own power. There is never so much as a hint in his teaching of dependence on God, and so there is no real power. He is always busy doing something, and he really does accomplish some things, but I don't believe he is making a permanent impact for good on any of the lives he reaches."

The two women sat in thoughtful silence for a moment, then Eleanor went on: "But, oh, Mother, I wish you could know old Dr. Cortland! He is impractical, and sometimes his absence of mind is amusing, but *he* gives real spiritual help. *He* knows where power comes from. He depends entirely on the Lord's leading. Philip King—well, he acts first, then expects the Lord to ratify his work."

Mother wove the needle in and out of the sock in her hand. Then she spoke slowly. "I've never seen Philip King, but I know he has been acclaimed for his work among young people. What you say disappoints me greatly, for our young people today need their hearts and lives really transformed by the Spirit, and He cannot work through one who is not yielded to Him. Eleanor, Philip King needs prayer. We must pray that God will deal with him to stir his heart and cleanse it completely of self."

"Mother, I know that if you pray for him, he will be helped," said Eleanor impetuously. "And while you are remembering him, I wish you would pray for his wife's health. She is beginning to seem like a sister to me—but I fear for her life sometimes. She has one of the sweetest dispositions I have known, and all her trouble and pain haven't embittered her one bit. I don't blame Dr. King for adoring her. She is adorable! But she is dangerously ill."

"I will pray for her too," promised Mother Stewart, with a look of faith on her face, which testified to many experiences with a Lord who answers prayer in a mighty way. "I am sure the Lord is using you to help both of them. Sometimes God uses sharp tools to shape the lives He wants to use, but we can trust His hand. If he has chosen Philip King for a special task, He will prepare him."

"You're such a comfort, Mother," said Eleanor warmly. "Oh, I want to tell you one more thing about Philip King, and then we'll change the subject. Did I tell you that I have recognized him at last?"

"Recognized him?" repeated Mother Stewart, puzzled.

"Yes," replied Eleanor. "Remember that I told you about the church service Chad and I attended together the last Sunday before he left me? When the preacher delivered such a powerful sermon on 'The Bond Servant of Jesus Christ'? Well, that preacher was Philip King."

"How does it happen that you didn't recognize him before?" asked Mother in surprise.

"He has changed so much," replied Eleanor. "He is thinner and older-looking, and that newly acquired lock of white hair has changed his appearance. But one Sunday at the institute he preached that same sermon. I was shocked when I realized it all.

But the thing that hurts, Mother, is that one who has the gift of persuasion as he has should not live what he preaches. He isn't yielded to Christ! He follows Philip King's will, not God's!'' Eleanor paused for breath after this outburst, then added anti-climatically. ''No wonder his baby is stubborn! He came by it naturally.''

''My dear, Bethel College surely needs our prayers,'' said Mother Stewart, deeply moved. ''That place was born in prayer and has been nurtured by the Spirit, and it has done a powerful work for God. Man's wisdom must not crowd out the Spirit now!''

''You must have an extremely long prayer list,'' remarked Eleanor, respectfully. ''How do you find time to pray for every-thing?''

'' 'Pray without ceasing,' '' came the answer. ''I have found that I can pray at any place and at all times.''

''I must try that too,'' mused Eleanor.

A stray kitten wandered into the room. Seeing the Christ-mas tree, he immediately began to pat with his paw at the dan-gling icicles. Eleanor chuckled, then removed an icicle and be-gan to tease the kitten with it. Mother Stewart looked on, smiling affectionately. Suddenly she sighed deeply, leaned her head back, and closed her eyes. Her mouth tightened. Eleanor looked up in sudden concern.

''Mother, are you well?'' came the insistent question. The kitten, forgotten, began pulling the piece of tinsel across the living room floor.

''I am a bit tired, dear,'' replied the older woman, with a patient smile. ''We have been in such a hurry-scurry to get the fireplace built before you came. I'll be all right again before long.''

''I hope so,'' returned Eleanor with loving ooncern. ''I don't like to see you looking so weary. I am afraid you worked too hard getting ready for Dick and me.

''Oh, no! The girls did it all. I'm just a bit tired. I'll be all right.''

''It was grand of you to give Bob and Marilyn the little house and ground for their own,'' said Eleanor a few minutes later. "They will be happy in their own place—but what will you do without them?"

"Oh, Bob will continue to run the farm. I can't spare him from that. But now that their little family is growing, they should have their own home. Bob has been such a good son he deserves all I can give him. We will get along here fairly well—and next year, unless the Lord has other plans, you can stay with me while Connie goes to school."

"I'd love that!"

"I think God sent you to us when we needed you," said Mother Stewart, patting Eleanor's hand lovingly. "You are a comfort to us all."

"Thank you, Mother. I love you all and want to do all I can for you to show it. You don't know how much you've done for me."

Then silence reigned, broken only by the snapping and crackling of the blazing logs on the hearth.

Outside the snow glistened in the morning sunshine, and in the distance, on the hill behind the church, two tall pine trees decked in gleaming white mantles stood firmly against the blue winter sky.

Merry shouts were heard outside, and Eleanor and Mother hurried to the window to see the fun. Connie and Marilyn, returning with the group from sledding, had tripped Bob, rolled him in a great drift, and were washing his face with fluffy handfuls of the snow, while Dick and Mary Lou looked on in glee. Bob finally shook himself loose from his tormentors and made a lunge at Dick, knocking him into the deep snow. Over and over the two rolled. The girls stood and hurled snow at them until there appeared to be five animated snowmen running around the yard, chasing each other with snowballs. Then the rosy cheeked snowmen tramped on to the front door, only to be met by an adamant Mother Stewart.

"Into this parlor with all that snow on you? The very idea!" She laughed. "Down to the basement, all of you, and sweep off before you set foot in my house."

"Woe is me!" Bob drew a doleful face. "Turned out of my home by my own mother! Come on, girls and boys—let's not subject ourselves to any further inhospitality *here*."

"Oh, Len, you missed such fun," said Mary Lou, the first up from the basement.

Eleanor only smiled, then Dick, who had just emerged from the regions of banishment, rubbed his cold nose against her cheek and whispered, "Eleanor, I'll never thank you enough for bringing me. This has been the greatest fun I ever had!"

He smiled cryptically, then dashed off to his room to brush his hair for dinner. "Now what has he been up to?" pondered Eleanor, observing the cocky tilt of his retreating shoulders. "Homesick, indeed!"

Mrs. Hunt covered herself with glory when the Christmas feast was set on the table. Turkey, cranberries, squash, potatoes, gravy, biscuits, salad, fruitcake, pie, nuts, were all there, in tempting and aromatic array.

"Oh, boy!" exclaimed Dick with enthusiasm. "Eleanor, just think of the poor souls who had to stay at school over the Christmas holidays and are even now gazing upon cafeteria trays in the deserted lunchroom."

"Poor things!" echoed Eleanor.

After dinner Mother went to her room for a nap. Bob tucked Marilyn and baby Patty into the sled, and they set off to see Marilyn's family. Mary Lou curled up in a chair with *The Swiss Family Robinson*, and Connie and Dick donned snowshoes and returned to the woods to gather some bittersweet and glossy greens they had admired.

Eleanor was left alone. She donned her heaviest wraps and slipped out the side door into the clear cold winter air. Drawing deep breaths to fill her lungs, she realized how invigorating it was in comparison with the smoky city air to which she had been accustomed.

Her footsteps turned toward the road leading to the pines on the hill. Less than a year ago she had fled down this same road in lonely desperation, and now—how changed her life was! The despair and grief were gone. In spite of the separation from Chad, she was not even lonely, for she had found the companionship of One who had filled her life with joy again.

Eleanor found the little church closed and silent, and the ferns and flowers she had last seen on the hillside were now blanketed with snow. But the faithful little evergreens stood firm, vivid against the white background.

Snowdrifts covered the steps, but Eleanor felt her way up carefully. At last she stood at the top, and there before her were the two graves that she sought, covered with freshly cut boughs of cedar and spruce.

Bob and Dick must have done this when they went with the milk this morning, thought Eleanor. *It was kind and beautiful of them to remember Chad and Father Stewart amid all the festivities.*

With mittened hands Eleanor brushed the snow from the bench and seated herself. Many were the quiet hours she had spent in this peaceful place last summer. Now the vast expanses of unbroken snow, the mantled hush of the winter woods, and the cedar-covered bed where Chad lay sleeping, even while his soul was rejoicing in the glory of a better land—all brought Eleanor to a sense of nearness to God. She bowed her head and prayed.

As she thus communed with her Father, all her burdens and small cares slipped away, and she realized a new gladness in being even a small part of God's plan, a tool in His hands to be used as He saw fit. The old willful Eleanor was gone—buried, perhaps, in the grave under the cedars. A new Eleanor was now truly the bond servant of Christ, voluntarily yielding to Him a life full of talents, ready for service.

A cardinal fluttered to a branch close by and began his message of "good cheer, good cheer." Eleanor started and realized it must be high time to start back. Before leaving, though, she knelt by the stone that said "CHAD" and prayed again.

"Dear Father, I thank Thee for loving me and saving me and bringing me out of my darkness into this place of peace and service. I thank Thee that I had Chad for a while and that he is now with Thee. I thank Thee for my baby—our baby. I know that he is in Thy care. If it be Thy will, may I find him some day. But if not, then please let me trust Thee that he is safely in Thy care. Take him and me and use us both for Thy glory. Amen."

Eleanor patted the cedar boughs. "Good-bye for now, darling," she said. "You do know that God has healed all my willfulness, don't you?"

27

One morning in late January Eleanor met Dick as he came from the school post office. His hands were bulging with mail.

"Did you leave any for me ?" she asked gaily.

Dick shook his head. "Nope. I got it all."

"It looks as though that fat envelope might be for me," continued Eleanor. "I surely recognize the handwriting."

Dick's face reddened, and he slipped the telltale letter into his pocket.

"How often does Connie write?" continued Eleanor with a sisterly interest.

"Not often enough," growled Dick. "Don't tease me, Len. I can't stand it. I thought you knew I had heart trouble."

"Since when?" asked Eleanor, suddenly concerned.

"Oh, Christmas time," replied Dick airily and started away. Eleanor called him back.

"Please forgive me, Dickie boy. I won't tease you any-more. In fact, I give you my blessing. I'll bake pies for your wedding."

"Perhaps we'd better just elope," replied Dick, making a wry face. "I don't trust your pies. But on the whole—" he began to walk away, so that his words merely floated back to Eleanor's eager ears "—it's—not—such—a—bad—idea!"

"Well, I never!" she exclaimed to herself happily. "I really started something, I guess." Then she went on into the post office.

The clerk handed her a letter addressed in Mary Lou's distinctive handwriting. She smiled at the sloping letters, but the smile faded from her face as she broke open the envelope and read the contents.

Dear Len,

No one knows I am writing this, but I think you should know that Mother is sick. She says she isn't, but she doesn't smile much anymore and Connie cried last night and Bob said he didn't care if we all had to go hungry but Mother *must* go and have an operation. And Mother said there wasn't enough money to pay for that and for a nurse to take care of the saniterrium while she was gone and she would be all right. It makes me afraid and I think you should know. If we had not built the fireplace and bought a new truck we would have more money, but God can fix it anyway, don't you think? I prayed last night and at recess at school today, but I am pretty little and I'd like for you to help me pray. Don't you think if we all pray God will send the money to make Mother well? Patty has a new tooth and took her first alone steps today.

Your loving sister,
Mary Lou

Eleanor found it impossible to concentrate on her next class. *What will they do there with Mother sick?* she pondered, while the lecture droned on and on. *And how will they ever pay for the operation? But Mother must have it, if I have to—why, of course! I will help pay for it myself! They've done so much for me, here is my opportunity to repay it a little.*

Quickly Eleanor sketched out a plan in her mind. As soon as her classes were over she sped to Dr. King's office and excitedly confronted that startled young man.

"Dr. King, I know you will be surprised at my coming here like this, but I had to ask you an important question," Eleanor began. "Would you still like to find a full time nurse for the baby?"

"Sit down, Mrs. Stewart," came the cordial invitation. "Yes, I certainly would. Lorraine is definitely not improving in health, and unless she gets more rest she will never gain strength. I am—much concerned about her." Dr. King walked to the window and looked out.

In a moment he turned back. "Have you any suggestions as to a nurse?" he asked briskly.

"Yes—myself," smiled Eleanor.

"You?"

"Yes, I. Don't look so incredulous, please. I meant it. Would I do?"

"Why, yes," came the answer in delighted tones. "You would do admirably. But how do you have time to take on a responsibility like that—and, if I may ask, why do you wish to?"

"As for the first question," began Eleanor, "you know I don't really need the credits on all the classes I am enrolled in. I could drop everything except Bible, which I do need in order to graduate. Surely your maid could care for the baby during that hour every day. Then all the rest of the day I could care for him, and Mrs. King needn't be worried at all."

"This sounds like a direct answer to prayer." Dr. King smiled. "But why have you made this sudden decision?"

"The truth is," said Eleanor, her clear eyes looking straight at her questioner, "I need the money. Mother is ill and needs a very expensive operation, and this was the only way I could think of to earn extra money to contribute. And you know I love to care for the baby. I believe I could get him to eat—to bring his weight up to normal. And I have hopes of erasing his tantrums from the scene."

Dr. King sat in thoughtful silence for a moment.

"May I try?" persisted Eleanor.

"You certainly may," he said finally, in a tone of relief. "I believe that the Lord is answering our prayers through you. Lorraine is nearly worn out. So shall I tell her you will come?"

"Yes. I'll come today if you want me."

"Fine!" The brown eyes beamed. "Come in early this afternoon and find out all about what there is to do. I can't tell you anything about that—you know fathers are rather stupid when it comes to naps and formulas and understanding children in general."

"Not all fathers," Eleanor could not resist remarking. Then, lest she appear rude, she quickly said, "Thank you so much. This means a great deal to me."

"Thank *you*, Mrs. Stewart," said Dr. King, rising to open the door. "Not every baby is as privileged as ours—to have an eminent botanist for a nurse!"

Eleanor laughed, and they parted. Then she hurried to her room, took out her writing materials, and wrote:

Dear Bob:

Today I am stepping into the role of big sister and am asking you to let me have my share of the family responsibilities and burdens. If Chad were here, he would want to do whatever he could in any family crisis. Won't you please let me take his place now?

A little bird—if birds wear pigtails—told me of Mother's illness today. Why didn't any of you mention it before? You probably didn't want to worry me. I could scold you. But that's not why I'm writing so quickly.

I know that the operation and nursing care, plus extra expenses for help at home, will cost a great deal of money. At one time I could have paid for the whole thing outright. I can't do that now, but I intend sending—if you will let me—as much money as I can spare each month until this thing is all behind. I may be able to send as much as a hundred dollars a month.

Here is the reason why—I've got a job! I am to take care of the King baby full time now, and they will give me room and board and fifteen dollars a week. Part of this, plus Chad's insurance checks, can now come to you. Will that make it possible to have the operation? Please, please tell me the truth. For if it still isn't enough, I have another plan.

Please don't object to this, Bob. Make Mother see that I must do it. I feel that God has definitely provided me with this opportunity to help.

Let me know all about Mother. She is so dear to me that I get shaky every time I think of her being ill. If you need me in person, I'll come and bring the King baby with me.

Love to all,
Len

Eleanor walked briskly back from the mailbox and straight up the steps to the King apartment. There lay Lorraine on the sofa.

"Eleanor Stewart!" she cried joyously, sitting up with sudden energy. "This is too good to be true."

"I think so too," smiled Eleanor. "I'm going to enjoy it, I know."

"You're a direct answer to my prayers," continued Mrs. King. "Last night I was so discouraged I felt I simply couldn't go on another step but would have to go home to Dad and my sister Edith, who would take care of the baby. But I don't want to leave Phil! So all alone in the middle of the night I knelt down and asked God to send someone I could trust with the little chap. And He sent you!"

Eleanor sat down cross-legged on the floor beside the couch where Mrs. King lay and said, with a squeeze of the thin hand that had reached for her own, "Mrs. King, God answered both our prayers. I need the work, and you need my help. I am sure that He planned it. Now if you'll just tell me what is expected of the full-time nurse to His Royal Highness, I'll try to get settled before His Majesty wakes up."

By the time Little Chap awoke from his nap, all the instructions had been completed and Eleanor was ready for their walk in the park. She walked into the nursery smiling. The Little Chap laughed in glee and held out his arms. She lifted him and held him close for a moment before she spoke.

"Let's go for a walk now."

The air was cold, so Eleanor tucked several robes around the little boy before starting off. As she did so, the blue eyes met her gaze with a loving, trustful look.

"You adorable little laddie!" she exclaimed. "You surely have changed! When I first knew you, you were a screaming little skeleton. Now you look like a sweet baby. Soon I'll have you walking around like a big fellow. Do you want to do that?"

The baby laughed and bounced up and down with eagerness to start.

"All right, we're going," said Eleanor, beginning to push the carriage down the street. "And by the way, angel boy, do me a favor, will you?"

The blue eyes looked around in uncomprehending amusement.

"Just when we're alone," said Eleanor, with a catch in her voice, "may I call you little Chad?"

A few days later the mailman left Eleanor a letter from the farm. It was addressed in Mother's handwriting. Eagerly Eleanor tore the envelope open, then held the letter on her lap and tried to read while she fed the Little Chap his breakfast.

Dear Daughter:

Your letter came yesterday, and that you may know that you really belong to us and have a part in our burdens as well as our joys, I want to tell you first that we didn't even argue about accepting your help. Your check, with what we have in the bank, will take care of the hospital bills nicely, and the money you can send each month will pay for a woman to take my place here in the sanitarium until I am able to work again. I couldn't refuse it, dear, for I had left the matter in my Father's hands and told Him I would follow as He led. So I accepted it as His leading.

Bob and I drove to Woodstock last night and made arrangements for me to enter the hospital Friday. The operation will be on Monday. Don't worry, dear. I am not fearful. I know the surgeon. He is an old friend of my husband. And I have great confidence in him. But better than that, I have absolute confidence in my heavenly Father, and I am sure that all will be well. Connie will keep in touch wish you.

I know you are happy in caring for the King's baby. The experience may be trying for you in some ways, but if you are convinced that you are following the Lord's leading, there is no other thing to be done. God will bless you, I am sure, and as you give loving care to the little boy who needs it, somehow and some place your own little one will be cared for too.

Write me often, dear. Your letters will cheer my hospital room.

Love,
Mother

Eleanor's heart was reassured. Mother was in God's hands, and He would care for her. As she went about her work—cooking the baby's cereal, sitting by him as he played, tidying up his room and putting away his clothes, taking him out for an airing—her heart was lifted almost constantly in prayer, yet there was no real anxiety. Whatever came would be all right because it was God's will.

Monday morning while the Little Chap banged with his toys in his play pen, Eleanor and Mrs. King knelt together in prayer for Mother and for the surgeon whose hand would perform the operation. Together they waited through the hours until a messenger boy brought the telegram, "All is well." Then together they wept for joy.

Lorraine King had learned many hard lessons during the months since her baby's birth. She had been a sincere Christian for many years, but life had been easy and she had never had to learn how to lean on One stronger than herself for constant help. But when the storm clouds piled high in the heavens, when the winds of adversity blew strong, she learned to cling close and ever closer to her Rock of Safety and had found in Him comfort and strength. Trial and testing had refined her, and the pure gold of her character shone through all the weakness and pain that handicapped her frail body.

No wonder her husband worships her, thought Eleanor. *I almost could myself.*

As the weeks flew past and the Little Chap grew strong and sturdy under Eleanor's loving care, he learned to toddle about on his own chubby legs, and gradually Eleanor came to have more and more time to devote to Lorraine, relieving her of the oversight of Nellie, the maid; reading to her, running errands—and gradually taking over the full care of house as well as baby. For it was evident to the anguished eyes who watched her that Lorraine was not getting better. Rather, as spring came on, she grew weaker, and the agonizing heart attacks became more frequent. Often it was suffocating for her to lie down, and Eleanor knew that many nights Philip sat all night with Lorraine cradled in his arms. He never complained but frequently he arrived at school with dark rings under his eyes, and he lacked some of his old jaunty self-confidence as he went about his teaching and his institute work.

His indifference to the Little Chap infuriated Eleanor. She wrote one day to Mother:

I still have a red-headed temper, I fear. I had hoped it had rusted thoroughly through disuse. But P. K. has revived it. Mother, *why* should any man dislike his baby? I believe sometimes that he would like to let himself go with the Little Chap—that he finds himself loving him in spite of himself—but he seems to draw back willfully. The Little Chap will toddle across the floor and hurl himself at the honorable P. K.'s legs, calling, "Daddee, Daddee," and for a few minutes P. K. seems to enjoy it. Then he will deliberately disengage the little arms, put the Little Chap in his play pen without saying a word, and proceed to forget that he exists. Perhaps I oughtn't judge him so harshly, for I myself have much to be forgiven. But I can't understand it.

It isn't jealousy. As much as Lorraine loves the baby, he never comes between her and Phil for a minute. She enjoys the Little Chap all day, but when it is time for Phil to come home, baby and I do a vanishing act and those two almost forget that anyone else exists.

I am glad, though, that they enjoy each other's company. For I fear Lorraine will never be strong again. The doctor said recently that there was no *immediate* danger—but I don't like what that word implies.

Did I tell you what my newest name is? It is Miss Honor. Nellie, the maid, calls me Miss Eleanor, and last week the Little Chap began calling me Miss Honor. It amused Phil and Lorraine so that he repeated it, and now I am Miss Honor all the time. I have more names than I need—while that poor baby has none. When I'm alone with him I sometimes call him Chad but won't allow myself to do it often. No more heartbreaks, if I can help it.

Love,
Len

28

Through the daintily curtained open window the scent of blooming lilacs came into the room where Lorraine lay still on the bed. Several weeks ago was the last time she had felt able to sit in the big easy chair. Now when the hours of pain came, she was propped up in bed with pillows. Her eyes were shadowed and full of pain today as she watched the Little Chap toddling back and forth in his play. For several days she had insisted on his playing in the bedroom as much as possible, and Eleanor's heart ached for both the mother and the child—the mother knowing that separation was coming soon, and the child not knowing.

Sensing Eleanor's unvoiced sympathy, Lorraine finally said softly, "Eleanor, you have been like a dear sister to me this spring. Somehow I know that you understand. It must be because you've suffered too!"

"Yes," came the halting reply, "I have suffered, and I have found help in my suffering. I know that His grace sustains you, too."

"Yes, His grace is sufficient for me," replied Lorraine, leaning back and closing her eyes. "But sometimes I feel that I have had more than my share of suffering. Then I pray to have that sinful thought taken away. Eleanor—you are strong in spite of anything you may have suffered."

"No, Lorraine, I am not strong—in my own strength. But God has been doing wonderful things for me, and it is His strength that keeps me going. He forgave me so such that I shall never be finished praising Him.''

"Could you tell me, Eleanor?'' the sick girl asked softly. "I've always felt that there was some great tragedy in your life, and I feel that it has something to do with the two pictures on your dresser—your husband and your baby. The baby is cute. He looks a bit like the Little Chap.''

Eleanor's face went white. Then, with a prayer for courage, she said, "Lorraine, that isn't my baby's picture. It is my husband as a little boy. My mother-in-law gave it to me, and I keep it to help me realize how my baby may look. I never saw my baby.''

"Never saw him?'' exclaimed Lorraine, now frankly interested. "Why?''

"Because—I—oh, Lorraine, I never expected to tell this story again. But somehow I feel that God wants me to tell you today.''

The Little Chap, tired of play, had wandered over to Eleanor's chair and was tugging fretfully at her skirts to be picked up. She lifted him into her lap and began to rock him slowly as she began her story. She would have preferred not to take a stranger into her house of memory. But God seemed to be constraining her to do so. Perhaps somewhere in the story was a message of comfort for the sufferer on the bed. So down the corridors of memory they went together.

The shadows were long on the lawn outside, and the Little Chap was sound asleep in her arms, when Eleanor finally finished the narrative. Lorraine looked at her with eyes bright with unshed tears and then spoke with a quivering breath.

"God did lead you to tell me that story, Eleanor. Some day you will know why. His ways are wonderful, and His love is so kind that I want to shout for joy. I hear Phil coming. Take your little Moses and put him to bed. I'm so *glad* you told me.''

Eleanor looked with alarm at Lorraine as she rose to comply. Could she be delirious? Perhaps the story had excited her unduly. Softly she walked out of the room with the sleeping boy and bent to lay him in his crib. As she did so her eyes rested upon the picture of baby Chad on her dresser. "He does look a bit like the Little Chap,'' she conceded. ''Dear God, please take care of my baby, wherever he is.''

The next morning Lorraine seemed better and asked for her writing materials.

''I don't think you are strong enough,'' Eleanor protested dubiously. ''Why don't you let me write your letters for you?''

''Sorry, not this time,'' said Lorraine, smiling sweetly. ''Please, just a note or two. I won't overdo.''

So Eleanor propped her up with pillows and swung the bed table around in front of her.

''That will be fine,'' said Lorraine, happily, taking up her pen. ''You can put Moses to play in his pen while you go to your Bible class.''

''Moses!'' exclaimed Eleanor. ''Have you really named him at last?''

''Surely. Don't you like it?''

''Well, not exactly. It doesn't fit his appearance.''

''I'm sure Phil will think it is quite fitting.'' Lorraine smiled.

Eleanor left in perplexity and did not pursue the subject further. When she returned at the end of the hour, the writing materials had been put away, and Lorraine lay sleeping contentedly.

A few weeks later Mother Stewart walked slowly down the pathway leading to the mailbox. Gradually her strength was returning, and she was drinking deeply of the beauty and fragrance of the spring flowers this lovely May morning. Opening the box, she found a letter from Eleanor. Seating herself on the bench under a blooming apple tree, she tore open the envelope.

Dear Ones at Home:

Lorraine has gone from us. She fell asleep in my arms last night, with Phil on his knees beside her. It was *hard* to bear!

Today she looks so happy and sweet and peaceful that I couldn't possibly wish her back. But, oh, Mother, pray for Phil. He has been shut up in his study all day. Lorraine's father and sister came, and I caught just a glimpse of Phil's face as he opened the study door to let the father in. It was so pitiful! I went back to my room sick with the memory of a night when I suffered a similar loss. I wish I could comfort him, but only the Lord can do that.

I thought perhaps at last his heart would open to the Little Chap, but when I suggested this to Lorraine's sister (Mrs. Carder), she feared it would only antagonize him more to see the baby now. Pitiful, isn't it?

Mother, what ever will become of the Little Chap? I wish they would let me take care of him permanently. Pray that somehow God will care for him and give him a mother.

I'll write more later when I feel better.

Love to you all,
Len

Mother walked slowly back to the house, the letter in her hand. Already she was trying to think of some way in which she could help this perplexing situation. The whole family became greatly concerned for poor, motherless Little Chap, whose father did not love him, and many prayers were offered for a solution to the problem.

The following week another letter came from Eleanor.

Dear Mother:

I know you must think I have forgotten you. I am so glad you are getting well and strong again. But please don't try pitching hay this summer. I'll be home soon to take over all the work. Last year I was an invalid, and you bossed me about. This year our situations are reversed. And what a boss I'll be!

Only one week more of school, then I will walk out of here with my sheepskin. It has taken me six long years to get one little degree! Wouldn't my good aunt be ashamed of the child she thought was so brilliant? Well, I've learned a lot of other things besides, and, though I'll never have a diploma to show for it, I have become an expert in finding "joy out of sorrow, peace after pain."

Just now I'm glad I'm so busy, for I don't want to be homesick for the Little Chap. Mrs. Carder took him home with her. Lorraine's father lives with her, and he seems to feel a special attachment to the baby. Phil, true to form, paid no attention to the whole procedure, but I have the queerest impression of having seen him crying over the baby's crib the night after the funeral. I had a severe headache and Mrs. Carder had given me some medicine and put me to bed on the cot in the nursery. I seem to remember waking and seeing Phil there with his head in his hands and his shoulders shaking with sobs. But next morning he was as indifferent and cool as usual, so I must have been dreaming.

That day they took my Little Chap away, and he cried and kicked and reached out his little arms for me until it almost broke my heart. Yes, I'm paying the price now for letting myself love him so much But the joy was worth it.

I'll be home on June 7, and I feel now as though I never want to leave again. Oh, I almost forgot to ask—Dick wants to know if Bob doesn't need an extra hand for the summer. He thinks an Arizona rancher could learn to be a dairyman without too much difficulty. Or perhaps he wants to learn to help can. Ask Connie if she would like to teach him. He is most desirous of finding some work on our farm.

Love to you all,
Len

29

It was June again on the farm. Eleanor had come home late the night before, and now she sat with Mother Stewart in the morning sunshine on the big porch swing, drawing in long breaths of the fragrant country air.

"You look tired, dear," said Mother Stewart, patting the small hand with her own toil-worn one. "You are emotionally exhausted, I'm afraid."

"Yes, Mother, I *am* tired," Eleanor admitted. "I do live intensely, and seeing Lorraine fade away has wrung my heart. Then it was hard to have to give up the Little Chap just when he was getting so strong and sturdy and full of mischief."

Her eyes brimmed with tears, and her voice was tremulous.

"But you have help in your trials, don't you?" probed Mother Stewart.

"Yes, I do—and I need a lot of it. I haven't any strength of my own at all. But the Lord gives His, and I go on. Somehow I feel that it was all His will, and so I have no regrets. Now I want to get busy with the work, and soon I'll be fat and sassy again."

Baby Patricia toddled out of the screen door that Marilyn held open, and Eleanor held out hungry arms for her.

"Bless her heart, she's out bright and early to see her Auntie Len. I was going to come over and inspect your new home this afternoon, Marilyn," said Eleanor, cuddling the little girl close.

"Come right ahead," was the invitation. "I can't stay long now, for I have bread rising. But I wanted to say hello, so Patty and I rode over on the truck with Bob."

"You and Patty both look so sweet," exclaimed Eleanor impetuously. "No wonder Bob has the air of a millionaire."

"I've never noticed that." Marilyn laughed. "Next time I see him I'll look for it. I'm eager to show you our house," she said, changing the subject. "My father and brother painted it for us, and Dad says he will put in a furnace next fall. And I begged clippings and seeds and roots from both of my mothers until my garden is almost as nice as theirs—given a little time to grow."

"Given a little weeding, too," added Bob, coming up the steps. "That garden has enough weeds to keep our eminent botanist-sister busy for a year classifying them. Some day I'm going in there with a scythe," and he looked teasingly at Marilyn.

"Oh, no, you're not," she retorted, smiling. "I'll handpick those weeds. I've been so busy with my vegetable garden I have neglected everything else, but next week Patty and I will tackle those flower beds. Won't we, precious?"

"Pull flowers," murmured Patty ecstatically, nodding. Everyone laughed.

"Truer words were never spoken," commented her father. "Come on, Marilyn. I have visions of the bread running down and out the door. Eleanor, come see us soon. In fact, come for supper—how about tonight?"

Marilyn added her invitation, so Eleanor consented, and the little family walked down the path, Patty waving a happy goodbye over Bob's broad shoulder.

"What a good-natured baby she is," Eleanor commented. "So different from the Little Chap. He wasn't really naughty, though, Mother. He was just determined. He didn't particularly want to do bad things—he just wanted to have his own way."

"And therein," remarked Mother Stewart, "lies the essence of original sin. We all do that until God renews our hearts."

"And I am the chief of sinners in that respect," confessed Eleanor. "Perhaps that is why I feel so strongly that the Little Chap should be carefully trained and disciplined. I know the distress that can come from willfulness."

Mother was always ready to give another the benefit of the doubt. "Perhaps Lorraine spoiled him because she was too ill to care for him properly," she said now.

"That's exactly it," agreed Eleanor. "She never had the strength to do battle with his stubborn little will. And Dr. King didn't care enough to do it. So the young tyrant ruled supreme—until I arrived. Mother, you should have seen the battles we had! Fortunately he loved me, so that helped—but it was a stormy time for everyone."

"How did his mother feel about it?"

"Well, she knew that his health depended on his being *made* to do certain things at the proper times—eat, sleep, and so on. Oh, yes, and take cod liver oil." Eleanor smiled reminiscently. "But she couldn't stand to see us differ. So all the disputes between His Royal Stubbornness and Miss Honor had to be conducted in the back of the house with the doors closed. Such times as we had! But the Little Chap soon learned that I could outdo him at his own game."

"Poor Little Chap," sympathized Mother. "Didn't he dislike you for this strictness?"

"No, he liked me better every day, and after he learned that I meant business he became quite obedient. But the little rogue knew that I wouldn't cross him in front of his sick mother. So when we were in her room he did as he pleased, with the *smuggest* look on his face. When we left her room he put on obedience again, just like a little suit. A little suit that didn't fit too well." Eleanor laughed.

"Oh, Mother, I miss him so!" she exclaimed suddenly. "And that makes me yearn more for my little Chad, too. The pain almost tears my heart in two. Will it always be so?"

"You know where to find comfort, dear."

"Yes, Mother, and I am ashamed to complain, for He does help me every hour. Out of my hardest experience He has brought blessing. But I am still inclined to want my own way sometimes, so keep on praying for me, Mother. I tried to teach the Little Chap submission—and my Lord is trying to teach me."

* * *

That night Bob and Eleanor walked home to the big farmhouse with a new and exciting plan in mind. They found the whole family sitting on the porch.

"Mother!" began Bob. "How would you and the girls like to go on a vacation?"

"Oh, vacation!" squealed Mary Lou. "Where?"

"Is your name Mother?" asked Bob in mock reproof. "Let's let the most important lady speak."

"Why—I don't see how I could, children," Mother Stewart hesitated. "Who would do the work here? And where would we go? And where would the money come from?"

"One question at a time," replied Bob, sitting down on the steps. "First, the work. Len and I can look after things, and you all need a rest—even Pest, here," and he pulled Mary Lou's pigtail affectionately.

"Where would we go?" asked Connie, with not too much interest. She had hoped to have a pupil in the canning factory before long.

"My cottage by the lake," spoke up Eleanor. "It has stood vacant for over two years now. It should be used occasionally, at least. The Fleets are going to rent it for July, and Billy is going to take a dozen institute children up there in August. But I want you folks to use it during the last two weeks in June."

"It sounds tempting." Mother hesitated. "But I don't like to go away and leave all the work piled on Marilyn and Eleanor and you, Bob."

"We'll keep Miss Knowles in the sanitarium for two weeks longer, which will help a little," he replied. "And we'll get along somehow. Any extra work will be amply paid for by the thought of you ladies down there in the woods basking in the breezes, doing fancywork, reading books—or anything else you may choose to do. What say, Mom—will you go?"

"Please, let's go!" and Mary Lou threw herself impetuously into her mother's arms. "It would be such fun."

Connie said nothing but looked eagerly into her mother's face.

"You could drive it in a half day," Eleanor went on, "and that oughtn't to be too tiring. It is one of the loveliest spots I know. There are deep woods, a lake with a grand beach for swimming, and everything for your comfort, except food, already in the cottage. At this season the other places on the lake will be full of vacationists, and so there will be plenty of young folk around to liven it up for Connie and Mary Lou."

"Eleanor, don't you want to go?" asked Connie, suddenly.

"Yes, I want to go," Eleanor said slowly, folding her handkerchief carefully into a little square, not looking up, "but I couldn't stand it. I was unspeakably happy there with Chad, and every corner has its own sweet memory. It would be a comforting experience to me if I could go, but—" her voice dropped low "—the day I left there the last time, old Hulda who had been living with me said, 'Will you be comin' back and bringin' the little one?' I can't go back there without him. So I'll stay here."

As none of the others spoke, Eleanor continued. "The cottage isn't mine outright. It is only mine for my lifetime, then it must become the property of my oldest heir. My lawyer and the lawyer who arranged the adoption papers both know this. So some day, when I am gone, my boy will receive the cottage and go back to the place where his parents learned to love each other. While I live, I hope to use it wisely as my Lord would wish. But I can't go back there without him."

The family sat in sympathetic silence. After a few moments, Eleanor spoke cheerfully again. "But you haven't said yet that you will go. Please, Mother, won't you do it—for me?"

"Please do, Mom," begged Bob. "You need just such a rest cure to make you completely well."

"Well," Mrs. Stewart said slowly, "it does sound alluring indeed. So if you two are sure you can manage here, I am willing to go for two weeks."

Mary Lou jumped up with a shout and began to go around and kiss everyone in turn to demonstrate her joy. Connie's face reflected her pleasure.

"Then it's settled," said Eleanor happily "We'll all hustle with the work so that you can get off next Monday morning."

"Monday morning," chanted Mary Lou joyfully. "Monday morning."

"Oh, I forgot," remarked Eleanor casually. "One of the students at school needed a quiet place to work on a thesis, so I rented out one room at the cottage. You folks won't be bothered though. There's plenty of room for all.''

"Is it a he or a she?'' questioned Bob shrewdly.

"A he,'' remarked Eleanor, smiling.

"A theological student?''

"Yes.''

"Sings tenor, I believe?''

"Why, Bob, how astute you are!'' exclaimed Eleanor. "How did you ever guess it?''

"Because I don't trust that Dick Dunlap,'' replied Bob, grinning. "He's a sister-snatcher if ever I saw one. Connie, did you know about this?''

"If he bothers you, Mother, you can send him to a hotel to write his thesis,'' suggested Eleanor.

"Or perhaps I could stay home and help with the farm,'' continued Connie demurely.

"Children, stop your teasing,'' commanded Mother. "I like Dick, and, as we need a man in the house, I'll be glad to have him there. It's going to be a grand vacation.''

"I think so too,'' declared Mary Lou with exuberance.

A little smile that played around the corners of Connie's mouth made the others suspect that she thought so too.

* * *

After Mother and the girls left, Eleanor's days were busy ones. She helped Mrs. Hunt in the kitchen, she kept the big house in order, she cared for the tiny new chicks in the brooder house, and she worked with Uncle John in the vegetable garden. Every day was full, and every night found her too tired to lie awake and grieve over her empty arms. She had learned to leave her troubles "in the secret of His presence,'' but somehow there was still the memory of the tearful blue eyes and the quivering lips of the little lad who had not wanted to leave her.

On the second Friday afternoon Eleanor and Marilyn sat resting on the shady back porch. Suddenly Eleanor spoke.

"Marilyn, why couldn't you and Bob take a few days off and go to the lake too?''

"I'd love to," was the reply. "Do you think it would be possible?"

"Yes, I do. Bob said he wasn't going to start laying by the corn until Tuesday. We can manage nicely for three or four days. Mrs. Hunt can take care of the house, and Miss Knowles can keep on with the sanitarium. I can help Uncle John with the chores."

"I wish we could," said Marilyn, wistfully. "It would be a lovely change, and I haven't had a real trip since our honeymoon."

"Well, you need a change, and I'm going to see that you get it," Eleanor assured her. "Here comes Bob now. Let's see how good a persuader I am."

So successful was Eleanor that the next morning saw everyone up bright and early that the start to the lake might be made before the day became hot.

"While you're there, Bob," said Eleanor packing fresh vegetables and fruit into a large basket, "will you please do a few things for me?"

"If I can," replied Bob. "What would you like?"

"Look the house over carefully and see what needs to be done in the way of repairs. And I have a long list of things for you to bring back. Most of it is my photographic equipment. I am eager to get started at picture making again, although I must be sadly out of practice by now. Then these books I have listed will be in the case by the fireplace. That won't be too much, will it?"

"No," assured Bob. "We could bring back a whole library in place of all this food you are sending along. Do you think we'll eat this much?"

"I'm sure that the folks will have eaten all they took with them and that they must be paying fancy prices for fruit and vegetables and eggs if they are buying them there. The local folk take advantage of summer visitors."

As they were getting into the car, Mrs. Hunt emerged from the kitchen. She placed a large white can and several boxes on the backseat.

"Cookies and cake," she explained. "They will be glad to get them after eating store cookies."

Then Bob stepped on the starter, and, with Marilyn and Patty waving gaily, the car vanished around the turn in the drive.

30

Eleanor went slowly back into the quiet house. How she had longed to go with them! To roam once more through the woods she had loved since childhood; to see the blue sky over the lake at night; to sit on the beach listening to the little ripples swishing over the rocks of the pier; to dig in the garden she and Chad had planned; to lie on the hilltop and just rest. She was so tired. But it seemed as though the Lord wanted her here, and His way was best.

Eleanor wandered into her room, threw herself across the bed, and then, in spite of all her reasonings and her good resolutions, gave way to tears. The loneliness and pain were too much.

At last she lay exhausted and quiet, and the Comforter's voice spoke to her soul, bringing reassurance in place of sorrow and peace where the storm had raged.

"Oh, dear Savior, forgive me," she whispered. "I'm weak, and I keep stumbling, and I seem to lose my way again and again. But I do love Thee, and I do want to live for Thee, even though it means pain and sacrifice. Send me whatever will be for Thy glory, and help me to accept it joyfully for Thy sake. And oh, dear Christ, take care of my little boys—my Chad that I gave away, and my Little Chap who needs a mother."

After a while she arose, bathed her eyes, and rearranged her hair. Her face was peaceful again. Mrs. Hunt, in the kitchen, heard her singing:

"Oh, what wonderful, wonderful rest!
Trusting completely in Jesus I'm blest;
Sweetly He comforts and shields from alarms,
Holding me safe in His mighty arms."

Just before noon Eleanor saw the mailman's car coming up the road, so she ran down the walk to meet him. There were three letters for her, and she sat down in the porch swing to read them. First there was a letter from Carolyn, then a note from Dick describing the good times they were having at the lake.

The third letter was addressed in a strange handwriting, but when Eleanor saw the postmark she tore it open eagerly.

Dear Mrs. Stewart:
We have been distraught here by our inability to care for Lorraine's baby. He refuses to eat or sleep and has cried so much for Miss Honor that we decided to ask you if you could take him for a while. We reached that decision last night, and this morning before we could write you a package arrived from Phil, containing a letter which Lorraine had left in her desk, to be given to me after her death. There was also a letter for you which I am forwarding. It will explain itself, and no words of mine are necessary. All I can say is that my daughter Edith and I are almost overwhelmed at the marvelous way in which our Father works. We can only praise Him now.

We have a friend who will be passing through Woodstock (which is near you) next Monday afternoon. If convenient for you to meet her, she will bring the baby that far. Will you call me collect and let me know?

I know that Lorraine died happy in the knowledge that her baby would be taken care of. And I, her father, can only say, "God bless you and the little one."

Sincerely yours,
James W. Ferguson

Eleanor's heart pounded so hard she could scarcely see. Her hands shook as she opened the letter from Lorraine.

Dear Jochebed:
(What a thing to call me! thought Eleanor.)

225

The princess is too tired to care for your little Moses even though she loves him. And the heavenly Father knows that only one person can care for him properly—his own mother—yourself.

Eleanor ceased reading. The letter fell to the floor while the world reeled and swayed as the full significance of Lorraine's words dawned upon her. Jochebed! Moses' mother! Paid for caring for her own son!

When the sky and earth had ceased their whirling, and when the breath had consented to return to her body, Eleanor bent down for the letter and proceeded to read. Her eyes shone as the story of God's loving dealings with His children unfolded. For the first time she learned that the Little Chap had been adopted, in place of Lorraine's own baby, who had lived for only a few short hours and then slipped away to heaven.

Eleanor bowed her head, and through her sobs came the words, "Oh, Chad, He does fix things when we let Him."

On Monday afternoon two dusty cars rolled up the driveway to the big farmhouse, and the happy vacationers clambered out, glad to be at home again. Mary Lou ran into the house immediately, calling, "Len, oh, Len, we're home!" while Bob and Dick began to unload the bags and bundles. The ladies came up the steps, to be met by Mary Lou saying in a puzzled voice, "Len is gone."

"Gone? Why?" asked mother in disappointment.

"I don't know. She isn't here, and Mrs. Hunt says she went to Woodstock."

"Here's a note," said Connie, looking on the hall table.

They all clustered around while Connie read the contents of the note.

Dear Folks:
I received word that a boarder must be met at Woodstock so I'm going over today. Will be back on the four o'clock bus.
                                                    Len

"Bless her heart," said Mother, removing her hat. "She certainly is a dependable little helper. I wonder who the boarder is—must be someone from a distance. It's too bad she had to go on the bus."

"I wish sometime we could have a little boarder," said Mary Lou. "I get so tired of big ones all the time."

"Cheer up, sisterkin," said Bob. "In these days anything can happen. Maybe this is a dwarf or a gnome coming to live with us."

Mary Lou giggled.

"You're so funny sometimes," she remarked.

Mrs. Hunt came in from the kitchen. "Now I know you are all hot and tired from your drive," said she. "Here is a big pitcher of grape juice, and if I were you I would just sit down on the porch and get cooled off and rested."

So the whole party adjourned to the front porch and sat there reveling in the pleasure of being home again.

Mother looked strong and well. Dick, Connie, and Mary Lou were glowing with suntan, and even Bob and Marilyn looked relaxed and rested by the little excursion they had taken. Baby Patty trotted about, glad to be back in this familiar place, stealing sips of grape juice from first one and then another on the porch.

"Well, I guess we'd better be heading for home," said Bob, setting down his glass and standing up to stretch his legs. "Tell Eleanor I put all her things in her room. I hope I brought the right stuff. I'll be over tomorrow to talk to her about the cottage."

He swung Patty up to a perch on his shoulder, and they were just starting for the car when Mary Lou called out, "There's the bus!"

Seven pairs of eyes alighted on the familiar yellow and brown vehicle that had just pulled up at the dusty roadside. They saw Eleanor step down, then looked on in amazement as she came up the walk with a little boy in her arms.

"Oh, it is a little boarder!" exclaimed Mary Lou in glee. "It is!"

But no one paid any attention. All stood speechless before the radiance on Eleanor's face as she mounted the steps.

Then she spoke with a catch in her voice.

227

"Do you know our new boarder?"

"It must be the King baby!" exclaimed Connie. "The Little Chap!"

"Yes," replied Eleanor, her voice shaking. "The King's *adopted* son. Mother, oh, Mother, why didn't I guess it before? Look at him, Mother! Don't you know who he really is?"

The mother gazed with paling cheek at the smiling baby who had nestled his head against Eleanor's shoulder as if he couldn't get close enough to her. Then she looked at Eleanor's face. Her eyes went back to the baby's face, and as he met her gaze he gave her a smile, a three-cornered crooked smile that took her back a quarter of a century.

With a sob she held out her arms. But the Little Chap only clung the closer to Eleanor. So Mother Stewart clasped them both close, saying as she did so, with tears running down her cheeks, "I *do* know. He's *our* baby—our own little Chad! Oh, Father in Heaven, we thank Thee!"

* * *

Later, when the little boy had been persuaded to leave Eleanor's shoulder for his grandmother's eager arms, Eleanor read Lorraine's letter to the rejoicing family. At times during the reading her voice broke, as she remembered how dear Lorraine had been to her. Mother Stewart openly wiped her eyes once or twice, while the others listened in sympathetic silence.

Dear Jochebed:

The princess is too tired to care for your little Moses, even though she loves him. And the heavenly Father knows that only one person can care for him properly—his own mother—yourself. Oh, Eleanor, I am so shaken by my realization of how much God loves us, even in our weakness and sin, that I can hardly write.

This afternoon, when you told me your story and it dawned upon me that my little boy—the one that I have called my own ever since they brought him to me after my own tiny son died—was, in reality, your son, I wanted to shout aloud for joy. For I have lain awake many hours during these last weeks wondering what will happen to him when I am gone. It has become plain to me that I shall soon be leaving you, and I have been deeply troubled for my little nameless son. You must have observed that Phil has never cared for him at all. So I could not burden him with an unwanted child. Then, in my deepest distress, God sent you, the baby's own mother. It can be nothing but God's intervention in our lives that shaped events in this way.

Just think, Eleanor, when my father went to that sanitarium where you were, both Phil and I were in a hospital—he seriously injured by the automobile accident and I mourning for the baby that didn't live. Poor Father! He was frantic and did the only thing he could think of. Perhaps it did save my life, for I loved the Little Chap from the start.

But it was three months before we dared tell Phil that our little son, the Phil, Jr., we had longed for—had not lived and that a strange child was taking his place. When we did tell him, he had a relapse and almost died. Then, even after he got well, he never accepted the child he considered an interloper. I love Phil, but I've loved the little one, too, and at times my heart has been torn in two.

But now I am more happy than I have been in two years. I really don't mind going, but my heart aches for Phil. I know, Eleanor, that you and he seem to antagonize each other, but that is because you don't know him as well as I do. He has always been my "shining knight," and I love his proud self-confidence. It will be a sad time for him when I go, but God can comfort him.

My father will help you get the adoption papers fixed up for the baby. Edith and her husband signed the others, as we were both so very sick. Phil has never bothered to change them.

I have written a long letter to my father, explaining everything, and he will take care of the legal matters. Oh, Eleanor, I am so happy to be able to give your baby back to you.

I am asking Father and Edith not to tell Phil where the baby has been sent. That will be the only fair way for you. And Phil doesn't care. If he ever should get lonely for the little son he would not accept, I hope you can forgive him and be kind to him.

I am very tired, for I have written a long letter to Phil also, telling him many things I cannot say when I talk to him. May God bless and keep all my dear ones until we meet again by His throne.

Lorraine

As Eleanor finished reading, silence reigned. Everyone was marveling at God's goodness. Little Chad lay sleeping in his grandmother's arms, and she looked as though earth could hold no greater joy for her.

At last Eleanor broke the tension with a laugh. "This is the most humbling moment of my life!" she exclaimed. "I have just realized that this little person's willfulness, which I have sought for months to eradicate, is an inheritance not from the Rev. Dr. Philip King but from Eleanor Stewart!"

Mother swayed gently in the swing.

"Are you going to tell Philip King where the baby is—and who he is?"

"I will, if he ever wants to know. I would never inflict on anyone else the anguish I have endured. But I'll not volunteer the information. He can let me know through Mrs. Carder if he ever wants to see the Little Chap, and in that case he can visit him as much as he wishes. I owe the Kings a great debt for caring for my baby when I wouldn't."

"Poor Dr. King. I am sorry for him," said Dick from his perch on the porch rail beside Connie. "He looked haggard during commencement week."

"With good reason," returned Eleanor. "Lorraine's death came just before the close of school, and, with Dr. Hale ill, the burden of everything was on Phil's shoulders."

"How is Dr. Hale?" asked Mother solicitously. The president of Bethel ranked high on her prayer list.

"Not so well, Mother," replied Eleanor. "I doubt if he will be able to start school next year."

"I heard a rumor before I left," added Dick, "that the board was thinking of appointing an assistant to take over the work, a sort of president pro tem. I think that no one actually expects Dr. Hale ever to carry the whole burden again, but they don't want him to resign. The new assistant would be in training, as it were, for the day when Dr. Hale will be gone."

"Who are they considering?" asked Mother. "It will take a big man to fill that spiritual giant's shoes."

"Dr. Cortland could do it," remarked Eleanor. "I think he could accomplish a great deal in such a position. He never appears to be doing much, but somehow things happen when he is about. I think it is because he never does anything in his own strength, but relies wholly on the Lord."

"Well, campus opinion is divided between him and Dr. King for the position," said Dick.

"Oh, Dr. King is too young!" cried Eleanor in dismay. "He is clever and capable, but it would be tragic to make him president of Bethel College."

"Well, it hasn't been done yet," consoled Dick. "I was just peddling campus gossip. But he does have a reputation for accomplishing things, and for getting other folks to work, too. And Dr. Cortland is pretty slow compared to P.K., the whirlwind accomplisher!"

"I don't care if he *is* slow," Eleanor retorted. "He is a fine scholar and a dear old saint. I think he could be just as clever an administrator as Philip King if he desired."

"Better tell that to the trustees," said Dick. "For myself I'd vote for the dear old doctor, but I'm sure that Philip King will make a gilt-edged impression on the board."

"This is surely a matter to be prayed about," stated Mother, shifting the weight of the child in her arms. The action disturbed him, and the blue eyes opened, then gazed in sleepy bewilderment at the strange faces. The tiny chin began to quiver, then two pleading arms were lifted to Eleanor.

"Miss Honor, take!" he demanded, and with a surge of joy Eleanor caught her little son into her arms and smoothed his hair.

"Miss Honor it shall be today," she said. "But tomorrow I'm going to add a new word to your vocabulary. I can hardly wait to hear you say Mother."

31

For Eleanor that summer flew by on joyous wings. She had her little Chad, and was released from the ache and remorse that had never left her since they had been separated. She watched him grow strong and tall; she taught him and began to train the strong will into loving obedience. She learned to see the world anew through baby eyes just growing into observant childhood. Every day was a glad adventure.

Each morning Eleanor awakened with a prayer of gratitude in her heart when she realized that in the crib by her side lay the precious child who was left to her as a reminder of her life with Chad. Her whole being throbbed with the joy of God's great mercy and His love in returning her lost child. At work or at play, her heart was lifted up in thanksgiving. Life might bring more of trouble or of pain—it surely would—but the calm peace of her soul could not be disturbed. She knew her Guide and would rest confidently in His leadership.

Little Chad's lips soon learned to say "Mother," although occasionally he would forget and say "Miss Honor." After a few puzzled inquiries for "Mum-mum," he seemed to forget that lovely girl who had been mother to him. Several times he asked hopefully, "Daddee tum?" but as the days passed, the fascinations of the farm and the love and caresses of his new family crowded old memories from his baby mind. He was the darling of the family, bringing memories as he did of another Chad who was now waiting in heaven.

And he grew to love them all. He trotted after "Mammaw" as she inspected her flowers, he romped with Connie and Mary Lou, and he and baby Patty toddled about the lawn hand in hand, little Chad trying to help the "babee" as he called her. He rode Bob's shoulder to the chores. "I've long needed another man around here," Bob confided to him. "You and I will stick together for our own protection now."

In July Eleanor took little Chad and went for two happy weeks at the lake with the Fleets. In that lovely place where every corner of the house and even the woods and hills outside held memories of the other Chad, she rested as she had not been able to do before. And when she returned to the farm, Mother Stewart was happy to see the change in her. For the first time since they had known her, they began to feel that this was the laughing girl Chad had loved.

One day a letter came to Eleanor from Philip King, stating that Lorraine had asked him to give Eleanor the little pearl ring she had worn. He was having the set tightened and would send it later. After thanking Eleanor for her care of Lorraine during those last weeks, he scarcely mentioned himself except to say that he was well and learning to go on living. "One does somehow." Of the Little Chap he said nothing, and Eleanor tightened her lips at the neglect.

A letter from Billy told of days spent at the institute, of grand preparations for the trip to the cottage in August.

Dad and Mother are having as much fun as I am [she wrote]. Their problem child is a problem no longer. They are so interested in the work that if I wanted a yacht, all I'd need to do would be to tell Dad I needed it at the institute. Angela comes down occasionally but stays only long enough to get the files in a mess. She wouldn't come at all except for the fact that she wants P.K. to remember that she is still alive.

P.K. practically lives here. He is very sad and quiet and works hard with the boys. And his sermons on Sundays are great! Isn't it queer how decent and likeable he is here and how absolutely unbearable he is when he gets to strutting about the halls of learning?

Dick was back in the city working at an express depot during the day, and his evenings—well, Mary Lou insisted they were all spent in writing long letters to Connie. That young lady was preparing to start to Bethel College in September, and she and Mother were deep in wardrobe plans. Marilyn came often along the orchard path to help with the canning, while Patty and Chad played together under Mary Lou's watchful eye.

The first week in September Dick came up to the farm for a few days' vacation. The first evening of his visit he coaxed Connie out for a walk, and when they returned Connie held out her left hand to her mother in joyous delight. There sparkled a shining new diamond ring.

"I would have liked to get her a great big diamond," Dick said in bashful explanation. "But I had to get it now so that she could be tagged as mine before those other men at Bethel saw her."

"It's a lovely ring," said Mother. "I'm happy for my dear girl, and I'm glad that God has answered my prayers for her life. To know that Connie and you will be working and singing together for the Lord gives me great happiness."

Later that evening Connie and Mary Lou were helping with the dishes, while Eleanor and Dick sat in the porch swing and talked.

"Now do you realize the far-reaching effects of your Christmas invitation?" Dick said, unable to keep off the all-engrossing subject for long. "Future generations may rise up and call you blessed because of that little bit of charity."

"Could be," said Eleanor meditatively.

"Don't ever tell anyone this," Dick continued, "or they might think I was out of my mind. But before I had been here half an hour I had made up my mind that Connie was the only girl for me—and on Christmas Day she knew it! But she wouldn't say yes until last week."

"She probably meant to all the time," pointed out Eleanor, "but wouldn't give you the satisfaction. But she loved you at once. That's the Stewart way. Bob and Marilyn loved each other from first grade days. Chad and I fell in love at first sight. When the Stewarts love, it's for all time, and don't you forget it. I wish you long years of happiness, Dick. Connie will make a wonderful minister's wife.''

"I never thought of that,'' said Dick in surprise. "I just thought how much I loved her.''

"How are things going at Bethel?'' asked Eleanor, changing the subject.

"Oh, so-so. They have made some improvements on the campus during the summer. There are some dandy new tennis courts.''

"What about the vice-presidency?''

Dick looked more serious. "I saw Billy the other day, and she said Dr. King had been appointed vice-president, to be in active charge of Bethel under Dr. Hale's instruction. It's what a lot of folks have been expecting. He is no doubt in training for the presidency.''

"I'm so sorry,'' said Eleanor. "I wouldn't say that in public, and now that it has happened we must pray that it will work out for Bethel's good—and for Dr. King's good, too.''

"I will say this for him,'' continued Dick, "he has seemed different this summer, very quiet when on the campus. Bill Wilson says he has been living at the institute part of the time.''

Eleanor's face lighted. "Perhaps Lorraine's death has done for him the thing I have longed for—taken him out of himself and aroused him to really unselfish service. The thing that always troubled me about him was his unbounded egoism. He never seemed to forget self for one minute.''

"That's the way I felt,'' returned Dick. "In every speech and action he seemed to be concentrating on himself—on the impression he would make. Even his prayers seem to be arguments designed to convince God that Philip King's plans for the work were superior to any that He Himself might have!''

"Oh, Dick!'' reproved Eleanor.

"Don't you feel that way?'' he defended himself.

"Well, yes, a little,'' she admitted, laughing. "But I wonder why he is so willful. He is just the antithesis of Dr. Cortland, who lives so close to Christ that his own personality seems completely submerged. When he talks, it is not himself who is lifted up—it is Jesus Christ. And his classrooms become in very truth 'holy ground.'''

"Wouldn't it be fine if Dr. Cortland could be president?" asked Dick, wistfully. "I'd like to see him run an institution. It would be like George Mueller's orphanage."

"It surely would be a monument of faith," agreed Eleanor. "It could be done. Dr. Cortland believes that we should, in all the affairs of life, seek first God's kingdom and His righteousness and leave with Him the care of all our personal needs. He has lived that way for forty years. I'd like to see Bethel run that way, too."

"So would I. But Philip King is the one who will probably rule over Bethel's destiny and shape its future course."

"If we have sincerely prayed, Dick," said Eleanor, making room on the swing for Connie who was just coming out the front door, we do wrong to worry. God took my life and reshaped it, and He can work out His plan even through Philip King. Let's pray—not doubt!"

* * *

With two fascinating subjects to work on, namely baby Patty and little Chad, Eleanor found her interest in photography reviving. Uncle John fitted up a room in the basement where she could work, and she soon found her old skill returning. Pictures of the babies brought exclamations of pleasure from all who saw them, and Eleanor was persuaded to submit some of them to a children's magazine for illustrations. To her surprise and joy, they were enthusiastically received, and she soon had orders for as many as she could send.

In going about the farm and the woods, Eleanor found many interesting subjects to add to her collection of slides, and when Connie and Dick came home at Christmas time, she delighted a group of young people at the church one evening by showing many of her beautiful slides and giving an extemporaneous talk about God's works as seen through the microscope. Her only thought was to contribute to the evening's enjoyment and to give these country young people a glimpse into a fascinating world with which they might not be acquainted. But the results were far-reaching. In late January Eleanor received a letter from Philip King, to whom Dick had one day described the lecture and

236

slides. Dr. King had conceived the idea of having Eleanor present a series of lectures at Bethel, using the same topic she had used before.

> We have a fund for just such a purpose [he wrote], and if you can give the lectures, we will arrange to give you the chapel hour for two weeks. They would be a most fitting supplement to the science courses, and I am sure that all the students would be greatly profited by the lectures.

Eleanor was astounded at the offer and was somewhat inclined to refuse it. Mother, however, urged its acceptance. Eleanor could well be spared from the work just now (Little Chad would be cared for by herself) and—most important of all—this might be God's call to wider service.

Eleanor knelt down by her bedside and prayed over the problem, then rose from her knees feeling that God was indeed calling her to Bethel. So the letter of acceptance was written.

In preparing the lectures, Eleanor was brought back into the world of science that she had left three years before, and, though at times painful memories sprang up, she really enjoyed the study and preparation. Never before had she approached any study with the object of glorifying God through it all, and she soon found herself absorbed and thrilled with the magnitude and beauty of God's works.

* * *

In March she left for the city, promising to bring Chad the most wonderful toy fire-engine to be found in the shops, when she returned.

"And will you be a good boy while mother is gone?" she asked, almost tearfully.

"Yes, I will be good, Mother." Then he added for emphasis, "I truly will, Miss Honor." So Eleanor kissed him and was gone.

It was pleasant to meet old friends at Bethel. Eleanor had some talks with Dr. Cortland that inspired her with new courage. She visited the institute with Billy and rejoiced over the improvements there. Billy's father was growing much interested in the institute work, and Billy was planning a campaign of her own to get her father and some of his wealthy friends to endow the institute so that it could afford to hire a full-time resident pastor. Dr. King was still preaching on Sundays but had little time for weekday work there.

Yet with all the joy of being back at her old school, Eleanor had an uneasy feeling that all was not well there. The spiritual life of the school seemed to have lost some of its depth and fervor. Dr. Cortland's facial expression was sad, and many of the students seemed to feel dissatisfied with a vague something in the atmosphere. Yet no one could lay a finger exactly on the trouble.

Outwardly the school seemed to be progressing. There was talk of a building campaign to provide a new library and science hall. Everywhere was an air of brisk activity.

Eleanor saw Dr. King every day, but he was always busy. If his sorrow had had any deep effect on him it was not discernible. He looked as calmly self-sufficient as ever, and the only change in his appearance was an added amount of gray in the wavy brown hair. The one white lock was not nearly so conspicuous as before.

Dr. King listened to the lectures with interest, and, when they were over and Eleanor was ready to leave for the farm, he insisted on driving her to the station in his car.

"The train is late, I see," he remarked as they scanned the bulletin board. "That isn't surprising—and it will give me time to ask you something important."

"What is it?" asked Eleanor wonderingly.

"Would you consider a position on the lecturing staff at Bethel?"

"Oh, no!" she exclaimed without a moment's hesitation. Then, seeing his surprise she went on: "I do thank you for the offer, and I never dreamed of anything so big coming to me. But I don't wish to leave my little son in order to come back to school and live. He needs his mother—and she needs him."

"Certainly," Dr. King agreed, without conviction. "Well, I hardly hoped you would accept, but you can always remember that you once had such an offer. And some day Bethel is going to be a famous school where teaching will be an honor."

"As long as it stays a spiritual school, that is all I will ask," replied Eleanor soberly.

"Well, of course, it will do that, too. But you just watch and see our progress. Then when we are famous, think back that you might have been on the faculty—and perhaps it will help erase your shame at not knowing Jezebel from Beelzebub."

Then they both laughed, and, when the train pulled into the station, they parted with a friendly handclasp.

As Eleanor settled herself in the seat for the long ride, she thought, *He's still Lorraine's shining knight posing on his charger. How I'd like to shake him off it some day!*

Then her thoughts leaped ahead to the farm where a little boy waited for the wonderful red fire-engine that was even now reposing in her suitcase.

32

Once more it was spring in the country. New life was every-where—in the woods, where the flowers pushed the damp leaves aside; in the barn lot, where new calves walked slowly about on wobbly legs; in the brooder house, where peeping little balls of yellow fluff brought delighted squeals from the children. Up in the sunny south room of the sanitarium, the little son of Marilyn and Bob lay in his basket and voiced a lusty opinion of the world into which he had just been ushered.

Summer came with haying and gardening, and canning of fruits and vegetables— sunny days bringing work for them all, and occasional showers to remind them of God's provision and their need for both sunshine and rain.

Summer slid into autumn, and Connie returned to Bethel while mother and Eleanor carried on at home. As the days went by, Mary Lou changed from the roly-poly child Eleanor had first known to a demure girl with a slow smile and eyes that looked out on the world with serious sweetness. Little Chad grew tall and brown and more like the other Chad every day.

Through a long, snowy winter Eleanor helped mother in the little hospital, sewed with Marilyn, romped in the bracing air with Patty and Chad, cooked and baked in the big old kitchen, or spent long hours in study or prayer. The kind of happiness she had once dreamed of as Chad's wife would never be hers, but she had found a better and more lasting happiness—the joy of a surrendered life and will.

Then March came again, and she was at Bethel for another series of lectures. She found many changes in her beloved college. Dr. Hale had passed away in January. Although the new president had not been named, the general opinion was that Philip King would succeed to the position. Eleanor's hope for a change in Dr. King's attitude had not been realized. His self-confidence was apparently unbounded. He was full of plans for Bethel's advancement and sure of his own ability to lead the school into hitherto undreamed of achievement. In the chapel hours, which had always been a source of strength and inspiration to Eleanor, there was a restless bustle of activities that seemed far removed from the former air of quiet worship. There was much talk of spring sports, and interest in the coming interscholastic meets was high. Bethel had always had a balanced program of work and play. But this year, as she watched and listened, Eleanor wondered if there might not be much confusion in the students' minds regarding the relative importance of these things.

One evening Dr. King took Eleanor to a symphony concert. During the course of the evening, he described his plans with enthusiasm. The first thing to do, of course, was to raise money for new buildings, and for this purpose he planned to contact Angela's father and his friends.

"All these improvements could have been made long ago, given the proper cooperation," he said. "But there have been obstructionists on the board of trustees and in the faculty. Now I am overcoming that opposition, and I think I can see the way clear. Bethel College, my dear Mrs. Stewart, is going to awaken out of her hundred-year slumber and begin to take her rightful place in the educational world."

Eleanor was at a loss for an answer. Before she could reply, however, Philip King changed the subject and began to speak of the work at the institute. He had organized a boys' club here and had many other plans if only the right workers could be found.

Philip talked of Eleanor herself, asking about her life, her home, and her little son. She listened eagerly, hoping that he would say something of missing the Little Chap, but he never mentioned him, although several times he referred affectionately to Lorraine.

241

As he talked, Eleanor thought, *There are still two Philip Kings. This is the one who used to sit all night with his sick wife in his arms, and who is deeply interested in those ragged, pathetic boys at the institute. It's easy to see why they love him. The other Philip King is a self-centered egoist who wants to run the universe and whose self-pride will ruin Bethel College!*

So, as before, Eleanor returned to the farm with a heavy heart, determined to forget Philip King and the whole unhappy situation. But it was not easy. The Lord had laid upon her heart a deep burden of prayer for the self-surrender of Philip King, and she was constantly constrained to lift up her heart that he might forget his talented self and grow into the stature of full Christian manhood. Eleanor was learning the lesson Mother Stewart had taught her by example—that of prevailing prayer.

She prayed that Philip might see clearly the necessity for self-crucifixion before he could be really used of God, and for herself she asked strength and grace and courage to tread the way Christ should lead her—even though it should prove a lonely one.

The annual meeting of the board of trustees of Bethel College was scheduled for early June. As the date approached, Eleanor was increasingly burdened. One day, while she was on her knees in prayer for Philip, she seemed to receive a direct injunction, "Write to Philip."

Write? she wondered. *What shall I write? What can anyone tell him?*

"Write to him," directed the Spirit. "I will speak to him, through the letter."

So that night, after little Chad was asleep and the whole house was quiet, Eleanor took out her writing materials and began a letter to Philip. It was not an easy letter to write. Several times she tore up the pages she had written and would have given up the task in despair had not the urging of the Spirit been so strong within her. She prayed as she wrote:

Dear Dr. King:

I have been hearing much lately of your prospects in connection with Bethel, and there has come to me an ever-increasing urge to write you. To make the situation clear to you, I must tell you of an incident that deeply affected my own life.

Several years ago at Thanksgiving time, you preached a sermon on a Sunday morning in a little place called Meadville. Your topic was "The Bond Servant of Jesus Christ." You will remember the sermon, for you preached it later at the institute. It was a powerful message. My husband and I attended the service and heard the message and went out of the church with our hearts filled with its inspiration. Neither of us would forget that sermon or ever be quite the same after hearing it. My husband was already a consecrated Christian, and it served to deepen and sweeten his fellowship with Christ. It charged me with responsibilities of which I had never before been conscious. Because of that sermon, I was forced to make a decision of great importance involving the future of my husband and me. If I yielded to the Lord, I must make material sacrifices that would make impossible a career I felt we must follow. If I refused to make the sacrifice, I would be turning my back on the Lord who loved me. Chad, my husband, saw only one thing to do—to yield all to the Lord and trust Him to care for us. I was willful and refused to listen to the Spirit's pleading. He wanted full surrender, but I hardened my heart.

Two days later my husband was taken from me, and I was left alone, bitter and rebellious. God had to lead me through deep and troubled waters before I finally yielded Him my life—before I was ready to give Him the full allegiance that was His by right of purchase with His own blood.

You wonder why I am telling you this, Dr. King. It is because *your* sermon stirred me and placed upon me the responsibility of surrendering to the Master. Because of what that sermon did in my life, I am claiming the right to say these things to you. When you read this letter you may be very angry with me. But whether you forgive me or not, I still must write this. Philip King, I challenge you to hear your own call! You preach surrender, but the months of close contact we had at Bethel have shown me that you are not surrendered. You are not yet a bond servant of Jesus Christ.

Am I too hard on you, dear friend, when I say that? Ask the Spirit to speak to you and show you His plan for your life. Ask Him to purge you from pride and self-will. Let Him lead you. Rely absolutely upon Him in *all* your ways and through all your days. I am sure you understand why this leading is so important just at this time. Do you remember another sermon you once preached deplor-

243

ing the folly of the Israelites who sought help from the Egyptians when they should have trusted God and triumphed? Oh, my dear friend, can't you see the enemy now tempting you to go down to Egypt for help for Bethel?

Writing you this is the hardest task I have had to do since the day I began to follow the Spirit's leading. But I *must* do it, and I plead with you again to let go of self and let God work through you. My days have become a constant prayer for you. Until I hear that the victory has been won, I shall literally "pray without ceasing."

Sincerely,
Your friend in Christ,
Eleanor Stewart

Eleanor laid down her pen. She was weary, utterly spent. But she had peace in her soul, so she knew that God was satisfied with the letter she had written.

After a few days had passed, Eleanor began to watch eagerly for the mailman's automobile each day, although she could not have told why, for she had no reason to expect an answer to her letter. She felt that the Spirit would use it somehow, but very likely at the cost of Philip King's friendship. A sense of desolation and loneliness came over her, but at the same time a sweet consciousness of having given something precious to her Lord whom she loved more than ever before.

Then a letter came from Billy.

Dear Eleanor:

I can't wait to tell you all about this choice incident, so am hurrying to write you before Dad begins to think the story should be hushed.

To begin at the beginning, Dad sprained his ankle last week and is confined to a wheel chair. So the meeting of Bethel trustees was held at our house. I had a sort of premonition that things would be interesting, so I offered to be steno and take it all down in shorthand. Dad didn't fall for that idea at all, so I don't have any verbatim reports.

The whole session was most stirring. You know that Dad and Mr. Davenport, Angela's father, never did hit it off very well, just on principle, I guess. I could hear argument after argument from out on the porch where I was. So by the time they got to the real purpose of the meeting, which was to elect a new president for Bethel,

I think Dad and Mr. Davenport were pretty upset. (I know how Dad felt. I roomed with Angela.)

I wish I could have sat in on the session so I could give a coherent account. I could hear Mr. Davenport doing a lot of talking and being interrupted by Dad now and then. Next followed a long pause that must have been a prayer by Dr. Cortland, and then an hour of argument of which I could get nothing but occasional phrases. At last Mr. Davenport stamped out, his back stiff as a rod. Then, soon after, the others left. They didn't notice poor little me, curled up on the porch settee, but I saw them and could hardly wait to find out what happened. All of the trustees looked as if they had been to a funeral, very subdued and meek. Dr. Cortland had, apparently, been crying, and his dear old face was a little swollen. Philip King looked like a little boy that hadn't any home or mother or even a dog to love him. Yet he was smiling, a kind of sick-looking smile, and he and Dr. Cortland went off in the car together.

So I went into the house. Dad was almost frantic because he couldn't get out of his wheelchair and dance a jig. He had to tell someone, and, happily, I was the person at hand. Now, from his rather incoherent ramblings here is the story as I have pieced it together.

Philip King refused the presidency of Bethel College! Instead, he suggested that the trustees choose Dr. Cortland, and they did! Oh, Eleanor, think of missing such a show as that must have been! Dad doesn't tell it so that it makes much sense, but it seems Philip King had had some sort of a jolt that Mr. Davenport is sure unsettled his mind. Anyway, he talked so convincingly of his own unfitness for the job that he had them all shaking with terror at the close squeak they had had. Mr. Davenport threatened to resign and called P.K. a quitter and said neither he nor any of his friends would ever give another penny to Bethel. So P.K. answered that as long as Bethel had the Lord on her side she could do without the Egyptians. "Does that make sense?" snorts Dad. "Well, I don't care if it doesn't. Davenport fairly wilted!"

Dad asked me to get him a Bible and a concordance, and he is down there now, the old dear, trying to find out what the Egyptians could have to do with Bethel. I slipped away to write you.

I wonder what P.K. intends to do now. I don't believe he will stay on as instructor or vice-president. Maybe he will come to the institute full time. That would be better than my wildest imaginings. Since hearing what he did at the board meeting, I could believe anything.

I'll let you know if I hear any more. In the meantime keep your fingers crossed, mainly that I don't wake up and find that this was all a dream.

Your pal,
Billy

Eleanor's heart sang! God had heard and answered prayer, and not only would God's power and glory be recognized at Bethel, but Philip had surrendered, and his life would now be given to God in self-forgetful service. He would be the bond servant now. Eleanor knew that her letter must have helped his decision, else why those references to the Egyptians?

And yet Philip had not written. Surely if her letter had been used to help him, he would answer it and tell her that her prayers had been answered. But one week after another slipped past, and no word came from him. Dick wrote that Philip King had not been seen on the campus since commencement, and no one seemed to know where he was or what his plans might be.

Now Eleanor was sure that Philip had been offended and that, although he might have yielded to the Spirit as regards the Bethel situation, he had rejected her as a friend. Her heart was sore, yet she could not regret her action. She had followed the Spirit's leading, and all would be well.

33

Mother and the girls were sitting on the porch one August afternoon, sewing some linens for Connie's fast-filling hope chest. Eleanor came out of the door looking like a little girl with her hair tied back from her face. She wore a fresh yellow gingham dress. She was followed by little Chad, who had just awakened from his nap, and now looked like a tanned little cherub in a blue linen sunsuit.

"Chad and I are going up to the church to weed the rock garden," Eleanor said. "I noticed Sunday afternoon that the purslane is trying to choke out the little new rock plants."

"I saw it too," contributed Mary Lou. "But it's not two weeks since Ruth and Jimmie and I pulled it all out."

"I know," said Eleanor. "But weeds are like faults. You just have to keep everlastingly at them. Our handyman once told me that I was meaner than purslane. I didn't realize the import of the compliment—then."

"That wasn't a very nice thing to say," said Mary Lou soberly.

"I wasn't a very nice child." Eleanor laughed. "I was just as uncontrollable as a weed. Someone should have pulled me. Well, sonny boy, give Grandma a kiss and come along."

Chad obediently planted a kiss on Grandma's cheek and submitted to her hug. Then he ran on down the path with Sport, his puppy, barking and running around him in circles.

Eleanor followed leisurely, rejoicing at the sight of the sturdy little lad who bore such faint resemblance to the sickly baby he had been a few years before. He was tall for his four years, with tumbled golden hair and the same sparkling blue eyes that had been one of the chief charms of the older Chad. Eleanor had never become dull to the joy of motherhood. Every day her son brought new happiness. She loved to work and play with him and whenever possible found small tasks that kept him near her.

When they reached the rock garden on the hillside, Eleanor showed him how to tell the purslane from the little plants and how to feel for the central stem and pull the whole weed without breaking it.

"We have to get the whole root, or it will grow again," she explained.

Then the mother and son spent a happy hour working at the stubborn little weeds. As they worked, Chad chattered gaily, and Eleanor drew him out in his conversation. She loved to hear of his doings, and she found opportunities in their informal conversations to plant seeds that would bear fruit later in Christian faith and life.

Then, when the last ugly weed had been uprooted, Eleanor and little Chad washed their muddied hands in the pool and sat down to rest on the bench by the edge of the water.

The fish pond was a new venture in the young people's landscaping campaign. Several hundred yards distant, a small brook flowed through the field and emptied into the larger creek across the road. One day a lad had remarked on the need for a waterfall, and together the young people conceived a plan for making a new channel for the brook and leading it down over the rocks. And now the brook tumbled down the rocks in a graceful spray and formed a sizeable pool at the foot of the hill. Thence it meandered off under the fence and across the adjoining woodlot to join the creek. It had been a real engineering feat, and the young people were justifiably proud of their handiwork.

The afternoon was warm, and Chad looked longingly at the cool water splashing on the rocks. He raised pleading eyes.

"May I play in the brook, Mother?" he begged.

"Oh, honey, I wish you could," she replied in a tone of regret. "But this is your third clean suit today. Mother can't spend *all* her time washing and ironing little suits, can she?"

"No, course not," came the resigned answer. But it was accompanied by a deep sigh.

"When we get home you can play in the big trough by the well," promised Eleanor. "I'll make you a boat to sail on it. How will that be?"

"That will be very nice, Mother." There was no enthusiasm in the tone, but no rebellion either. The lessons of obedience were beginning to be fruitful.

"I think I'll go around and get me a nice bunch of goldenrods, Mother," said Chad, after a few minutes during which they had both sat watching the fish swimming around in the pool.

"That will be fine, son," said Eleanor absently. So Chad slipped down from the seat and wandered away with the puppy at his heels.

Eleanor sat leaning her head on her arm, a far-away look in her eyes. The color came and went in her cheeks, as her mind traveled back to other scenes and days. Sometimes she smiled, then again her face wore a look of sadness. She had become almost oblivious to her surroundings, so deep in meditation was she.

Little Chad looked at her from time to time with speculation. Finally he approached the bench again quietly.

"It's hot, isn't it, Mother?"

"Yes, dear."

For several minutes there was silence, then Chad tried again.

"Do you like hotness, Mother?"

"Yes, dear."

"Well, I don't. Don't you like coldness better, Mother?"

"Yes, dear."

Chad gave her a puzzled glance, then spoke again.

"May I go and play with Patty and Bobby Boy when we go home?"

"Yes, dear."

"May I help Uncle Bob feed the calves ?"

"Yes, dear."

Chad looked anxiously at his mother for a moment, then said softly, "May I wade in the brook, Mother?"

"Yes, dear."

Carefully he slipped away and hurried around the corner of the church to the spot where the brook glided under the fence. Almost immediately, however, he was back at his mother's side and leaned against her knee. The pressure of his little body roused her from her reverie.

"What is it, son?" she asked.

"I guess I won't," came the answer.

"Won't what, dear?" She smiled.

"Won't wade in the cool brook, even if you did said so."

"But I said you *couldn't*."

"I know it. Then when I asked again you said, 'Yes, dear.' But I guess you didn't know what you said," Chad remarked.

"Did I really say that?" said Eleanor incredulously.

"Yes," replied the little boy. "I ask-ed lots of things, and you said, 'Yes, dear.' So I ask-ed if I could wade in the brook, and you said, 'Yes, dear.' But if you say that wasn't nice, I won't go."

Eleanor pulled her son up on her lap and pushing back the damp hair from his hot little brow she kissed him again and again. Then she spoke.

"You are your daddy's own little son. I'm proud of you. Now because you were such a good boy and decided all by yourself not to go, I will let you wade a little while. Maybe you can help Mother in some other way to make up for her having to iron all those little suits."

Chad's face lighted with joy. Quickly he slid from her arms and started for the brook. Soon Eleanor heard him shouting merrily to Sport as they splashed together.

Left alone on the bench again, Eleanor gazed quietly at the fish darting between the rocks in the little grotto and wondered what lay ahead of her in life. She was busy and peaceful on the farm, and God had been good to bring her here. Once she had thought that she would never want to leave this haven. But of late there had been a mysterious restlessness in her heart and a loneliness that even the love of her Savior and little Chad's companionship did not dispel.

Perhaps it was the preparations for Connie's wedding in the fall that had stirred her heart with longings. Perhaps the Lord was trying to lead her out into greater service for Him. Perhaps it was the knowledge that things would change on the farm with the passage of time. Bob had been trying to get Mother to give up the sanitarium, and yesterday Mother had disclosed a plan that pleased them all. She wanted to fix two small kitchenettes in the upstairs, and thus have two apartments. These apartments were to be rest homes for missionaries on furlough. It was like Mother to think of such a thing. But in that event, Eleanor would really not be needed at the farm. Where would her field of service be? Surely some place God had a work for her where she could serve Him and raise Chad for Him. She wished she could discover what this vague restlessness was so that she might pray over it more intelligently. What did the future hold, anyway?

The sound of a step on the gravel interrupted her thoughts. She gazed in bewilderment at the man who approached. It couldn't be—this tanned and travel-stained stranger! Then he smiled, and she sprang from the bench with face alight.

"Philip King!" she exclaimed. "How—where—"

Laughing at her amazement, he clasped her outstretched hand in both of his and said, "I came past the house, and the little girl in pigtails said you were here at the church."

"Oh, I am glad to see you!" she exclaimed impetuously.

"I had hoped you would be," came the answer, and she knew it was sincere.

They seated themselves on the bench, and Philip looked about him at this unusual setting for a country church, admiring its beauty and its peaceful charm. Eleanor told him how the labor of its achievement had been a unifying bond for the young people. They talked of various incidents of recent interest and exchanged news of school friends. But all the while there was an underlying consciousness of more important things that must be said.

After a brief silence Eleanor spoke hesitantly.

"Phil, you made me very happy by the step you took at the trustees' meeting. I am proud to be the friend of one who could do that."

"Who told you?" he asked in astonishment.

Billy wrote me immediately. I think I understand, as fully as anyone can, just how much it cost you, and I have been rejoicing ever since for I knew you were letting God have His way with you."

"It's a glorious way to take, even though it seems a hard one at times," he said soberly. "I longed to write and tell you, but the battle was still on, and I wanted to wait until I could report a full victory. That is why I am here today. I want to thank you for the thing you did for me. The letter *was* a bitter dose, but it was just what I needed and was sent at the right time."

"I didn't want to write it," she confessed. "I felt I might lose your friendship entirely. But I prayed and prayed, and still the Spirit urged me. I knew I must do it, but I was afraid you would be angry."

"I was," he admitted. "I was furious. If you had been at hand there would probably have been a battle royal. But you were not there, and my conscience was. I had not been happy for months. I've wondered since how many people were praying about me. I am sure that Dr. Cortland was, and my courageous friend who wrote the letter. When you two start on a fellow he might just as well get in line at once, for he will eventually! God had been dealing with me, and I had been running from Him, trying not to hear the Spirit's voice. But when you put it all into words, I could evade no longer. I had to stand and fight."

He hesitated, as if even now the memory of the struggle was not pleasant. Then he drew a long breath and resumed.

"Before the meeting of the Board I had to face the issue of the presidency. It was not easy. I didn't want to give it up. For years I had pulled strings and played politics to get that position. I honesty thought I was the best man for the place. But your letter, on top of all the turmoil I had been in for months, was too much for me. The night before the meeting I walked the streets all night. When morning came, I knew what I must do. Even then I didn't like it. And I had no idea what the future held for me. I only knew I must leave Bethel and let Dr. Cortland take over. So—I did.''

"Oh, it was a big thing," said Eleanor unsteadily. "It was a real victory, and I have been rejoicing in it ever since. I could not bear to see you fail yourself and the Lord.''

"Well, it was not a complete victory yet. I had given up my prideful dream, but my heart was bitter with resentment at life and anger at you. Never in all my life have I been so angry at anyone. You see, it was the first time any person had torn off the—veneer, shall we call it—and shown me what the soul of Philip King really looked like. It was not the beautiful, shining thing I had pictured it, but a poor, miserable, deformed soul, and the sight of it sickened and shamed me. I did not feel that I could ever face myself in a mirror until I had done what had to be done. I knew that it would have to be complete surrender, and I dreaded to face all that such surrender implied.

"When I left the Board meeting that day I felt more lonely and disconsolate than I can tell you. But God was working. A letter came that very day from an old uncle in the west suggesting that I use his fishing cabin on a Minnesota lake for a quiet vacation. It was a heaven-sent idea, I am sure. I have been there all these weeks in conference with my Lord—just He and I alone. I knew I had to find peace to rid myself of the resentment against you—to seek out all the phases of my life that were yet unsurrendered. I was resolved to make a thorough and complete job of it this time. Oh, Eleanor, it's much easier to preach surrender than it is to live it! No one but God Himself can ever know the heat of that struggle. I slept only from sheer exhaustion and awoke each time to begin the same fight over again. It was an ordeal of prayer and self-crucifixion that I hadn't dreamed a man could endure. But the Lord won, as He always will if given a chance. The old Philip King is gone. The new one is today and forever a bond servant of Jesus Christ.''

His voice had broken on those last words as if the depth of his feeling were almost beyond expression. Eleanor, too, could not speak for a moment. Then, laying her hand on his arm to show the sympathy she could not put into words, she sat in silence as she tried to realize the import of all that she had heard.

"Oh, I am glad," she said at last, softly. "I know how you feel now, for I lived through that same struggle myself. I felt I could not let go of self. Yet when I did, I was happy beyond words. I felt so clean—and alive—and so rested!"

"That's the word—rested!" he agreed. "The struggle past, the battle won—by Him! It's a glorious peace."

"And where now?" she questioned, after a few more minutes of silence. "Will you still be reaching at Bethel?"

"I haven't gone so far in my thinking that I can answer that. I thought a few weeks ago that I should never enter its doors again. But now I feel that I might count it a privilege to go in as a student and learn of Dr. Cortland how to live."

"He's a grand old saint," agreed Eleanor. "More times than I can count he has helped me to get up and go on when I felt defeated and ready to quit."

"I must see him soon and lift the burden from his mind. I have had several letters from him, forwarded from the city, and I know he has a real concern for me. But I had two other matters to attend to first."

He looked straight into Eleanor's eyes, and she flushed under his steady gaze.

"The most important was to thank you for what you did. I tried to write you but found it difficult and decided to come instead. I do thank you from the depths of my heart."

"Oh, don't please," protested Eleanor. "I can't feel that I should have any credit at all. I had my orders, and I had to obey. but I didn't want to!" Her voice shook, and her hands twisted her handkerchief.

"I know that. It was that realization that finally broke me down," he admitted. "I realized that that letter hurt you just as it did me—and yet you had sent it."

Silence fell. Eleanor folded and unfolded her handkerchief carefully. She dared not look up, fearing that her eyes would betray how dear this humble Philip had suddenly become to her.

Philip sat tearing a catalpa leaf into shreds. His head was bent. At last he drew a deep breath, threw the leaf away, and spoke again.

"One more thing yet remains to be done. If I have time after it is accomplished I shall come back, if I may, and tell you good-bye. Eleanor, this is a hard thing to say. But—here goes! I am going to see my father-in-law and find out from him where the Little Chap is."

Eleanor was speechless from surprise. Her heart beat tumultously as he continued. "I know I don't deserve to see the boy again. I don't ask anything for myself. But I must know that he is all right and being taken care of properly. They told me that he is with his mother, but that isn't enough information to satisfy me. She may be some wanton girl of the streets—she may be mistreating him for all I know. He may be hungry—he may be dirty. Eleanor, there hasn't been a night since they took him away that I haven't gone to sleep wondering where and how he is."

"God is taking care of him," said Eleanor consolingly.

Philip brushed this aside with his hand. "I grieved for Lorraine, but God gave me peace and comfort there. Dearly as I loved her, I couldn't wish her back. I know she is with Jesus, which is far better. But where, where is he? I tried hard not to love him, but after he was gone I found that he had wrapped himself about my very heartstrings. I tried to forget him, but the effort was useless."

"How will you find him?" Eleanor questioned soberly.

"Dad Ferguson knows where he is, and I intend to find out. I will make no claim on him, for I have none. But before I go out into my uncertain future, I must know that he is all right."

Eleanor's breath came quickly, and she wondered what to say. Her prayers had been answered in fullest measure, and the thing for which she had longed had come to pass. She spoke quickly, with an excited catch in her voice.

"Oh, Philip, I'm glad! I used to feel that you would love him if you would let yourself."

"May God forgive me," he replied, with his face buried in his hands. "I don't quite know why I felt so toward him—probably grief over the loss of my own son, resentment at Lorraine's love for him, jealousy— Oh, why name all those sins? I know now that I would give all I own for the assurance that he is well cared for."

"It will be all right," said Eleanor consolingly. "When the mother understands, she will be reasonable, I am sure. Now I

255

want to show you my own little boy. He is playing with his dog on the other side of the church.''

Eleanor puckered her lips and gave the clear whistle that Chad had learned to obey. He did not appear, so she called, ''Come here, son, instantly.''

There was a sound of running steps. The boy and his puppy bounded around the corner of the church. At the sight, Philip burst into laughter, and Eleanor sat in speechless dismay, her face crimson. The little blue suit had been removed, and the child's only clothing was a tiny pair of cotton shorts. From head to foot he was muddy and wet. Even the golden curls were plastered with mud. But on his face was a satisfied smile as he said to Eleanor, ''I tooked off my suit, Mother, so I wouldn't get it dirty.''

Turning to Philip, Eleanor said with an embarrassed laugh, ''Will you excuse me while we go back to the brook for a few minutes and try to make a little white boy out of this apparition?''

Philip nodded his amused assent.

''Would you like to borrow a big handkerchief to use for a towel?'' he said.

''Please,'' Eleanor replied. He gave her the handkerchief, and Eleanor and Chad started off, the muddy little hand tucked inside the firm, maternal clasp. As they walked away, Chad looked up anxiously into his mother's face and said, ''Was I naughty, Miss Honor?''

* * *

In another fifteen minutes Eleanor and Chad returned. The brook had proved an adequate bathtub, and the little boy fairly glistened with cleanliness, even to the damp, freshly-combed hair. The little blue suit had indeed been well cared for and bore no traces of mud. Back on a bush by the fence the little pair of shorts was drying in the sun.

''This is my Chad, Philip,'' said Eleanor. ''Shake hands with Dr. King, son.''

Philip took the little brown hand in his and tried to say something, but his face twisted with emotion he could not hide, and he drew the boy close. Clasping both arms about him, his shoulders shook with sobs. Chad looked at Eleanor in bewilderment. He could not understand why this strange man was crying, or why his mother was shaking her head at him with her finger on her lips. And Mother was crying too! It was a perplexing world.

At last Eleanor drew Chad gently away from the broken Philip and said, "Dr. King had a little boy of his own once, Chad, and you are like him. Why don't you and Sport go play by the steps while we talk? See if you can find some acorns for Patty."

"Come on, Sport!" Chad called gaily and raced off.

Eleanor turned to Philip, who was wiping his eyes.

"Forgive me," she said, laying her hand on his arm. "I did not realize that you would recognize him—he has changed so much. I was going to tell you later."

"I knew when he called you Miss Honor."

"Bless his heart," said Eleanor fondly. "He still does that when I am disciplining him. I want you to know, Phil, that I would have let you see him anytime if I had dreamed that you cared."

"Oh, it is all my fault," declared Philip. "But Eleanor, how in all the world did this come about? I never dreamed—I am absolutely amazed—it's the most stupendous thing I ever heard of." He was at a loss for words.

With her eyes fixed on the gravel path under her feet, Eleanor told again, with faltering voice, the story of her marriage, Chad's death, the baby's birth. She did not try to minimize her own attitude of willfulness, knowing that Philip would now be able to understand and sympathize with what she had once been. Then she told how God had led her to Bethel, and to Lorraine; of her confession to Lorraine, and its result.

As she talked, both her heart and her listener's were lifted in gratitude to God for His direction and shaping of their lives. Philip's arm lay along the back of the bench, and when the story came to a close he drew Eleanor's head down to his shoulder and wiped away her tears.

"Eleanor," he said tenderly.

"Yes?"

"God has led us marvelously along separate paths until now —but don't you think that His will for us is that we go the rest of the way together?"

"Do you really want it that way, Phil?" she asked.

"Oh, Eleanor—I want it so much I can't even express myself." His arm tightened around her shoulder. "I hadn't intended to tell you this just yet. But the obstacles are all cleared away. I know now that the Little Chap is all right. Although—" Philip smiled teasingly"—the condition I found him in left something to be desired in the way of cleanliness."

"We have that remedied," she retorted, laughing unsteadily.

"Eleanor, I love you," said Philip. "Can't we serve our Master together, if He is pleased to spare us?"

She drew a long breath, then lifted her eyes to the pines on the hill above them, and the shadow of an old pain crossed her face. Philip saw it, and his eye held sympathy and understanding. Softly he spoke.

"I know what you are thinking, dear one, and we must speak of it now so it will never trouble us again. Because of the sorrow that has been the share of each of us, we can help each other. My own grief over Lorraine makes me capable of understanding what the loss of Chad meant to you. But they are gone now. Their memories will always be a blessing to us. They are safe and happy in that land where there is neither marrying nor giving in marriage. You and I are left behind. Why God took them and left us, we will never know. But we do know that there is work to be done here, and the way will be harder if we have to go alone. God, who gave us each a beautiful experience of love once, can do so again. I believe both Chad and Lorraine would want us to marry if we love each other. I do love you, and I'm daring to hope that you love me a little bit."

She turned to face him fully, and the shadow was gone as she spoke quietly.

"Not just a little bit, Phil. I love you dearly, and if we can go on together here, it will make me happier than I ever expected to be again."

Then his arms were around her, and his kiss was on her lips.

Sometime later Eleanor asked softly, "When did you begin to care, Phil? If you were so angry at me, how could you learn to love me?"

"I think I really started to love you in March, when you last came to Bethel. I felt you didn't approve of me, and it seemed tremendously important that you should. That started all the questioning and self-analysis. I resented it and you, but up in the woods I knew that I loved you. And I had a sign that let me hope you loved me, though you might not know it."

"Why—what—I don't know what you mean."

He laughed at her confusion, but his tone was serious as he said, "One night when the battle was hardest, and I was losing, it came over me with a rush that if I lost that battle, I'd lose your friendship. And I could not bear that. When I thought how empty life would be without you, I knew I loved you. Then, in almost the same instant came the realization that our friendship meant much to you also, or you would never have written a letter every word of which must have caused you pain. That knowledge broke me down. I cried like a baby that night, and the next day I started back. And here I am."

"Yes, here you are, and here I am, and God willing, we'll travel the rest of the way together."

The shadows were lengthening across the church lawn, and still they sat and talked. The barriers that had always been between them were gone forever, and they could face together whatever the future might hold.

"Perhaps God will want me to go back to the institute," said Philip. "I think that is the only really unselfish work I ever did. When I was down there, the needs of those poor, ragged, hungry boys and girls growing up in that ugly district pressed upon me until I forgot myself. If God wants us to go back and live there, will you mind?"

"Oh, no! Often I've longed to be back there. Perhaps God *is* calling us to that place. Working there with you I would be supremely happy."

"There is a movement to get a full-time resident superintendent. That would mean living there. Would you take Chad down there to live? It isn't an ideal place in which to raise a child."

"Other children just as dear to the Lord as he is are born and reared there," came the quiet reply. "We would always have our own home, which would be Christ-centered and guarded by His angels. If God wants us to go there, it will be the safest place in all the world for us, for it will be the center of His will."

The arm across Eleanor's shoulders tightened as Philip said huskily, "With you as a helpmeet I am ready for whatever service He has for me."

"Where are you staying now? You can wait a few days before going back to the city, I hope."

"I had planned to take the late bus back to Woodstock and catch the midnight train. I can take a room at the hotel there and come out and see you and the Little Chap again. I don't have to be in the city until Friday. That would give us three days to visit and make some plans. Is that all right?"

"It certainly is not! Mother Stewart has plenty of room, and you are going to stay with us."

"They might resent my being there," he said slowly. "They are the family of your husband, and—"

"Oh, they're not like that! Mother will be happy for me, and so will they all. If I came home without you I would have to bring a better excuse than that. You will come, won't you?"

"It certainly is an unorthodox situation, but if you say it is safe, I'll risk it. It's worth some risk to be near you."

Little Chad returned, tired of his play. Philip lifted him to his knee, and Chad leaned trustfully against the friendly shoulder.

"Where *is* your little boy?" he asked.

"In heaven with his mother," Philip answered simply.

"My daddy is in heaven, too," Chad informed him. "I guess he'll take care of your little boy there."

"Perhaps he will. How would you like to be my little boy while we live here on the earth, and let me be your other daddy to take care of you and mother?"

"Oh, I'd like that," Chad exclaimed, his eyes shining. "Patty and Bobby Boy have a daddy—he's Unka Bob—and I'd like one. Will you be my daddy right away?"

"Not right away, dear," said Eleanor hastily. "It will mean that you and I leave Grandma and live in the city. We will have a great many things to do first. You and I will have to work hard to get ready.''

"And I have to go back to the city and get a home ready for you to live in. But I'll be back before long.''

Chad's lips quivered, and a disappointed little voice said, "But I want a daddy. Can't Mother and I go with you? You could help with our work, and we'd go fast. And then Mother and I could help you get the house ready. I have waited so *long* for a daddy.''

Philip and Eleanor laughed, then Eleanor started to explain to Chad, but Philip interrupted.

"Oh, Eleanor, you could! Why wait? We have both suffered so much that it seems a shame to waste even a day.''

"I don't know what to say. I am confused. It seems so—''

"Just say yes,'' Philip suggested. "Finney once told his students that a man is just half a man without a woman. Help me to begin without delay to do a whole man's work.''

As Eleanor hesitated, Chad, not knowing quite what it was all about, but sensing her indecision, leaned over and hugged her, whispering, "Please, Miss Honor!''

Eleanor laughed shakily and said, "I don't seem to have any choice.''

"You have the entire choice,'' Philip assured her gravely. "I want you to do exactly as your heart dictates.''

She sat quietly for some minutes, watching the lengthening shadow of the pines. Philip and Chad sat waiting. Her face was very serious, but when she looked up the sadness was gone.

"This is no time for subterfuge,'' she said. "I do want it as soon as possible.''

Chad, realizing that a momentous decision had been reached, was ready for a change of subject.

"Let's go home. I'm hungry.''

"Oh, we should,'' said Eleanor, looking at the sun now low in the west. "I'm afraid we'll be late for supper.''

They started down the gravel pad. As they passed the church door Eleanor turned to Philip.

"Come and see our little 'church in the wildwood.' The door is never locked.''

They walked reverently into the cool sanctuary and stood in silence at the altar. The setting sun shone in through the plain glass windows and lighted the three faces with its glory. Philip slipped to his knees and drew Eleanor down beside him. There, in the quiet of that sunset hour, two who had learned obedience through the chastening hand of a loving Father thanked Him from full hearts for His love and faithfulness and laid their lives on the altar in service for Him.

Then with little Chad walking between them, they turned toward home. Service and love were ahead of them, and God would lead the way.